WANJĨRA

For Akshata, who will
write her own book someday!
With very best wishes,
Ms. Wambui,
CRLS June, 2008

A novel

Wambui B.Githiora

First published by Dog Ear Publishing
4010 W. 86th Street, Ste H
Indianapolis, IN 46268
www.dogearpublishing.net

ISBN: 978-159858-310-6

This book is printed on acid-free paper.
This book is a work of Fiction. Places, events, and situations in this book are purely Fictional and any resemblance to actual persons, living or dead, is coincidental.

Printed in the United States of America

For my parents—
Mr. Raphael Githiora Wa Wamunyu,
and the late beloved Mwalimu Alice Wambui Githiora,
who loved stories.

Acknowledgements

With thanks to the readers who offered suggestions and corrections: Ms. Emily Donaldson, Dr. Chege Githiora, Dr. Wanyagi Githiora, Ms. Yvonne Githiora, Mrs. Margery Kabuya, Dr. Matunda Nyanchama, and Mr. David Updike. Special thanks to Ms. Zeituni Onyango for her help with Dholuo.

WANJĨRA

CHAPTER ONE

Wanjira woke up at the first ring of her alarm clock. She had set it for a quarter to six, knowing she needed an early start this morning. She looked out the window, and was pleased to see the light of the early morning shortly after sunrise. It would be a clear, crisp, morning, another lovely day in September, she thought. The neighbours too were up for the day, and she could hear the usual morning commotion in the house next door. The roosters in people's backyard coops were crowing loudly, announcing the new day, and the familiar sounds of Municipal buses, *Matatu*, and private cars passing by, headed for the city center and beyond, left no doubt that Harambee Estate and the entire Eastlands was up, ready for another day.

In a few minutes Wanjira was out of bed, into the shower, and was soon sipping a cup of tea as she began to dress in her matching *Kitenge* skirt and loose fitting blouse. She had carefully picked out everything the night before, deciding on the look she would have today. She liked the earth colours on her outfit, and the writing along the edges of the blouse, which declared, *"Dunia ina mambo."* She had chosen the outfit purposely for the occasion, feeling, as the cloth designer had obviously felt, that the world was truly full of wonder. She had had this feeling for the last few months.

Wanjira then put on her silver earrings, and, carefully examining herself in the bathroom mirror, and liking what she saw, thought, "not bad." Indeed the dark brown face that met her gaze in the mirror pleased her. Though not especially vain, Wanjira, like many women her age, liked to wear nice clothes and accessories, and she had come to care for her appearance when she stepped out in public. She was an attractive woman, a fact many eyes affirmed whenever they encountered her. Wanjira had a shapely, medium build, and her figure was strong and firm, not yet distorted by extra fat or loose muscles, a common fate of many older women, and her face had no notable excesses of nose, eyes, forehead, lips or ears. Although such extra endowments could sometimes be attractive, lending interest to a face otherwise considered odd or uncomely, regular features like Wanjira's were thought more beautiful, certainly at first glance. But maybe people really noticed the young woman because of her striking eyes which came with long, black, eyelashes and thick, equally black, eyebrows. When she smiled her whole face lit up, showing her very white teeth with a slight gap in the middle of her upper teeth, set in dark gums. She was a true *Nyarari,* as many older people had often remarked to Njahira, her mother, who always smiled at the compliment but said little to the admirers. Njahira was a modest, quietly ambitious, woman who had high hopes for her daughter succeeding in school and going on to do what she thought of as "great things," and who privately worried that too much focus on her daughter's good looks might bring on misfortune. Didn't her people say a beautiful child could get the "*Githemengu,"* the curse invoked by people of jealousy and ill-will? But she kept these thoughts to herself, even as she privately felt grateful to Ngai, Lord of the Universe and the giver of all things, and proud of her daughter, who was truly a beautiful girl. It was, perhaps, such quiet and muted reaction to her physical beauty by her own mother and the rest of her family that had helped Wanjira go through her teenage years more interested in her education than in her looks, a common preoccupation of many of her age mates.

This morning, however, as she examined herself in the mirror, fixing a touch here and there, Wanjira was clearly focused on looking good. It was, after all, a special day, and all her energies of the last few days had gone to preparing for it. There was much to do yet and hardly enough time!

It was time to check her nails. They were neatly filed, and shone from the clear nail polish she liked to wear. She had worked on them the day before, but one must always double-check things. Her hair, with fresh zigzag patterned cornrows done two days earlier, pleased her. Since leaving school, where girls weren't allowed to wear braids, or cornrows, she had indulged in various hairstyles done by friends, or by hairdressers in Nairobi's burgeoning beauty salons, thoroughly enjoying the experience of someone's fingers working methodically on her head for an hour, sometimes even three, depending on the style's complexity, and relishing the conversations in the beauty salons. In the days that followed Wanjira would feel wonderful, her facial features and general appearance affirmed, enhanced, by the patterns on her head.

From his bedroom, her brother, Kairu, called out, "Are you ready, Dada? Be sure to leave soon. You don't want to wait in line all day."

"I'm almost done," Wanjira replied. "Thanks for the tea." Kairu had made the tea earlier, and had also scrambled some eggs, and cut up some bread. Wanjira went into the kitchen and poured herself a cup, but ate nothing, feeling too excited. She was not used to eating so early in the morning anyway.

Kairu, now ready for work, said good-bye. "Don't forget to ring me tomorrow or the day after," he told his sister. "I'll see you at St. Paul's on Sunday." A recent pharmacy graduate of the University, he worked at a pharmaceutical company in Industrial Area. Wanjira felt lucky to have a brother with a house in Nairobi and had appreciated the chance to spend the last three days at his place.

Her preparations over, Wanjira checked her teeth one last time. She was careful about her teeth, nature's own special gift to men and women. Dull, unbrushed teeth always made her cringe. Satisfied she was totally presentable, Wanjira now surveyed her belongings, packed carefully the night before, and felt prepared to leave. And oh, before she forgot, she quickly unplugged her radio-cassette player from the wall, and put it into her *kiondo.* Everything was all set. She was ready.

"I'll never forget this month's events," Wanjira had written into her journal the night before. She had developed the habit of keeping a journal since secondary school. Sister Margaret, her English teacher in Form Two, had encouraged her students to keep journals, and they had. Since then whenever she had a chance Wanjira recorded her thoughts, observations, favourite songs, poems and passages from books into special exercise books she carefully guarded from her younger siblings' curious eyes. Now, in the privacy of her bedroom in Kairu's house she wrote, *"September 1976 will always have a special place in my heart. The month I complete two decades on this earth! The month I set out on my own for life as an adult. 1976!! Is the year I will realize my life-long dream!"* She had underlined the last sentence

Wanjira was on her way to the University of Nairobi. In a few months she would turn twenty, like so many others in her class, a group of Kenyan youth who had entered school in 1963, the year Kenya became independent from Britain. They were the *Children of Uhuru*, beneficiaries of many different programmes established by the government to help improve education throughout the country. Often referred to by politicians and others in positions of authority as "The Future Leaders," most of these young men and women were the first generation of high school educated members of their families, and the fact that they would soon become "graduates" was awe-inspiring to one and all. The one thousand or so students in her year had a bright future ahead, an assured future, everyone said. All their lives the young men and women had been urged to prepare themselves to become the country's leaders, but it was also known that the really attractive prize ahead of them was an identity as privileged elites with good jobs, money, and unlimited opportunities. Their classmates who did not make it to university would always be aware of the fact that they had been excluded from such privileges, mostly through no fault of their own. The system simply ensured that only a select few could enter the university, and had designed examinations that eliminated all poor and nervous exam takers, most students from poor, ill equipped rural schools, and anyone but the brightest and luckiest.

Wanjira had qualified for entrance into the university following her successful A-level performance nine months earlier. It had been an exhilarating six months since the announcement had been published in the newspapers, and since, shortly thereafter, she had received the official notice from the University that she had been admitted into the Faculty of Arts, her first choice! She was later to learn that she was one of slightly fewer than three hundred women from all over the country admitted to the university that year.

Her family and friends had been very pleased, as had her History and Literature teachers. Many people sent her congratulation cards, telling her they had always known she would "make it." Some people had given her "something small" to celebrate her success. An elderly aunt had given her twenty shillings, a touching gesture, for the woman had very little money. Her brother had bought her a dress at Deacons, and given her two hundred shillings for pocket money. What generousity! Wanjira assured her parents that she was really fine, and they should not bother themselves about giving her anything, but they had given her fifty shillings, anyway. Everyone had been very kind. Just that past weekend her cousin Kuria had taken her and her friend Julia to a celebratory lunch at the Hilton, the first time she had ever stepped into the grand place.

In addition to what she had saved from her teaching job, which she had been offered shortly after completing her A levels, Wanjira now had six hundred and fifty shillings, the largest sum of money she had ever had in her life. She looked forward to even better times since all university students received an allowance for books, clothing, and living expenses. It was part of the loan every student received from the government to cover living expenses for the entire university course, and was known as "Boom," as she would soon find out. She felt very happy, ready for whatever lay ahead.

Wanjira took bus number 22, which wound its way through Harambee Estate, past Jericho, Jerusalem and locations in between, right across the Eastlands, into the city center, and on to the University, where she alighted. The bus continued its route to Kabete.

Her brother had been right. The line was long. First Year students, eager to start their new life, had arrived early. They came from all over Kenya, some arriving by bus, *matatu*, or train the night before, or that morning. Those, like Wanjira, who had siblings or other relatives in the city, had arrived over the weekend, washed off the dust and fatigue of long journeys, and were now ready for university life.

Wanjira lined up behind a male student with a medium size, well combed Afro, gray suit, white shirt, maroon tie, and brown platforms. He looked good. In front of her were about five hundred men and women, all finely attired, the men in formal wear or in casual trousers and short sleeved shirts, the women in dresses, skirts and blouses, or in jeans and trousers. Wanjira noted the women's hairstyles—braids, cornrows and straightened hair. What variety, she thought. What beauty! She surveyed the men and women around her, admiring them, and feeling she was in the midst of some special gathering. Her generation had come of age, she thought, remembering her father's words. He had once said to her and her brothers that each generation's coming of age is its chance to make a difference in the world. He had remarked that in the olden days young men and women came of age in publicly witnessed and much celebrated circumcision ceremonies, but all that was gone, and the completion of secondary school was the modern exit point for the young. Now her generation had reached its point of exit from its early youth, and was entering the final preparation stage. After three years the world would be waiting to see what they could do. But for now the future leaders waited patiently to file by the university employees who would ask them to sign forms, and lead them to a photographer to obtain their identity cards. Following that they would find their way to the halls of residence, their homes for the next three years.

The morning dragged on. She had arrived at the main campus of the university at nine thirty in the morning, and now it was nearly mid-day. The line appeared to be crawling. The sun was gradually climbing to the center of the sky, and it was getting hotter. A cool breeze blew, helping make what might have been an uncomfortable situation a bit better. People sat on their suitcases, or on the grass, making sure to keep their places. Conversations could be heard all around, especially by those who seemed to know each other. Wanjira herself had begun to converse with her gray-suited neighbour, whose name was Samuel Baraza, and who came from the Coast. He had attended the famous Shimo La Tewa Secondary School, and as they talked Wanjira felt herself relaxing despite the fatigue she had began to feel. He was admitted into the Law Faculty. They soon found they knew two people in common: he knew her cousin Kimani, who had been at Shimo two years earlier, and was now a third year student of Economics at the university, and he also knew Maria Mtema, a girl she had gone to secondary school with. His family and hers had known each other for years, he told Wanjira.

"What a small world!" Wanjira said, laughing. Samuel also laughed, emitting a loud, vibrant sound from his mouth. Wanjira noted the sound with pleasure, and made a mental note that he had beautiful, brilliant, white teeth. But yes, it was a small world indeed, and soon the two were talking as if they had known each other all their lives. She enjoyed taking with him, noting the way he inserted many Kiswahili words into the conversation in English. She wished she spoke Kiswahili fluently, like Samuel, and people from Nairobi, or the Coast. People from Coast, especially, gave Kiswahili certain cadences and lilts that made it sing and dance in their mouths. Wanjira loved hearing Coast people speak, and could always tell which Voice of Kenya announcer was truly from Pwani, or from Bara, the hinterland, her own home.

Wanjira and Samuel were so busy talking that they hardly realized they were reaching the end of the line. Soon enough they found themselves signing forms, and fully enrolled into their respective faculties. Together they walked toward the residence halls, suitcases in hand.

"I am very pleased to meet you, Wanjira, and I hope to see you around," Samuel said to her as she reached the women's halls. His residence was farther down the hill from hers.

"I am, too," Wanjira told him with a smile. "You're my very first friend in this place," she said. "Please come visit me sometime." He was soon off to his new home and she to hers, which she was to learn, soon thereafter, was called the "Box", and that she and all the other female students were called "Boxers" by the male students.

By the end of the first month Wanjira had got into the rhythm of her new institution. Lectures, tutorials, meals, friends, and events on campus kept her busy. She had become comfortable in her new room and with her roommate, Jessie, who had been in the same A-levels program with her. The two women had lived in different houses in secondary school and had not known each other well, but finding each other roommates now they found they had a lot of friends in common. It made sharing the same space a bit better, even though each woman privately wished she didn't have to share a room with the other. But there was so much to do during the day, and little chance of getting in each other's way, and in any case Wanjira found it more interesting to spend her days on the main campus, where there was much activity throughout the day. She loved sitting on the grass outside the library reading her book under the shade of a large *Mukinduri* tree, or simply watching students go back and forth between their classes, the library, and the halls of residence. She was especially intrigued by the frequent student meetings at the main campus' open quadrangle, the main public space for the university community, known to all as the Great Court, where, it seemed, some lively and obviously highly intelligent Second and Third Years had a lot to say about the university administration, and the country's political situation in general. These meetings were known as *Kamukunjis*. Kamukunji was an open field in the City where, during the 1950s, Africans held open meetings to agitate against British rule in Kenya. Someone must have thought it appropriate to adopt the name for meetings at the Great Court, and the name had stuck. Wanjira would observe these *Kamukunjis* from afar, not quite knowing what to make of things. "The place is so lively!" she would think, full of wonder, but also fear, a quickening of the pulse. She had heard that the special riot squad, whose headquarters were conveniently located across from the university's main campus, often forcefully interfered with such meetings and clobbered students with a vengeance born of rage that such privileged youngsters could be so ungrateful to the government that fed, clothed, and educated them free of charge! These spoiled brats, authorities felt, should be disciplined, and maimed, if necessary. They should be taught a lesson! Her brother Kairu had suggested she avoid such gatherings as much as possible, and she planned to follow his advice. But she was impressed by the student leaders' audacity, their apparent strong belief in certain ideas, and the energy they seemed to possess. She noticed that no woman spoke at these Kamukunjis, but that there were many, like herself, standing at various points on the Great Court, listening, laughing at times, and seemingly quite involved in the goings on. Wanjira thought some of these guys who rose to speak about the need to fight corruption, and to limit the excessive powers of the presidency, looked really handsome, and she admired their command of language and ability to express their ideas. Such confidence, such power!

During these first few weeks Wanjira met some of her old classmates from secondary school, many of whom she had not seen for nearly three years.

Five of her friends from Saint Gonzaga Gonza School, commonly known to all as Saint GG, had made it to the University, and fifteen girls from The Advanced Levels Preparatory, where she had studied after Saint GG, were there as well. She also met friends of her friends, some of whom were taking classes with her. In the evenings she visited friends in their rooms, and the young women would talk, laugh, trade experiences of their first few weeks, and comment on their lecturers, some of whom seemed strange, though interesting. A few main campus lecturers stood out: they were handsome, recently returned from Europe and the United States, PhDs in hand. The first year women in her faculty found the lecturers intriguing and even Wanjira seemed quite taken with the handsome lecturer who had made the first few weeks of thinking about African politics a real adventure. Who would have thought the topic could be so interesting, and make so much sense? She had looked forward to the lectures with this handsome lecturer. Some of the girls in her class groaned when they heard he was married. "What a loss," they said, laughing mischievously. "I wouldn't mind hooking one of the handsome ones for life," one of the girls, Judy, said loudly one afternoon as a group of girls sat on a bench near the Great Court, observing students, administrators, lecturers and others on their way to and from classes, the cafeteria, or on their way to town. "Watch me, girls, and see me hook one of these guys! Just watch—I'll find myself a lecturer." Judy seemed serious, and Wanjira thought she detected a scheming, shrewd, calculation in her face, but the moment passed quickly and all the young women laughed and laughed, more from the thrill of imagining themselves linked romantically with such distinguished men as the handsome lecturers than from any consciously dismissive thought that Judy was simply dreaming. Wanjira felt some excitement course through her body at the thought of befriending a college lecturer! Aah…the thought…!

Wanjira and her fellow year mates looked forward to attending classes by the famous writer, Ngugi wa Thiong'o. Imagine that! Most of them had read at least two of his books in secondary school, and Wanjira had had an especially wonderful experience teaching *The River Between* to her Form Two students at the *Harambee* secondary school she had taught in following her A-levels. The novel had led to passionate discussions in her classes, and she had enjoyed the experience. To think now she would actually sit in the very writer's classroom! But that would have to wait till Second Year. For now there were the handsome lecturers as well as the renowned Ugandan writer, Okot P'Bitek, whose course in African Oral Literature she would take during the second term, and others like Malawian poet and scholar David Rubadiri, and Ugandan playwright John Ruganda, whose courses she would take during her first year. She felt privileged and proud to be in the company of such competent and highly qualified teachers.

There were only two women lecturers in the entire Faculty of Arts, one of whom, Wanjira learned, would be her lecturer in second and third year. Dr. Muhoti was a senior lecturer, a fact that impressed the young women in Wanjira's class, and each time she walked by they would observe her in a respectful, awed, manner, stopping any conversation they might have been involved in to let the woman pass. This very beautiful woman enhanced her beauty by wearing colourful, well designed, African clothes and always had an elaborate hair style. The patterns on her head always looked fresh and creatively designed. Looking at Dr. Muhoti, Wanjira would think to herself that African fashion beat the "London Look" any day, and yet most women in Nairobi preferred the latter, and would go to great lengths to get the very expensive and less well fitting clothes that clearly did little to complement their beautiful brown skins and generally ample figures. And what about hair! Most women in Nairobi would pay dearly to change the texture of their hair using expensive chemicals, or by use of the hot comb, and did not seem to value the beauty of unique patterns the very skilled hair dressers could make on their heads, or the ways in which natural hair could be beautifully maintained by use of coconut and other hair oils. But as soon as the beautiful woman was beyond hearing someone might say, "Hello! aren't we impressive today," or "Give me that figure and hairdo any day!" Once someone said, "Beauty with brains," and from that day on Dr. Muhoti became "Beauty." Wanjira always felt encouraged by the sight of this woman on campus, and each time she observed her from afar she looked forward to being her student. She wondered if the woman was as strict and as aloof as she seemed, but still looked forward to what a Third Year she knew said were interesting and well delivered lectures from Beauty.

The other female lecturer was less elaborate, if also very good looking. In the two women, as well as in the few women administrators at the college, who also looked quite personable, Wanjira realized that all the things she'd heard about "educated women" were untrue. In secondary school one of the girls had said, as if stating a fact, that highly educated women were rough, ugly, and unmarriageable. Such talk had always worried Wanjira because it seemed to suggest that a woman was making a mistake if she planned to go to university. Once Wanjira had remarked to a group of her secondary school friends talking in this fashion, "Don't you think it is strange that we are being encouraged to study hard, pass our exams, and help build Kenya, and at the same time being told we will be ugly, and unmarriageable if we do exactly what our parents and teachers want?" The conversation had gone on for a long time, with many of the girls saying they did not care if they became ugly, they just had to pass their O-levels, and others saying they would go into training right after their O's, and not bother with continuing with A-levels. Such talk always made Wanjira sad and confused, but she had held on to her dream of making it to the campus, and here she was! Her excitement knew no bounds.

Two other lecturers and a few graduate students on the main campus were also noticed by the First Years: these ones because of their long, shaggy beards and somewhat intimidating personalities. One wore army fatigues, as though he were permanently going to war. Another spoke of different "plitcl purdies" in Africa and other parts of the world. It was said he had an American accent. He spat out his words with a powerful mixture of arrogance and disdain, intimidating everyone. One of the students remarked, loudly, that the lecturer should remember he was supposed to be teaching, not pushing hard on a toilet. "How irreverent!" thought Wanjira, but she had laughed and laughed. And then there was the other lecturer Wanjira and her classmates soon realized was unreliable: he had come to the second lecture twenty minutes late, and had actually not shown up for the third week's lecture!

One evening, during her second week, Wanjira visited Farida, a former housemate from her secondary school, and there she met two other First Years who would, in the coming months, become her close friends. Through the two she would learn some of the most important lessons that life, and her university experience, had to offer. Wangu was in the Faculty of Arts, and hoped to concentrate on sociology, and Wahito was in the Faculty of Medicine. The two women, though very different in personality, had been very good friends since high school. That evening Wanjira was instantly attracted to Wangu's loud, boisterous laugh, and her lively personality, and to Wahito's quiet nature and amused eyes that seemed to say much, though she actually said little. In the months to come Wanjira was to realize that Wahito's quietness belied her powerful analytic mind and a strong personality. Wanjira felt she was in good company. She was very happy.

CHAPTER TWO

It was now nearly three months since Wanjira had entered the university. She felt at home in her new environment, and thought she had developed a good schedule that helped her lead a balanced academic and social life. But some nervousness had crept into her life lately, and for the last two weeks she had been gripped by a feeling that she was not doing well academically. She had mentioned her concern to her cousin, Kimani, and he had told her to relax, that it was common for first year students to feel this because they were new to the system. "You'll get used to the idea of reading on your own, discussing ideas with others, clashing intellectually with them, and holding on to your own position. Just read. That's what you must do in this place. You must wean yourself from high school where many teachers spoon-fed you." Wanjira had been somewhat comforted, and had stepped up her efforts, making sure she was keeping up with all assigned readings. But the feeling that she was not doing well persisted. She wished she had had the courage to tell Kimani the truth: that she was absolutely terrified of participating in discussions during tutorials. Something was not right.

The Christmas holiday was in two weeks, and Wanjira had submitted a paper on each of her three subjects. So far she had only received one back, a paper discussing the rise of nationalism in Africa during the 1920s. She had found the subject interesting and had thoroughly enjoyed her lectures delivered by Dr. Mwangi, one of the handsome lecturers in her Faculty. In his lectures Wanjira began to think about things she had not thought of before: nationalism, the struggle for independence, and the conditions of post-independence in Africa. For the first time in her life she began to think about the fate of the African continent. Until entering university she had not thought of other African countries, except Nigeria, after reading Chinua Achebe's *Things Fall Apart* and Elechi Amadi's *The Concubine* in secondary school, and Uganda, where, according to news filtering in through newspapers, radio, and the many Ugandan refugees in Nairobi, Idi Amin had ruined everything since coming into power a few years earlier.

Things she had heard from her father, who fought for the British in India and Burma in the Second War, began to make sense. She had once heard him say that it was in the jungles of Burma and Ceylon that Africans from Kenya, Uganda, the then Gold Coast, Nigeria and other British colonies, made up their minds to fight the British to the end. "To begin with," her father had said, "Africans from the British colonies got to meet for the first time. That in itself was very interesting, and in those terrible war conditions one also got to think hard. Most of us realized we were fighting a war we had no business fighting," Her father had sounded angry when he said this, and for a while he had seemed lost in thought. Then, in an even angrier voice he had said, "And to make matters worse, when we returned home we were mistreated by the colonial authorities. Former soldiers did not get compensation they had been promised. I mean the Africans, but the British Johnnies got a lot of land. Oh yes, they did! People were dissatisfied." Wanjira was young at the time, and though she never forgot his words, and the angry and passionate voice with which he had spoken about his war experiences, she had not heard her father say much else about the Second World War. In this class she now had a chance to read what scholars said about the things her father had alluded to. She planned to talk to him over the Christmas holiday.

Wanjira had woken up at four in the morning for a whole week to write this and her other two papers. She loved the early morning; it was the only time of the day she could think, and read, without interruption. When the papers were returned she had a B+, and the grade disappointed her. She had wanted to earn an A, a letter grade she had got used to throughout high school. But her lecturer had written many comments on her paper, and this pleased her. She felt that he had responded to everything she had thought and written about in her paper, and she examined his comments closely, hoping and planning to write a better paper next time, and in spite of her disappointment in the grade she had liked his final comment: "An interesting and well written paper. You have delved into the complexity of African nationalism and I look forward to future papers from you. Keep up the good work!"

Akili, the bearded graduate assistant in war fatigues she had found intimidating at first, was her political science tutorial fellow, and by now Wanjira had come to feel comfortable about him. She hardly noticed his unconventional style, or his clothes. These garments and his manner were just part of his personality. She found him interesting, animated, and it was obvious he knew a lot about his subject. She had come to admire and respect him. This Friday morning he was discussing the nationalism issue, but the room appeared unresponsive. Wanjira wondered if it was because papers had been returned already. Perhaps no one cares, since it won't make a difference to their end term results, she thought.

"Let's hear from someone," Akili said, hoping to break the silence. He searched different faces, waiting. "People, let's not be so silent," he said. "I need a few ideas from you. Don't let me do all the talking." Wanjira felt personally challenged. For the last few months she had said nothing during tutorials, fearful of appearing ridiculous. It was a strange feeling, this fear, for throughout her academic life she had always been able to put her points across, verbally, and in writing. All through secondary school, and throughout her A-level course, she had enjoyed speaking up in class, and had acquired a certain reputation as a particularly confident and able student. But now things appeared somewhat different: something about the very idea of university, the seemingly brash male students, their sense of confidence, and the fact that she had never been in the same classroom with boys until now, had intimidated her. In her journal earlier that week she had expressed her fears: *"I have become someone else. I no longer recognize myself. Things frighten me, and I don't know why. I must do something . I must begin to speak up or else..."*

"The only thing I'd like to note is the difference between the response to colonialism and subsequent nationalist response in Francophone and Anglophone Africa." The voice came as though from someone else, and even Wanjira seemed surprised at herself. She took a deep breath, trying to avoid all the eyes now focused on her.

"Yes, what about it?" Akili looked interested, and Wanjira felt encouraged.

"It appears the French speaking Africans were more interested in appeals, and in proving to the French that they could, indeed, become a true extension of France. They believed in the idea that they were French, albeit African Frenchmen. The nationalists in British colonies simply wanted the British out, and were determined to fight them. They had no illusions about becoming British. Its clear from all the readings that the French duped their colonial subjects in a way the British did not..."

There was silence in the room when Wanjira finished. Akili smiled. No-one said anything until he said, " A most astute observation, and I couldn't have said it more eloquently than...eh...please remind me your name?"

"Wanjira. Wanjira Kamau"

"Yes, my sister Wanjira here. I like what she has just said, for she has hit the nail on the head, so to speak. She has articulately pointed out the difference between the so-called Assimilationist Policy at the heart of French colonialism and the overtly exploitative but clear British idea that its colonial subjects were just that: colonial subjects. Their role was to produce raw materials for Britain, to keep the colonial machinery going. They were definitely British subjects, nothing else."

The conversation soon became quite animated, and the hour passed quickly. Wanjira felt good because she had at last conquered the fear she had felt ever since beginning university, but as she walked back to her room, something nagged at her a little bit: why had Akili called her "my sister"? It had not felt right that a man who did not even remember her name could so quickly give himself the right to call her "My Sister." She felt irritated, feeling that Akili had patronized her. But had he? She could not shake this feeling, even as she realized that the morning's tutorial had marked the beginning of the end of her self-imposed silence during class discussion. "Or I'm I imagining things?" she asked herself later that evening as she prepared for an evening out with Wangu, Mercy and Kimani, at Furaha nightclub, where the popular band, Mangelepa, was playing that night. She longed to share her thoughts with someone, to hear of other people's experiences in lecture halls and tutorial rooms. What, exactly, did it mean to be a university woman? Did other women feel intimidated in the tutorials, and what were they doing about it? Did anyone else share her reticence to speak out, and had they, like she had done earlier that day, plucked up all courage and spoken their thoughts out loud, asserting themselves, finally? Wanjira longed to know what other women at *Chuo Kikuu,* the nation's main University, felt. She would ask someone, perhaps Wahito. Was it the same in her faculty? And what about Wangu? Despite all the friendly conversations the women had had in the past, they had not said anything about their actual experience of university life in the lecture and tutorial rooms. Thinking about this Wanjira suddenly found herself wondering why no-one she knew spoke of the specific things he or she was learning at the university. Why? Before leaving for the nightclub she wrote into her journal, in capital letters: *THE SPELL IS BROKEN!*

CHAPTER THREE

The Christmas break was over. Thank God, Wanjira thought, relieved to be back in the residence halls. It had been especially crowded at her home that holiday: some of her cousins had visited for a few days, and many other visitors, her parents' friends, had streamed in day after day. She and her younger sisters had stayed busy, offering the visitors tea, *mandazi*, *githeri* and other hot meals, and generally seeing to the running of the home. It had been exhausting, and she was pleased to be back in her own space, to enjoy some peace and quiet before classes began.

Despite all the work, though, the holiday had been interesting in many ways. For one thing she had had an opportunity to hold long conversations with different family members: her brothers, sisters, and cousins. She had also had a chance to speak to her father about the Second World War, and he had impressed everyone with his tales from "That horrible war."

"Ai! the jungles of Burma are terrible! Terrible!" He paused, and seemed lost in his own world of memory and pain and despair. "Our clothes were so damp for so many days and tore off if you as much as scratched yourself...and the Japanese! Those people are no joke. Do you know that many killed themselves rather than be taken prisoner?" They would actually open up their stomachs and commit suicide—they are no joke, those people, no joke." As he spoke, Wanjira's father's face seemed full of awe; his eyes took on a glazed, intense, look, and his hands, demonstrating all the hardships, had a taut, hard, look. He seemed ready to grab something and hold it in a tight grip. As she watched her father speak, his face tortured by the memory of a hard and terrible war, Wanjira realized there was so much about him she did not know. For years she had simply taken him for granted: he was her father, and that was all. Sometimes stern, often tipsy after consuming many bottles of Tusker, generally warm and kind to his children. He had not seemed to bother very much with her and her siblings' schooling; somehow he took Njahira's word that the children's grades were often good. Wanjira now remembered that her father had visited her in boarding school only twice in the six years she lived away from home. But he was always at home during the school holidays, and so the non-visits had not really bothered her. The thought had only now hit her, years later. But she had been impressed by, and had keenly noted, the fathers and mothers who visited their daughters in boarding school often, sometimes musing at the whole idea of people riding in uncomfortable *matatu* and over-crowded buses for the long and difficult journeys on poorly paved roads, simply to visit their daughters for two or three hours on Sunday afternoons. One particular father had impressed the girls at Saint GG's because he visited every Sunday. So regular were his visits that the girls could almost tell when he would arrive: an hour and a half after lunch. If he arrived late it was noticed, as was the exact moment of his alighting the *matatu* at the end of the drive, from where loud voices could be heard announcing; "Rita, Rita," for that was his daughter's name. Rita would shyly emerge from wherever she was to greet her father, hear news of home, and receive his weekly gifts of orange squash, raisin cinnamon bread, tinned margarine, sardines and Marie biscuits. These foods made Rita one of the most envied girls at Saint GG's, and it is true to say that Wanjira and many of her classmates experienced at one time or other some envy toward Rita, and also a certain measure of regret at the lack of a father like she had, a man who could be depended on to show up every Sunday, rain or shine, carrying lovely gifts and treats for his daughter from the best shops in Thika town.

This Christmas Wanjira and the others listened to her father's tales of long ago and faraway places and marveled. Wanjira found herself imagining her father as something other than the ordinary father she had grown up with. She looked at the photographs of him and a few friends hanging on the living room wall, all taken during the war, and tried to imagine the terrors these men had faced, even though the pictures showed the men either smiling, or with serious, intent looks into the camera. All that terror, and for what? For the almighty British empire? She felt dissatisfied, and could feel the slow, steady rhythm of her heart as she listened, especially when her father said, his voice hurt and mystified, "And then we came back to Kenya and were ill treated by the Colonial Government. Ahh, those people mistreated us! We were soldiers in Burma and Ceylon but back in Kenya we became nobodies. They watched us....many of us...ah...These are harsh things to remember..." and he said no more after that, and everyone in the room realized the reminiscences had come to an end, for that time at least. Wanjira's curiosity was aroused and she knew she would be asking her father about the war when a good chance came up. Perhaps next holiday.

A week later Wanjira learned that her roommate, Jessie, was pregnant. Ah, now it made sense, Wanjira thought, for Jessie had been acting rather strangely before the Christmas break. Wanjira had found her on many occasions taking a nap in the afternoon. She had also noticed that Jessie ate very little, sometimes not even bothering to go to the dining hall at all. She seemed content to simply drink tea, which she made in the room using her electric kettle. "I just don't feel well," she had told Wanjira once. But then she had seemed to recover. The two roommates had seen very little of each other because Jessie went to visit Munyua, her boyfriend, almost every evening and all weekend. He was a bank employee who lived in South C, a graduate of the Faculty of Commerce at the university, one of those graduates considered to have a truly bright economic future. He would pick Jessie up in his white Datsun in the evening, shortly after she had returned from the Library, and drop her at the main campus in the morning, where she would head into the library to prepare for her lecture or tutorial for the day.

When Wanjira learned of these arrangements she wondered how Jessie could possibly enjoy such a life, so programmed, so controlled by her relationship with Munyua.

On a rare evening when Jessie was in the room, Wanjira asked her about her life on and off campus. Jessie told her she enjoyed staying in Munyua's flat, and that the residence hall was just a pleasant alternative. "I'm a woman with two homes...lucky, don't you think?"

Wanjira agreed she was lucky indeed, but it was just a way of talking. She really did not think Jessie was as lucky as she said she was, but for different reasons.

"Jessie, wouldn't you just like to spend your evenings here, visit old friends and make new ones? How about just staying in your room in the morning, especially when you have no class till late in the morning, or early afternoon?"

Jessie just smiled, saying that she liked it this way. She said nothing in the university was as important as her life with Munyua, and that she felt very comfortable about him and their relationship. That was about a month before Wanjira learned Jessie was pregnant.

"Are you sure?" The news shocked Wanjira.

"Of course I am" Jessie smiled. "Five months." Wanjira made a quick mental note. It had happened before they entered university then. Goodness!

"What are you going to do now?" Wanjira must have sounded alarmed, for Jessie laughed out loudly, as a way of reassuring her, before saying, "Of course we'll get married. During the holiday we got things moving. His family will visit mine in two weeks, and we plan to hold the wedding in April."

Wanjira felt numb. Pregnant! Marriage! All the things she had sworn to avoid until finishing university. What a nightmare! But Jessie was smiling.

"Wanjira, I'd like you to be one of my bridesmaids. Please say yes." Wanjira smiled, surprised at this invitation. She had always thought bridesmaids were special friends or relatives, but she had also known of others invited to this honour for practical reasons, such as the forging of future friendships and cementing of family bonds, especially with the bride's sisters in law or special cousins of their husbands. Could she turn the offer down without deeply offending Jessie? She quickly thought no, and when she said yes she had a happy smile on her face in spite of her inner turmoil and confusion. Jessie quickly went on to tell Wanjira of her wedding plans: "I'll have eight bridesmaids and four flower girls." She seemed quite animated. "And Munyua will also have eight men with him, one for each of the ladies." The two women laughed. Wanjira was getting into the excitement.

"What colour will the women wear?"

"I'm thinking light blue, some light material, perhaps chiffon, pale blue hats, and white shoes. What do you think?

"It sounds wonderful!" Wanjira felt like a hypocrite for sounding so enthusiastic. "And the men?"

"Munyua thinks navy blue suits, light blue shirts, and black shoes. Someone will buy the shirts and hats in London."

"Ehe! It'll be quite the wedding, Jessie. London Look for sure." Wanjira said this with a mixture of admiration and cynicism. She remembered a wedding she had attended recently, her friend Lucy's cousin's wedding. All the bridesmaids had worn short *Kitenge* dresses, and their hair was done in beautiful cornrows with extensions. The men had worn short sleeved *Kitenge* shirts and navy blue trousers. The bridal party had been quite colorful, and lively. A new idea in Nairobi, many had remarked. The bride, visibly pregnant, wore white, and the man wore a light blue suit. Wanjira thought she would mention this to Jessie.

"Have you considered *Kitenge*? Its affordable, beautiful, and the tailors could make any style you desire."

"Oh no, not *kitenge*," Jessie said frowning. That won't do. I could not imagine my wedding party in *kitenge*, though I'm hearing about it these days. Forget it."

Wanjira dropped the subject. After all, she really did not know Jessie much, or her ideas about things, and besides, she was all set, having obviously planned everything already. She agreed to accompany her to Biashara Street the following Saturday to go look over some material. "We don't have much time," Jessie said, "I have to get the material, then arrange a time for all the maids to get the tailor by mid January. He's told me he needs a month for the order."

Jessie's news had actually shocked Wanjira more than she dared show. All she could think of was her roommate's fate: she was headed into her husband's home. So shortly after being her parent's daughter, she would now be someone's wife, having so quickly interrupted the brief pause life provided between home, boarding school, and married life. "Why do women do this?" she thought, almost angrily. "What is wrong with waiting a little bit? We'll all get married, sooner or later, so why rush? The thoughts raced through her mind. She said nothing to Jessie, however, for she did not think it would be useful. And it was not as if expressing such thoughts would change anything, anyway, for now Jessie's life had changed. A baby was on the way, and that's no joke, Wanjira thought. A baby would change everything. From now on Jessie's life would be focused on nappies, maids, baby clinics, relatives everywhere, shopping, cooking, cleaning, cooking, shopping and cleaning again. *Taabu, taabu!!*

And there was something in this for Wanjira, despite her misgivings, for she had actually come to enjoy her roommate's frequent absences. Jessie's many visits to Munyua's flat gave Wanjira a chance to relish the privacy of having a room to herself, something she had come to appreciate at the Advanced Levels Preparatory, where she had had a cubicle all to herself. Alone in her cubicle she could relax, or read, for as long as she liked. Despite the tiny space and thin cubicle walls Wanjira had felt very lucky, never having slept in a room of her own, or by herself, until then.

That night Wanjira had bad dreams. She was at a wedding, but there was no bride. People waited and waited, and just as they were about to leave, a huge car drove up. Wanjira did not know whose wedding it was, or who was in the car. She suddenly woke up with a start. She was sweating. After trying to get back to sleep for what seemed a long time, she gave up, made herself a cup of Nescafe, and began reading Ousmane Sembene's *God's Bit of Wood,* one of her assigned literature texts. She had already read it, but wanted once more to read about Penda, a woman who was not afraid to do a few unconventional things. Wanjira longed to be brave, and strong, but on this night she felt weak, adrift, and unhappy. Jessie's news had stirred up feelings inside of her that had recently started to nag her—the fact that she had no boyfriend. She had turned down many boys in the past, feeling that if she became attached to any one of them she would be trapped, and entangled in an emotional situation she could not extricate herself from. She feared becoming pregnant, which invariably happened to most of the girls she knew who had serious boyfriends, a reality that would inevitably interrupt her education. "No, that just won't do," she would tell herself. But a small thought had lodged itself in her mind that maybe it was time. The thought came to her after she completed her A-levels, and as if reading her mind, her mother, Njahira, had told her one Sunday afternoon as the two rested in the shade of two large *Mikinduri* trees at the back of the family house, "Wanjira, the heart knows what it wants. Just concentrate on your education. When you meet the right man you will not need anyone to point him out." Mother and daughter had been talking about one of Wanjira's cousins, Nduta, whose marriage had been announced a few months after the completion of her teacher's certificate course. The discussion had led to the topic of suitable men, and Wanjira had got the feeling that her mother was eager to hear that there was someone her daughter thought special, but Wanjira had assured her mother there was none. "One of these days, Mami," she had said, laughing out loud. "Don't worry, I will keep my eyes wide open at University." Her mother had said other things, which left Wanjira encouraged and reassured. One of them was that it was important to enjoy herself as a young woman and not rush into marriage. "Make sure you get a chance to earn your money, and to buy all the platform shoes you want. Marriage will come in due course because a good woman is always in high demand." Her mother had always given her good advice. But this morning, even as she marveled at the beauty of the dawn, the soft light that now filled her room and the ever beautiful colors of the bougainvillea that lined the wall outside her window, Wanjira felt discouraged.

CHAPTER FOUR

Jessie's wedding took place on a rainy Saturday in April. It was the season of the short rains, and farmers all over the central highlands of Kenya were busy tending the newly planted and rapidly germinating maize, beans and potato crops. The young plants created a carpet of green all over the region and Wanjira, sitting in the back of Jessie's cousin's red Datsun, was struck by the beautiful sight: on some plots the maize plants of a daring farmer were already half a foot high, having survived what had seemed, three weeks earlier, a lingering and persistent dry spell unsuitable for planting the crops, a fear unalleviated by the rain clouds that had gathered in the distance. The rains had come, however, and farmers who had hesitated to plant their seeds a week before the rains must now be full of regrets, Wanjira thought. She observed, to her right and left, the contrast between the food crops and the extensive coffee farms between Ruiru, and Juja towns, many of them now owned by cooperative societies and the banks that had loaned them the funds to buy the farms from Europeans who chose to leave Kenya after Independence. So much land devoted to one cash crop, Wanjira thought, wondering if the areas they were travelling along would not have healthier children and adults if more land were used to grow food. Her own area, Ngumo, had such large coffee farms, and many emaciated children who ate only one meal a day, after sunset, when their tired mothers returned home from their low paid contract work on the farms. As a young girl, Wanjira had felt sorry for many of the children she knew in her village and at school who lived this difficult life. She felt both lucky and guilty because she had better clothes, and her family always had enough to eat. It just was not right, she would think, but then did not know what to do about the children.

In Kahoti, Jessie's home, Wanjira and the other bridesmaids mingled with many happy relatives from Jessie's mother's and father's side of the family. Jessie's paternal grandmother was especially pleased that her namesake, whose *real* name was Wagio, her own name, was getting married. By custom, Jessie was named after her paternal grandmother because she was the first daughter in her family, and many in her village called her Wagio. Like many Kenyans however, Jessie had become accustomed to going by her so-called Christian name, a practice that began with colonial and missionary education years past, and which had not abated more than a decade after independence. A few people, for example Wanjira, her brother Kairu, and others at the university and in many other places around Kenya were beginning to use their African names in their formal and informal worlds, but the majority of Kenyans, especially those who considered themselves truly "modern," preferred to continue using their western style names.

Jessie's grandmother's joy was echoed by her aunts, who were excited by their niece's upcoming marriage. They plotted to get many presents from Munyua's family the next day.

"*Hii, hi!* we can't just give them our soon-to-be graduate," one of the aunts declared. "They must give us proof that our valuable daughter will be in good hands," another added. Spontaneous singing punctuated these utterances, and there was much merrymaking. Wanjira noticed that some of the women were sipping beer from large glasses, and that as the evening wore on, the noise level went up, as did the many bursts of laughter from the jolly women. Only Jessie's mother was quiet. She seemed lost in her own thoughts, and although she smiled and spoke with the guests the sadness on her face was obvious. Wanjira had heard it said that a bride's mother is often sad for she is losing a daughter, and fears for her daughter's future. A mother in-law, on the other hand, is always happy because she is gaining a daughter and a helper. She wondered if a mother-in-law did not think of losing her son in a significant way, but then again sons could not quite be lost to their mothers: for the most part they built their houses right next to their mother's houses and somehow managed to keep away from the not uncommon struggles that almost always developed between their mothers and wives. That way they remained their mothers' children forever. Ahh! marriage!

Wanjira had learned to associate weddings with these complex feelings and expressions of sadness and joy, and had always felt moved by a bride's tears. Brides generally wept in church and during the festivities afterwards. As a little girl Wanjira had wondered why brides agreed to marriage in the first place: why go into something that made you so sad? Once, on remarking this to her mother after they had been to a cousin's wedding Njahira had said, "Wait until your own day comes. You also might want to cry." But she had said this with a smile. Wanjira had felt a shiver go down her spine.

But this evening in Kahoti Wanjira and the other bridesmaids tried to make themselves useful. They served drinks, and helped bring the food from the makeshift kitchen outside for the ever growing number of visitors. They did all they could to make Jessie feel pampered on this special evening, her last night in her parents' home. A few final touches needed attention this evening: the white-lace bridal gown examined, and put away in a special place in Jessie's parent's bedroom; the bridesmaids' dresses pressed and re-examined for any possible flaws, their off-white shoes and stockings all ready and carefully stored away; everyone's nails and toes painted, the bride's in her favorite ruby-red colour, the other women's in a less dramatic but nonetheless beautiful beige-pink colour; every woman's hair pressed with a hot comb for tomorrow's shiny and smooth look. Wanjira had agreed to the style only because every other bridesmaid would have it: It was Jessie's wedding, after all, she had reasoned. She had had her hair pressed with a hot comb at a boutique near the university a day earlier, and later in the evening would curl her now soft, limp, and quite dead hair in readiness for the curly uniform look all the women would have as they escorted the bride to her new life.

"Tomorrow you will have a new home," someone said, and Jessie laughed loudly. There was a nervous sound to the laughter, and Wanjira did not miss it. She was busy painting Jessie's toenails, and now decided to tease the *muhiki*, the bride, herself: "Now remember, no tears tomorrow. No outbursts. We are modern brides, and we don't cry. We choose marriage and so we are happy brides!" Everyone laughed, and then Nyathira, one of the other bridesmaids said, "The tears only come because of our mothers. We feel we are abandoning them and our younger brothers and sisters too. Its just painful, Wanjira. You'll see when your time comes." Nyathira, Jessie's cousin and close friend, now a student at the Science Teachers College, had married only five months earlier. She already had a three month-old baby who was in the next room with his grandmother, Tata Mugure.

As the evening progressed it became clear that there was an agenda to be followed and that it was being directed by the older women in the other room. The noise level in that room had risen to such an extent that now there was a kind of din, a palpable sense of excitement. But somewhere in that din a voice was heard asking loudly for the bride. "Where is our *Muhiki*? and her bridesmaids? *Nimooke othe*! We want them all here! It was Tata Mugure, who, Jessie had told Wanjira, was quite a character, and a favorite aunt of hers. She was her mother's younger sister and was a nurse at a very busy clinic in Thika. She also owned a number of buildings in town, from which she collected handsome amounts of rent. Jessie had told Wanjira and the others that Tata Mugure was tough, generous, and a straight talker.

The young women brought the bride into the room, which all of a sudden went quiet, ready, waiting. Wanjira felt excited, wondering what was coming next. She looked around the room at the faces of Jesse's aunts and mother's friends. This, then, was Jessie's family inner circle: the special female group that formally releases a bride to her new family. This group that gives a bride her last, relaxed, yet formal, address before the more ceremonial ones of the actual wedding day. Those ones were formal, and public. This group gave a formal, but private, sendoff. Wanjira had realized there was a clear sense of order, mixed in with all the seemingly structure-less days and evenings related to weddings and associated events. You had to pay attention to the subtlety of things, and not rush to judgment. The seeming effortlessness in moving from one aspect of a marriage to the next was all planned, after all. A few women were the silent directors of all these activities and now Wanjira realized that Tata Mugure was the general manager of the whole evening. Chief of protocol. Even as she sipped her beer she had a strategy for how the evening would go, and of course she had a master plan for the following morning, when she would act as the family's chief spokeswoman. She would negotiate Jessie's final exit from her parents' home with admonitions and demands, and it was up to her to control the timing of everything. Tata Mugure could delay the official wedding time for as long as two or three hours if she thought it fit, and Wanjira hoped she wouldn't. She would have loved to know how Tata Mugure and the others had conducted themselves during the formal marriage negotiations, which had gone on for well over three months, and only been quickened because Jessie became pregnant. Those events were run by men and women were relegated to the background as the men of each family negotiated on behalf of sons and daughters ready to become husband and wife...Ordinarily the talks would have gone on for at least half a year. I suppose its not a joke, Wanjira thought, suddenly smiling because she suspected bride and groom must have planned the pregnancy to avoid, and hasten, the protracted meetings between their two families.

Wanjira's thoughts were interrupted by an "*iiiiiii, riu niguo,*" yes, the time has come, from somewhere in the room. The room became silent. Altogether there were fifteen women present, young and old. Tata Mugure cleared her throat, and began:

"Our *muhiki* is here." It was just a general statement. Everyone could see Jessie, who sat next to her Tata Grace. She looked radiant and happy, if somewhat tired. Someone gave her a cup of tea and she took a sip. As if on cue, Tata Mugure said, in a loud voice:

"Let us thank the Lord for giving us this day." All bowed their heads, and the older woman reeled off a long prayer of thanksgiving for life, happiness, and generousity. She thanked God for the lives of Jessie and Munyua and their offspring, whom the good God of the Agikuyu, of all Kenyan people, the God of Abraham and Serah and Isaac and Jacob and Ruth, the Great Jehovah of the heavens and the earth, ruler of the universe, King of Kings and Lord of all Hosts, in his kindness and mercy and love and understanding and hope for the future of families, of generations to come throughout the country and the world, had seen fit to put side by side the hearts of these two beautiful people who tomorrow would announce their love to the whole world and who would forever be blessed and supported by their love of the Lord and their families. It was a long and beautiful incantation and Tata Mugure's voice sounded strong and vibrant and lovely as it smoothed over the words. Everyone said a loud "*Aaaamen!*" when it was clear she was done, and the prayer over, it was time for business.

"Jessie," Tata Mugure said, "We are happy to be here tonight to help escort you to your new home. We are happy with your choice: an educated man like Munyua will understand a well educated woman like you. We are glad."

Loud ululations greeted these words. "*Aaariiri riiii riri riri ii ! Aaari ri ri ri riiiiiri riiiiiiii!*"The room had come to another life.

"There are a number of things to be said tonight, and now is the time to say them." Everyone was silent, with heads looking at some undefined spot in the distance. Some faces had smiles on them; others were still as masks, and it was hard to imagine the thoughts going on in these women's minds.

"First of all," Tata Mugure said, "We need to tell you about one of the most important duties you will have as Munyua's wife. Indeed it is the most important thing we want to tell you this evening." She paused dramatically, and surveyed the whole room. Wanjira waited to hear of the important duties, always spoken about at weddings: "Take care of your husband, children, relatives, and your home. Mind your reputation. Always have a good word for your in-laws; treat everyone with respect. Above all conduct yourself with dignity. Let people know when you pass them on the roadside that you are your parents' daughter and your husband's beloved, his *ngatha,* and he will continue to treat you as such; avoid loudmouths at the marketplace; avoid women who might secretly wish to cause mischief by going after your husband, they are often simply jealous of the harmony existing between a man and his wife, and often do not even really want him. A *muunjuga* should be unwelcome in your home; and don't tell us someday that we did not warn you. Wanjira expected to hear all other do's and don'ts brides were reminded of on their wedding day and assumed this litany of responsibilities was now going to be recited by

Jessie's aunt. She soon found out how mistaken she was for the woman, after a dramatic pause, said, in a loud, strong, voice:

"Jessie!" Tata Mugure and many of the women present tended to lengthen the syllable to Jesse's name so that it came out as "Njessay," and this time, what with the gravity of the situation, the name came out of Tata Mugure's mouth full of color and meaning. "Njessay, the first, and really the most important, thing you must always remember as Munyua's wife is this: *you must take care of your money!.* "

As if on cue, a loud ululation burst out from every woman's mouth. "*Arri riri riri riri! Ariri riri ririri!*"

"Let's say six for the girl child!" It was Tata Wagio who said this, and everyone, recognizing its significance, raised her voice and produced some of the most beautiful trilling Wanjira had ever heard. Women had now refused to be given only the four ululations traditionally given a girl, while a boy got five! They would give their daughters six! They ululated in unison, with beauty. After giving Jessie this special recognition it was time to listen to Tata Mugure.

"Let me repeat: You must take care of your money! Money is not life, but it is very, very, important in life!"

The other women nodded vigorously. Someone made a loud trill, and the room burst into laughter.

"Yes ! Yes!" Jessie's Tata Joyce shouted. "*Thikiriria biu!* Pay full attention to what's being said," she turned to face Jessie, and she had a big warm smile on her face as she spoke. Tata Mugure continued, "You must keep a separate bank account, your very own, and *never* let Munyua see it." There was much laughter from the women. "Never," Tata Mugure repeated, "Unless you want to be a fool, like your cousin Wahu." The women's faces fell, and little "tss" sounds could be heard everywhere, for everyone knew of Wahu, Tata Wagio's second daughter. She was a primary school teacher whose husband, a lover of alcohol, and women—three others, in fact, all in different towns—had convinced her to open a joint account with him before marriage, and now the poor woman could not even afford two pairs of shoes, let alone other things for herself and her three young children. For a long time she had kept the one pair for school, and walked barefoot, or in Bata slippers, the rest of the time. She had also tried hard to mask her poverty, not wanting her family to know about her husband, but her mother eventually found out what was happening and began to help her daughter. The story of how Tata Mugure, acting on behalf of her sister, had confronted her niece's husband—an encounter that had included two hard slaps on his face to teach him a lesson—was still fresh on the women's minds.

"Wahu is a fool," Tata Mugure said, her face crumbling. Her voice trembled as she added, "If you hold on to your money, and do things to let it grow, your children will never know want, and your husband will respect you."

"But Tata Mugure," Jessie said," How can I keep such a secret from my husband? Doesn't that make me a liar? What if he ever finds out about such an account?"

"*Haaiya*, what is this we're hearing?" The voice came from Justina, one of the quieter women in the room, and a cousin of Jessie's mother. "What is our bride telling us?" She clapped her hands loudly as she rose from her seat, and moved to where Jessie sat. She stood over Jessie, imperially. "Are you telling us that up to now you have not seen what happens to women in this country? Where are your eyes? Is this why we sent you to school? So you could turn into a woman who cannot see things in front of her very own eyes? And you, a university woman with all this education, don't know this?" Justina's hands were on her hips. She seemed headed for battle.

"Listen, Jessie. It's not about lying. Let's just say its about keeping one or two things to yourself. Right now, as we speak, Munyua is also getting his last few words as a bachelor, and they are telling him that if he wants to have a peaceful life with you he must not pry into your private affairs, just as you will not pry into his. By that I mean that you will both take care of your family, to the best of your ability. Of course you are two working people, and you will have a joint family account. But you will also remain two people who can help their parents and siblings without causing animosity in the home. If you buy your sister her school uniform, should you beg or ask permission from your husband? Eh? And if you help your mother, or mother-in-law, with "a little something" for her pocket, some bus fare here, a school uniform there for a poor relative, must you beg from your husband? Ha! With your own money these things can be done. And you can buy yourself a handbag or shoes *whenever* you want. Its *your* money! That is what Tata Mugure is saying."

Justina's speech was received with nods of assent, laughter, and exclamations of "*Ta mwire*!" "Tell her!" "Let her tell you now," "Listen to these words," and "Never say we never told you." Wanjira and the other bridesmaids watched the women, realizing that they, too, were supposed to absorb this lesson. And indeed they were, for Justina suddenly turned to the side of the room where the young women were, and said, "And you, too, should remember this. We sent you to school so you could live a little better than all of us. Do you hear that?" Her voice was soft, and she suddenly seemed sad and ferocious at the same time. The young women nodded, their eyes wide with an unexpected anxiety evoked by the words and body language of the older women.

Jessie, a shy smile on her face, thanked Tata Mugure and the other women. "I'll remember your words. I will take your advice. And I will never forget this evening." She had a wonderful, shy, smile as she spoke "But right now I can tell you that Munyua is all I'm thinking of!" She spoke with so much feeling and her face shone with so much joy that the women simply had to smile, and all this encouraged a slightly changed tone to the conversation in the room.

"Of course, in the beginning its all wonderful, and with God's help it will remain so for a long time."

The words came from Tata Grace, who until now had been quiet. All evening she had sat in one corner of the room, a cup of tea in her hand, a quiet member of the gathering. "In the beginning all you see is him, and all he sees is you." She spoke in a matter-of-fact voice, as though she was simply affirming a well-known fact.

"Then what?" Jessie asked. Everyone's attention was now on Jessie and Tata Grace.

"And then the years pass, and a time comes when—how shall I put this ?—a time comes when…let's say you wouldn't want him to be ill, or meet with misfortune, but…her voice seemed to trail off, and she stared into the distance for a while. Then, in a burst of energy she had not shown in her earlier words, *"Nduramwenda! You really don't want him!* She paused, and then, her voice much louder than before, emphasized, *"Ai, you simply don't want him!*

Tata Grace's words were met with a burst of raucous laughter by the women. They rose from their seats, clapping their hands. They laughed and laughed, and such was the intensity of their mirth that most were soon wiping the tears running down their faces. Some slapped their thighs while others held their waists, heads thrown back, their laughter emerging from some deep, previously hidden, place. Looking at the women Wanjira suddenly felt uneasy. She had smiled when the laughing began, and then, like the other women, had started to laugh out loudly, more amused by the laughing women than by whatever Tata Grace had said. But now she felt that something about the laughter in the room was not quite right. She looked from face to face and could no longer be sure the tears in the women's eyes were all from their laughter. A chill went through her body.

"That may be so, Tata Grace," Jessie's voice was strong, confident, a firm disruption to the near-hysterical laughter. She too had earlier joined the laughing women, amused, like Wanjira, by the sight of these thick, aging bodies, so convulsed in what was clearly an older generation's private joke.

"But all I know right now is that I will love Munyua forever," Jessie continued. "He is the love of my life! The best man ever!" The bride had spoken, and moved them on to another thought, and Wanjira joined everyone in the ensuing laughter, which became more noisy than deep, and which opened the women's mouths, this time in song, in the old familiar bridal taunt:

Muhiki witu-i
Wa gututagahira maai-i
Na arega uguo-ri
Tukamucuuka—cuka- cuka!

Here she comes, our bride
She will fetch water for us
And if she doesn't
We will whisper about her
We will bad-mouth her!

And of course, as was customary at weddings, they could not stop teasing her:

No ndwakwirire
No ndakwirire Jessie!
Iceera ria Munyua
Iceera ria Munyua
Tigana nario!
Riu ni wahika
Riu ni wahika Jessie!

I warned you Jessie
About that Munyua!
I said watch his company
Watch that fellow!
Now you are married Jessie!
Now you are married!

They were clapping their hands, and some of the women had risen from their seats to dance around their *Muhiki,* who was also clapping her hands and moving in time to the song.

Other songs and ululations followed, each woman taking up the other's *ngemi* until the room was now full of merriment. *Aaririri riri ri ri ri ri!*

Aaririri riri ri ri!
Aari ri ri ri ri!

Wanjira wished she could ululate like the women, and made a mental note to practice the sound. All she could do was a trill that lacked the melody and smoothness of the sound these women made. When she ululated, now as eager to laugh as everyone else, her neighbor teased her a bit, "Yes, that's it, that's it," her wide grin showing Wanjira that she needed to refine her *ngemi.*

Now the send-off party was in full swing. Beers were passed around, and some of the women drank tea, while conversation filled the room. Wanjira felt warm and cozy in this room of women. The entire household remained abuzz with excitement as people came in and out, exchanged greetings, had something to drink, and set out into the night. They promised to gather early in the morning to await the groom's people.

After a while Wanjira left the room and sought Jessie's younger sisters and cousins. She found the girls sitting around a fire that had been lit outside earlier that evening. It was a cool night, and the young women draped their shoulders with sweaters or *Khanga.* The moon was out, giving a soft light to the compound. The air was fresh after the rains of the last two weeks, which had cleared the dust and left the soil everywhere moist and ready to nurture the young bean and maize plants all over Kahoti and the surrounding ridges.

A lively conversation was going on around the fire.

"All I'm saying is that I'll wait till I've enjoyed my money." It was Njoki, Jessie's younger sister, speaking. She was sixteen. Wanjira sat next to her and listened.

"Form Six is a must, of course," her cousin, Charity, also sixteen, said. "Like what Jessie has done. That will be the cue for me. It would be wise to attend University, or training college, as a wife and mother. That way one can be organized."

"What do you mean, organized?" Njoki asked.

"I mean, having a husband, a family, a purpose in life. A woman should have this by age twenty. After that things get tough."

"Meaning what?" Njoki sounded impatient.

"Meaning that a woman in her late twenties will not find a husband. A woman with a University degree, and her own money, will not attract a man. Men don't like women like that." Charity sounded smug, and sure.

"To hell with all that !" Njoki exploded. "Who cares about men like that anyway? Why should women not do what they really want to do?" She was so excited that she rose from her seat, and now started to gesticulate with her hands. She sounded passionate: "I don't care about what you call being organized. I want to finish school, work, spend my money, help my parents, and then, years later- when I'm about twenty eight or so, I will marry."

"*Hi, hi, hi*! are you out of your mind?" Charity's voice was loud, ready for an argument, and now she clapped her hands loudly to express her amazement. Everyone was laughing, waiting for the fireworks they knew were sure to come. "What a foolish idea!" she said, curling the corners of her mouth upward contemptuously. "Go ahead—do that, wait for that long, and get ready to wait a looooong time, for you will wait a long, long, time, my friend, and you will keep waiting..."

Charity did not complete her sentence because Njoki interrupted her, more passionate than before. "Say whatever you wish, but as for me, I don't care about being foolish. In fact, I will wait for as long as I want, and will marry whomever I want. He can be Luo, Luhya, or Maasai. I don't care! as long as I love him!" She was smiling, staring straight at Charity. "There you have it. And don't you ever say I didn't tell you!"

"Jehovah of the skies! This girl is mad! Come help this girl!" Charity clapped her hands together and then raised them up dramatically. The other girls started laughing. Everyone's excitement was rising. "You are a foolish girl, really," Charity continued, adding, "And please don't say such things again. Are you mad? Who do you think would allow you to marry a Luo, of all people? What's wrong with you?"

"Charity." The voice was that of Rakeli, another cousin of Jessie's who, until now, had simply enjoyed listening to the arguing girls without joining the conversation. "Charity," she repeated, in a calm, yet firm, voice, "There is nothing wrong with Njoki or any of us marrying anyone we love. The man can come from any part of Kenya. Or anywhere else. Even India! That would be alright with me. And who knows? Some of us will decide to never marry."

Rakeli surprised the group, including Njoki, who felt grateful to have someone come to her aid but who, like the others, perhaps had never contemplated the last thought Rakeli had expressed, and so calmly too—the idea that a woman might not get married, and by choice! It was a new thought for almost everyone in the group, especially coming from a young girl like Rakeli. She was fifteen, and only in Form Two, whereas most of the other girls were either sixteen or older. Wanjira, already in university, was the senior member of the group.

No-one spoke for a few seconds, so taken aback were they by what they had heard from Rakeli. Charity seemed too surprised to respond appropriately, and all she said was, "I...I don't understand you people, but I can tell you this: You, Njoki, and now I suspect even you, Rakeli, will never get married if you continue this way of thinking."

"And how can you be sure of that?" Njoki had a big smile on her face as she continued, "Let's wait and see...hm...maybe one day you'll get an invitation card asking you to attend my wedding to…hm…let's leave that to the imagination."

The girls laughed loudly, clapping their hands together, relieved that all was well, after all. Wanjira also laughed, quite amused by the laughing girls. Everyone loved a good verbal match, and maybe there were more interesting exchanges yet, for the night was still young.

The girls would have gone on arguing had Jessie's older brother, Maina, not joined them. He was a lot older than them, and the conversation had to change, for these kinds of things could not be said in front of a person so much older than the young women. They now turned to school, Maina asking how the young women were doing, and what they planned to do with their lives following secondary school. Maina was already a University graduate. He had studied architecture and was employed by an important firm in Nairobi. Jessie had told Wanjira all about him one evening in their room in the Residence Hall at the University. Wanjira now watched him, admiring his calm and respectful manner as he addressed the young women.

"The important thing is to fulfill your ambition. Don't rush into marriage- take your time. And whatever you do, be sure that you are in a position to support yourselves. Have a course you can depend on. You see, ladies, when a wife and husband can both support a family life is a lot easier for everyone." The girls nodded respectfully. Wanjira wished Maina had been around earlier, to give a male point of view to the discussion, but she liked what he said now. He reminded her of Kairu, her brother, and other guys she had met through him. They were the older generation, and they had good ideas about women's education. And yet she wished he had not joined them when he did, for his presence had changed the conversation, and the group's mood. Wanjira would have loved to hear more from the young women, but the moment had passed. Now she wondered: where did Charity get the idea of limiting herself so much? Why was she afraid to dare, to go beyond societal expectations? And was Njoki unhappy about her sister's marriage? Did she, perhaps, wish Jessie had completed University before getting married? And what about Rakeli? She was interested in that girl's mind. Rakeli had expressed a thought Wanjira liked: the thought that a woman in Kenya was free to do as she wished. This was a powerful conviction in a young secondary school girl, and Wanjira felt drawn to the young Rakeli. She shared her idea of a woman's right to marry whomever she wished, even though she had often heard people disparage the thought of "marrying outside." She had heard all kinds of remarks against people who did so, especially the few who married *Wazungu*, Europeans, but also those men who "dared leave all the beautiful women all around them" to "bring us" strange and ugly women from "strange places in the country," a complaint she had once heard a woman visiting her mother make. Like most other people of her generation Wanjira was aware that most older people approved of only those things that were familiar, and well known, to them, and feared new, potentially dangerous, unfamiliar ones. And yet they did not fear sending their children to school, a place that, inevitably, changed their children's ways of thinking, and certainly the way they spent their time, for they were gone from them for most of the day, and for most of the year once they entered boarding school. School was definitely the most dangerous place for any parent to send a child, and yet most parents throughout Kenya sent their children to the institution, for they understood that it was the one place that could help shape their children's lives and futures. Modern Kenya called for educated children, and with the exception of a few, parents had heeded the government's call to send their children to primary school. Nearly fifteen years after independence only the most unresourceful parents refused to send their children to primary school. Even though they could not guarantee completion of the first seven years of school, parents were determined that their children would learn to read and write. Working from sun-up to sunset they toiled on their own small plots or on richer people's land, or went to Thika, Nairobi, Nakuru, Kisumu, Mombasa and other cities to look for whatever work was available, so they could pay for their children's school fees, Building Fund, and uniforms. But maybe parents put all their faith in the expected benefits of schooling—opportunities for salaried jobs and expanded opportunities—and did not dare face the fact that they had no control over what happened to their children at school. For the most part parents had no clue about the daily goings on in school, and even if they knew, what could they do about it? They had no control over what their children learned, or did not learn, at school. They, therefore, focused on that which they felt they could control, in particular the big decision about whom their children should, or should not, marry. Through the enormous power of tradition and custom they possessed, parents wielded their strong influence on their children and generally only approved that which was familiar, time-tested, and in their view, safe because it was well known.

Wanjira had, however, not given the question of "marrying outside" much thought, for the "problem" had not been felt within her own immediate or extended family. She therefore had no particular feelings about it. If she had given the topic any thought at all, it would only have been to remark to herself that such unions were events and actions that affected others, often in faraway places. But this evening in Kahoti, Wanjira felt a jolt of recognition of something within herself: something that quickly told her that she fully agreed with Rakeli. There really was no good reason why one should not marry a man from any part of Kenya if one met, and liked, such a man.

Wanjira had gone through a lot this evening, what with the women, and now the young girls, Maina, and her own thoughts. Suddenly she longed to speak to someone her own age, and looking at the couples that came and went into the house and out for a walk in the moonlight, Wanjira felt an overwhelming sense of loneliness. She wished she had a boyfriend to go out for a walk with, to discuss things with, to argue with, even.

CHAPTER FIVE

Wanjira's life at the University was becoming more and more interesting. She was learning so many new things that she thought her head would burst. There were more and more reading assignments, and she found herself working late into the night. Her A-level courses had prepared her for university, she thought, but no one, really, could have adequately told her of the heavy work load ahead, of the high expectation her lecturers had. Each one seemed to think his or her course was the only one on the syllabus, and every day there was a new article, a new chapter, to digest. Reading assignments on reserve in the library was a special challenge, for often there was only one book to be shared by many. But students had no choice; the lecturers, after all, were loaning them their personal copies to ensure everyone had a chance to read all assignments. But everyone was serious, and took turns, and the librarians were strict in enforcing regulations: two hours, and only two, students would be told; no late returns; others are waiting; you will be fined. On weekdays Wanjira generally read in the library until about eight o'clock, after which she would walk back to the Box, have a cup of tea, take a shower, and then begin phase two of her evening work, another hour or two. At times she would put everything aside, and wait for morning. She felt refreshed then, ready for the day. Luckily she still had the room to herself as no new roommate had been assigned Jessie's vacant space. She continued to enjoy her privacy and hoped she would not get a new roommate soon.

Sometimes Kimani walked back from the library with her, and they would catch up on each others' news. He was one of her favorite cousins, and both had happy memories of holidays spent at their grandparent's home in Matemo. There the children of her grandparents' daughters had spent many happy and carefree days punctuated by hard work imposed by their grandparents. The girls mostly worked with their *Cucu* on her special sections of the land, weeding or adding manure to the bean plants, or in the maize fields. Other times they worked on the potatoes, always making sure to follow her special instructions. "Be careful! there! Do not expose the young ones or they'll dry up. There, there, *one uguo*, that's the way to do it." Their *Cucu* was good to be around; she laughed easily, and hard. She seemed rather carefree, always ready to respond to their *Guka's* admonitions or comments with strong and sure words of her own. Sometimes she held her hands akimbo and called her husband *Githuuri giiki*, you old man, and the children tittered in their seats though they were sure to not laugh out loud. As a young girl Wanjira often wondered why her grandparents related to each other as adversaries, but never asked anyone about it, for after a while she took it for granted that this was their way of being.

Guka had the boys help him prune the coffee plants, or with tending the cows and goats, and when, twice a week he picked up his special meats from the *king'eero*, which he owned, his special compensation as provider of the slaughter house, the boys helped him roast the delicious livers, kidneys and pancreas on specially prepared hot coals. What enjoyable treats they were! The old man would say, "This gives you strength," and emphasize even more, as he chewed, looking happy. "Strength!" The children admired, but kept him at a distance because he was stern, taciturn, and was always working, working. Now Wanjira and Kimani, remembering some of those days sometimes, laughed, recalling their *Guka* and *Cucu* and how there was no way of resting in their presence: you had to keep doing something. Always. No wonder Wanjira's and Kimani's mothers were the same; always working. The women had inherited this from their own parents.

In the evenings the children shared stories from the different parts of the country they lived in. They spoke of their friends, their teachers, and taught each other songs, jokes and riddles. Their grandmother often told them traditional stories of Hare and Hyena, of Fox and Elephant and Antelope. Wanjira loved these stories. But she also loved stories from books, narrated by Kimani, or Kuria, or Wanjiku, or Njeri, or Nyambura, cousins with a gift of storytelling, funny people who made her laugh till her sides ached. At her grandparents' home she learned you could love boys like Kimani and Kuria and the others because they were family; cousins, one's own male relatives, men who were, but not quite, like one's brothers, young men with whom one could be safe. You loved them dearly, and passionately, but not like boyfriends, and not like your brothers either, whom you loved with all your heart and soul, but they were your brothers. Your mother's sons. Cousins were a bit more exciting than brothers because you could share secrets with them and they did not scold like brothers and they did not look at you with strange, passionate, longing, eyes like some of the boys one met in the village, or later, in high school during school debates and dances. At these gatherings the ground shifted and there was admiration of a different kind, a different tension; a heart-warming, dangerous, somewhat frightening energy from boys one could possibly agree to become friends with; boys who wanted your address and who then wrote long, heavy, letters full of declarations and demands. But cousins! They were special.

Kimani and Wanjira had continued their friendship and she loved it whenever they bumped into each other on campus. One evening, after he had waited for her outside the library to walk back to the halls with her he said, his face all serious, what a pity it all was for despite all this hard work Wanjira and all others at *Chuo Kikuu* would not acquire the "power to read" until the very end, on their graduation day, when this power would be bestowed upon them by His Excellency himself! Wanjira laughed and laughed, and said she longed to see Mzee himself at close range. "Remember those days at *Cucu*'s when he passed by every evening? What magic that was!" They laughed at their excitement when, every evening during the week, Mzee's motorcade, announced by six or more loud, motorcycles manned by colorful riders, passed by the road near their grandparents' home and how all the children along the route rushed to the road, so excited, so awed by the great man, and how they raised their index fingers in the well-known party salute, and how the amazing, charismatic and well-liked president, the great liberator, the father of the nation, *mzaliwa wa karne iliyopita*, raised his left index finger and waved his famous flywhisk with his right hand, his famous salute. Wanjira had, years earlier, been captured by the lyricism and beauty of radio announcer Leonard Mambo Mbotela's reference to Mzee as mzaliwa *wa karne iliyopita*—he-who-was-born-in-the-previous-century. It had been one of those occasions when the radio brought into people's homes the pageantry, pomp, and ceremony of Independence, or Kenyatta Day, making young and old tremble with excitement and longing. Mbotela, in an awed, reverential voice would lower his beautiful and melodious voice an octave lower when Mzee's motorcade was in sight, and inform the listener glued to the radio: *Ameingia, ameingia, shujaa wa Kenya, Kiongozi wetu, Mpendwa Raisi Mtukufu, Mzee Jomo Kenyatta, Baba wa Taifa, Mkuu wa majeshi, Mlinzi wa nchi yetu, Baba wetu, Mzaliwa wa karne iliyopita, Mzee wetu*... By which time goose bumps would be crawling all over Wanjira's body because such a voice, such use of language, and the man it described, were out of this world. *Here he comes, he is here now, Kenya's Hero, Our Leader, Our Great and Beloved President, Our Old Man, our Mzee Jomo Kenyatta, Father of the Nation, Commander of the Armed Forces, Defender of our Nation, Our Father,*

He-Who-Was-Born-Last Century: and then the Police or the Airforce Band would play the magnificent tunes of *Kenya, Kenya, Kenya Taifa Letu, Kenya, Kenya our Nation*, and life would feel, for that one moment, extraordinary, and very good.

He-Who-Was-Born-Last Century was of the same age as Wanjira's grandfather. The two men belonged to the same generation, of the very same Kihiu-Mwiri *riika.* According to tradition her Guka was the great man's comrade for they came of age in the same year and thus shared a link enshrined by custom and tradition, a bond that was forever. But to Wanjira that thought was far from her mind as she joined thousands of others in what was clearly a semi cult-worship of Mzee. Her Guka was one thing, and Mzee was quite another. As a child, by the roadside, she'd felt the power and mystery of Kenyatta, and like all other children, convinced herself that he had looked straight into her eyes, and had smiled at her. Years later many girls in her high school made the same claim: Kenyatta had looked directly into their eyes while they danced for him, or as his motorcade had passed them by on some road or highway and they'd stood by, in awe, their index fingers declaring unity with the old man's one and only party, and had smiled sweetly at them.

Wanjira had actually seen Mzee, years back, at his home in Icaweri, near Gatundu. Her primary school, which was located some eight miles from the big man's home, was often scheduled to dance for him. Other schools in the old man's constituency were also on the dancing roster, and often the songs one heard in the primary schools in Wanjira's day were praise songs for Mzee.

"Gaka kagica-a kagica
Nguku iria iri kwanyu yuugaga atia?
Gaka kagica-a kagica
Yuugaga muthini ni athii wiira
Nakio gitonga gitigwo toro…
Gaka kagica-a- kagica
Ngari ya Kenyatta yaathire ku?
Yathire Nairobi kubatithio
Yabathithio yeetirwo atia?
gaka kagica-a kagica
Yeetirwo "Mukuui wa Munene"

My little kagica, kagica
What does the rooster in your homestead say?
It says: the poor man should go to work
and the rich man stay in bed
my little kagica, kagica

Where did they take Kenyatta's car?
My little kagica, to Nairobi to be baptized
and what became its new name?
My little kagica they called it
"The Great man's carrier"

The children would whirl and twist their waists and shake their shoulders and dance to specially choreographed steps. At the end they would stamp their feet in unison to fully declare, and affirm, Mzee's greatness. Sometimes the songs and dances were wild and beautiful and even Wanjira, who did not always like these trips, would get into the spirit of things:

Eetagwo Kenyatta! Eetagwo Kenyatta!
Ngaagera Icaweri
Kana ageetwo Baba wa Taifa
Ngaagera Icaweri ngigeithagia Kenyatta
Nitumugeithie! Nitumugeithie!
Ngaagera Icaweri
Twirigaine mweri ikumi na inya
Ngaagera Icaweri ngigeithagia Kenyatta!

His Name is Kenyatta, his name is Kenyatta!
Or Father of the Nation!
Let's go by Icaweri to greet him
We salute him! We greet him!
Yes, let's go by Icaweri
And greet him
We last saw him on the Fourteenth!

Sometimes the children had seen him on the Fifth, or on the Twentieth, and their lyrics would change accordingly. Wanjira loved the song's rhythm and tempo, and the energy of the dance movement required to sing and dance to it perfectly. It called for an enthusiasm and spirited expression not often felt in some of the more stylized dances she and her classmates practiced on break, or in physical education classes, and the children loved it. But one day, while singing and dancing happily to *Ngaagera Icaweeri* out in the family yard she heard a loud hiss from her mother, and a warning: "I never want to hear that song in this home ever again!" Wanjira was astounded, and it was only afterwards, when she told one of her friends that her mother did not like the song, that she learned its tune was that of a famous circumcision song, and many older people, even Christians who had given up the formal circumcision rituals of old, loved and admired the song and could be seen nodding and smiling whenever they heard it. "That is why Mzee loves it so much," her friend Nyathira had said. "Haven't you seen how his eyes glint with happiness when we do this dance? Its because he is from the old days." Ahh, *Mzaliwa wa karne iliyopita,* Wanjira remembered, and smiled.

The trips to Mzee's home had been exciting, but the all too regular dance sessions also tired the children. The lorry that came to pick the children from her school would arrive at about five o'clock, right after study time, and return them to their various homes after midnight. She hated these night rides along the winding Ngumo-Gatundu dirt road, in the back of a lorry with singing, or sleepy, children. Once her mother had complained bitterly that no young child should be required to sing for anybody, no matter who, well past the normal bed-time. At such times Wanjira had bitterly regretted being from Mzee's constituency, and wished she had been born far, far, away, like the boy she once spoke to at Gatundu one Saturday afternoon. His name was Hassan, and he was from Garissa, and was also in Standard seven, like herself. She had liked him, and had offered him some of the pancakes her mother had packed for her in a paper bag, but he had politely declined her offer, and then offered her an orange from his own food bag. She had accepted it with a smile, and thanked him. She wondered if he was shy. She had never met anyone from Garissa, or from anywhere beyond her own district, before then. He was so handsome! He had soft, brown skin and black, curly hair, and his teeth were very white. When her group had to go Hassan kept on looking at her, intently, and she returned the stare, trying hard to put an intense look on her face. But then she felt herself frowning. Soon his group also had to leave, as did hers, but she had thought of Hassan for a long time afterwards. She wondered if she would ever see him again.

Wanjira's introductory course to Government Studies the previous term had aroused in her a special interest in Mzee's ideas, and in the history of nationalism in Kenya and elsewhere. She felt a strong passion developing inside of her. She was now studying a follow-up course in African politics, and was studying African and European literature as well. These days she felt a strong, almost overwhelming, passion toward something, but she did not know what this something was. She read all assignments and tried to think hard about what she was learning; only she did not feel that she understood very much. She was taking in a lot of information. So many things, so much to learn, so many new feelings to deal with! Her mood these days alternated between shock and amazement in lectures and tutorials on the workings of the modern African state. Things were complex, she was learning. Corruption and bad leadership were the order of the day. Unscrupulous types were everywhere, and the poor had no chance. Freedom was just a word. The African writers she was reading provoked many thoughts inside her, but also showed the beauty of the villages and of African men and women. Into her mind many images gathered: ugliness, beauty, power, control, abuse of power, betrayal. She often wanted to shout, to scream at the injustice of it all whenever she read of African states' repressive methods of operation, in particular the silencing of those considered enemies. She now thought of Kenya differently, and often felt like one who had been asleep for a long time. She remembered the story of Rip Van Winkle waking up from his seventy-year nap to find a world that baffled, frightened, and probably intrigued him no end. It seemed she was only now awakening to the realities of the world around her.

Some weekend evenings she and her new university friends went dancing, or to the movies, and she was learning a lot about Nairobi's night scene, which was teeming with young people like herself, tourists from Europe and America, all looking for a good time in the nightclubs. For the first time in her life she saw a lot of Indians—families walking together along Kenyatta Avenue, Mama Ngina Street, and the other posh areas of town, going to and from the movies at the Indian and other cinema halls. She had not realized that Indians had such a social life, having associated them only with working in their shops and going to study in England and Canada, or being doctors, pharmacists and opticians. They were Kenyans but far removed from the ordinary toil of daily life. At these night clubs Kenyans of European descent also could be found, another group of people she had never really seen. What did they do for a living? Where did they live? Did they still live on the farms their grandparents had taken from Africans, urged on and supported by the British government? She wanted to learn so much about so many things!

Wanjira was fascinated by the night clubs and their revelers. But even as she enjoyed dancing she could not help feeling like an outsider. She did not belong to these places her friends were introducing her to. So many tourists! So many painted Kenyan women! So much smoke! She disliked, yet liked, these nightclubs. Girls in secondary school had spoken of them—Club 1900, Star Light, Florida, and others—in awed voices. "We were at 1900, you see," they might say, "When who showed up but So and So." So and So would be well a known boy from some of the high cost schools of the city, Lenana, or Nairobi School, and this boy was supposed to be *the* boy of the year, the one so very many girls wanted. Now Wanjira felt upset when she saw Kenyan women with tourists. She disliked the way most of these women were handled by these strange looking men, and the way the women were handling the men. The men touched the women in bold, suggestive, ways, and the women appeared to like being touched, but their smiles seemed cold, forced. Once Wanjira looked directly into one of these women's eyes and was surprised to see the young girl's curl of the lips, an invitation to Wanjira to mind her own business. She was young, a girl who should still be in secondary school. Wanjira felt somewhat confused by her own feelings—she really had not meant to stare, or show disapproval, but she clearly had, and naturally the other woman did not like it. And yet she had meant to communicate something to the girl, but what? And why should she worry about this girl? She could take care of herself. This was Nairobi, not boarding school. One evening Wangu said to her, "Wanjira, stop being so judgmental. People just want to enjoy themselves." Wanjira had felt mortified.

Her social life picked up, what with all the new people she was meeting through Wangu and her other friends. She discovered that Nairobi's many bands could keep her and her friends quite busy on Friday and Saturday nights, and that she could remain on the dance floor for three to four hours seemingly without exhaustion. The music got into her heart and as she swayed this and that way wonderful feelings of lightness and strength and utter loveliness with everything and everyone would settle into her being, and she wanted to never stop but to dance all night long in the company of her friends, her Fanta or Ginger Ale the only fuel to keep her going. *Pamela ooh Mama, Pamela ooooh!* The song would send her to the dance floor the moment it started.

Umeonyesha juhudi kubwa o!
Kwa kumaliza masomo yako o!
Bila ya matatizo Pamela o!
Jambo la muhimu
Nakuomba Mama we
Twende kwa Wazazi nyumbani
Pamela mama o!

Pamela my darling
Your hard work has borne fruit
You have honored your parents
By completing your schooling
With no problems, dear Pamela
My dear let's now go see your parents
my darling Pamela!

At times it was Tanzania's Mbaraka Mwinshehe who sent her mind reeling and body moving with his guitar work and lyrics calling on the youth of Africa:

E Vijana, wa Africa
Tuzilinde nchi zetu
Na mapinduzi ya Africa
Vijana ndio roho ya Africa
Vijana ndio ngao ya Africa…

O youth of Africa
Let us defend our nations
With our African revolution
The youth are the spirit of Africa
The youth are the shield and defenders
Of Africa…

And who could remain seated when the bands started on *Sina Makosa*? The song electrified the dance hall and everyone, everyone, got up to dance. The warm up-would take about five minutes and the dancers would move, slowly, waiting, and then the words would come, and people would join in:

Hasira za nini wee bwana?
Wataka kuniua bure Baba
Yule si wako
Na mi si wangu
Chuki ya nini kati yangu mimi na wewe?
Wako hayuko
Wangu hayuko
Chuki ya nini kati yangu mimi na wewe?

Never mind the words, at least Wanjira and her friends did not stop to be critical of the song in any way, for the words were on everyone's lips:

What wrong have I done, my friend?
Why do you want to kill me for nothing?
She is not yours
And she's not mine…
Your woman is at home
So is mine
Why should we then fight, my friend?

At some point the guitar and horn would moan, each in its special language, and the drum would pound, and the people on the floor, no longer singing, their eyes closed, mouths slightly open, concentrated on the movements of their waists, hands, arms, and legs. Everyone responded to the instruments' commands, but if you looked at the dancers closely you could see that no-one did the same thing with his or her neighbor. The subtlety of each move was determined by the dancer's private communication with the instruments and the band members whose hands and fingers did the commanding. And the beauty of all this was that one did not need a partner to dance: this music did not ask you to come to Club 1900 or Starlight or wherever else with a special boyfriend or girlfriend. You could come alone, or with a group of friends, and go home having had a wonderful time. Sometimes the dancers, now completely lost to the music, gyrated and moved fast, or slowly, depending on their feelings, and some brought their swinging waists and bottoms slowly and methodically all the way down to the floor and then, still slowly and methodically, up, swaying this and that way, and might repeat the process for as long as their thighs could take it. No one spoke; all focus was on the body's moves, and all the while people emitted small grunts and sighs and exclamations of delight, releasing, at times, small, sharp, hisses from their mouths as they swished at the air with their hands and moved their arms this and that way. Only when the singer came back on, after five or so minutes of this intense dancing, and repeated his firm, yet, pleading, assertion, "*Sina makosa e bwana*," did the dancers emerge from their trance, and smile, or laugh, or clap their hands, wipe the sweat off their faces, and move to their tables to sip their Tuskers, Baby Chams, Martinis or soft drinks. Then they might sit, to rest a while before the next song, or return to the dancing area, released, happy with themselves and the world.

Weekdays provided a different opportunity for Wanjira to take in her surroundings. As she waited for an afternoon lecture or tutorial she would go to the university cafeteria, where a steady stream of students, university officials, and lecturers came in for coffee, lunch, or simply to read. She loved the buzz of the place: conversation, an occasional loud greeting, laughter, and always, the various styles the women had. She always watched the women, admiring their fresh looks, the way their bodies moved, some haughty, others shy, some with strange expressions on their faces, as though they were engaged in a tussle with something inside of them. She liked seeing groups of women come in, engaged in lively conversation, and envied them for their sense of confidence and seeming self-satisfaction. These women were loud, and seemed belligerent. Rumour about one such group had it that they were all into sugar daddies. Wangu had ferreted out some information from one of them, a family friend, and the woman had confided that she only liked older men because they could "show and give her a lot." Wanjira noted hairdos, trouser styles, blouses, dresses, sometimes making a note to have such and such a dress style of her own. Wangu had already introduced her to a very fine tailor in Kariakor, and her next door neighbor at the Box had promised to introduce her to her Goan tailor on Biashara Street who could reportedly make any style, and did such a fine finish that one might suspect the clothes were from Deacons, or even London. He charged a lot, but Wanjira had plans to take him some *Kitenge* material she had bought recently. The woman who sold it in the Box had a supplier from West Africa whose materials were beginning to attract the attention of many women in Nairobi. She planned to have a very well tailored short sleeve dress with a short jacket to match. All over the university women were experimenting with different clothes styles. Many wore blue jeans and light tops, often sleeveless. Others wore skirts, different coloured trousers, or dresses. They were like flowers in a field; red, white, blue, orange, burgundy, green, purple, lavender. They called attention to themselves, each one beautiful, unique. Wanjira was eager to wear fine things herself, and seemed completely biased toward the so-called African style. She found it more beautiful than anything else, and in any case *Kitenge* was a whole lot cheaper than some of the other fabrics. One had to be practical, after all. University had turned out to be just like her brother had said it would be: a place to meet as many people as possible, an opportunity to widen one's circle of friendships, a time to size up, and find a place within, one's generation.

CHAPTER SIX

Wanjira came to love her dance outings with friends on Saturday nights, but always took care to return to the Box no later than one o'clock because she needed to wake up ready for mass on Sunday mornings. Many of her friends also went to church, some to St. Andrews, right next to the Box, and others to different churches in the city. She had become quite involved in the St. Paul's church choir, which met an hour before mass to practice the day's program. She liked the men and women she had met there. The Chaplain at St. Paul's was a fascinating priest from Holland who spoke of peace, justice, and, always, about the poor of the land. Why were so many so poor in a land that could produce plenty? What were the responsibilities of individuals and governments to each other, and to all members of society? Jesus' commandment that we love one another was a practical idea. It was a revolutionary idea. It was the way to a just and fair society. The priest, in heavily accented English, would challenge the students to live up to the Gospel of Christ. "You have heard the words of John the Baptist: He has sent you the good news," he would announce to the Church, and the choir would sing:

God's spirit speaks in my heart
He has called me and set me apart
This is what I have to do:
He sent me to bring the good news to the poor
tell prisoners that they are prisoners no more
tell blind people that they can see
and set the downtrodden free
and go tell everyone the news that
the kingdom of God has come

Wanjira would sing along with other members of the choir, her heart pounding, her spirit soaring at the beauty of the voices around her and the comradeship of her peers. She felt chosen, special, and the priests' words tugged at some place within her. "You are special members of this society; the government is investing in you so that you can help lead the way. Your skills and talents are needed to advance society's well-being; use them wisely; learn all you can; help build God's kingdom in everyone's life." A challenge, a message to carry her through the week. But at times she wondered: "But what will I do? What can I do to bring this kingdom about?" She would feel bewildered, uncomfortable. Then she would remember her high school headmistress, Sister Benedict, and of the Bible study classes she had taught the girls. She had said, "The greatest commandment of all in the Christian faith is 'love one another.' It is our school motto, *God is Love.* If you can try to live according to this commandment you will be alright, and everyone around you also will be. It is the essence of Christianity. It is a very difficult commandment to fulfill. But we must all keep trying. All our lives."

In those lessons Wanjira would think of the girls she did not like very much, the ones she felt competitive with, and those she disapproved of. She would promise herself to try to like them, wondering if she could ever love them. Love was a strong word. The more she thought about it the more she realized how important the commandment was. It called for *a forever kind of thing,* a daily struggle, a constant search of conscience and an attempt to do the right thing. Sometimes while saying her prayers in the convent chapel after lunch, she would feel cheekiness come over her and she would tell Jesus, "But you know it is tough! You're expecting too much. I just can't like these girls. You made me this way...so you just have to bear with me." And then she would smile to herself, and feel good for most of the day. She felt she had been honest with Jesus, at least, and felt free to think of other things for the rest of the day.

But all that was in the past, in her days as a teenager. Now she was older, a university student, a young woman facing many new things, encountering new ideas, and meeting new people. She had, however, never forgotten those impressionable years of her life in secondary school.

Wanjira began to look at the streets of Nairobi intently, not quite sure what she was looking for. She felt good living in the famous city which she had first heard her father refer to as "Nyairobi" or "Gicuka," years earlier. Then it had seemed a place of wonder, adventure, and mystery. Through whispers she had learned that some people went to that city and got swallowed up by its ways. A much older female cousin of hers was said to have been thus swallowed up, as had one of her uncles. These relatives had simply vanished. Nobody ever saw them again, and it was assumed, after many years, that they had died. "Like dogs," her aunt once said, sadly. "No-one to bury my brother, and my niece!' She had then said, in a sad, yet firm, voice, "Nyairobi will destroy you. That's what it does to people. Its a big, bad, place."

Now Wanjira was in the big, bad, place, and excited to be living in it. She wanted to learn as much as possible about the city. She memorized names of shops, tea houses, and buildings. "*Jiburudishe Bar and Restaurant,*" "*Happiness Tea Shop,*" *Welcome Bar and Lodging," Uhuru House," "Kenya Cafe."* She studied people's faces, wondering about them. Who were they? Where were they going? On Koinange Street she thought she could tell who was from Campus, as many called the university; the village, or had a posh job in town. Students had a particular look. One could tell they were university students from the way they dressed: Short sleeved shirts on guys, T-shirts, blue jeans, Khaki trousers. The women had more variety, but she could still guess who was a student and who was an employee in a city firm.

A lot of people converged at the City Market at lunch time. Stall owners did their best to attract buyers to their goods, shouting this and that and sometimes even physically leading people to their particular stalls.

"Mama, this way, this way. *Mboga mzuri kabisa! Si unaona hii Mama? sema bei.* Look at this beauty of a cabbage! Name your price, Mama. I am giving it to you for free, really, Mama." The customer would name a price.

"Haai! Mama! You are killing me!" You might think the seller had been pierced with a sharp object right in his heart; such was the dramatic way he pressed his hand to the left side of his chest as he responded to his customer.

"But *you* are the person killing me! *Wanitesa* wee! You and your terrible prices. How do you expect me to feed the family at this rate?"

Smiles, frowns, more smiles. Customer and seller knew the appropriate facial expressions—of sorrow and pain, mostly, at the inevitable mention of how hard one was "squeezing" the other.

"Haa! Mama—see this? See all these fruits and vegetables? I tell you, the farmers are the ones killing us! You can't believe what we must pay them! Its a scandal! No-one can make a living in Kenya these days. Its terrible! Really terrible!

Each side would make the necessary hissing or *tss tss* sounds, as appropriate, the customer all the while picking and choosing whatever she needed for her basket. It was all market talk, and everyone knew how to talk this special language and delight in it, otherwise what was the point of going to the market? If one did not know how to bargain, and to exchange these bits of information that superficially, yet with much empathy, spoke about the shared pain of making a living, and affirmed the other's point of view even when totally opposed to it, half the pleasure of going to the market would be lost. Bargaining was essential to a satisfactory visit to the market, or to certain shops where prices were negotiable. It was part of an experience most girls had learned from their mothers and older sisters. They in turn would pass it on to their children, particularly their daughters. Nairobi women from all walks of life knew how to strike a good bargain at the market, or in Indian shops, for in these places the best price was the one with which each party finally agreed to. Such agreement was arrived at when one party made a concession, all the time reminding the other that the next time it would not be this easy, after which pleasant good-byes and promises to see each other soon were made.

As a child Wanjira had observed, sometimes with alarm, what seemed like endless arguments between her mother and the Indian shopkeeper in Thika from whom she bought the family's monthly supply of cooking oil, *Chapati Unga* flour, soap, milking supplies, cow-salt, and paraphernalia such as rat traps, glass replacements for the family kerosene lamps, the occasional addition to the pots and pans, plates and spoons, matchsticks—he seemed to stock anything her mother might need, including dress-making material. The two would bargain at length, each telling the other of the problems they were forced to face by the poor economy, now being excercebated by the other's unreasonable demands.

"*Muhindi,*" Indian man, her mother would say, "*Fanya bei.* Give me a price I can live with. *Unaona huyu mtoto?*" Do you see this child? Wanjira would cringe at the mention, at the possibility, that she was now part of the haggling.

"See her? There are others, and each must eat. And what about school? They must go to school. Uniforms, books, building fund. You want to kill me, I see. You must give me a good price!"

The shopkeeper would respond with a list of his own troubles. *"Mama taka ua mimi?* You want to kill me Mama? You should know the cost of buying and transporting these goods from Nairobi or Mombasa. Its terrible! And my children too must go to school.

Throughout his, and her, complaints, Wanjira's mother would be checking out this or that dress material, rubbing a segment of the cloth between her thumb and index finger to ascertain its value as a desirable type of cotton, to be sure it did not have too much starch on it; to be sure she liked the colour. Her mother had excellent taste, Wanjira thought as a young girl, and always chose beautiful fabrics for the clothes that were eventually made by Baba Akinyi, the best tailor at Thika City Market, and at whose stall her mother stopped by almost every month to deliver new material for a dress for herself or for any of her daughters, or to pick up the one she had left the previous month.

When she was satisfied with a particular cloth at the Indian shop her mother would say, "*Ai, Muhindi,* you have squeezed me a lot already. See? See? She would say, as she brought out the money from her handbag, or sometimes from somewhere inside her brassiere, having perused her list one last time and ticked off all she had come to buy. "*Haidhuru*...alright," and there would be smiles and good-byes, and promises to see each other at the end of next month. The shopkeeper would then ask one of his workers to escort Wanjira and Njahira to the bus stop, and the man would place everything in the big two-wheeled wooden cart, and off they would go.

Wanjira always wondered why her mother and other women called the Indian shopkeepers, *Muhindi.* Indian. The Indian men didn't say, *Mwafrika,* African. It was something Wanjira did not understand but never asked about. It was just the way it was. "*Muhindi, Muhindi.*" and "Mama, Mama." Each one seemed to understand the other's position and did not put up a quarrel.

After they had stored everything at another store—this time where her mother bought different kinds of flour—*Muhia, Ugimbi, Mwere,* all this for the family breakfasts, mother and daughter would take off for the city market, about a mile away, leaving all their purchases under the care of Mama Muiru, the shop owner. She and Wanjira's mother were old friends, and Wanjira's mother was one of Mama Muiru's most reliable customers.

At Baba Akinyi's there was no hard bargaining, just a pleasant exchange of greetings and news of each other's family. Then came the trying on of new clothes, and comments about their fit, and discussions about whether the new skirt or dress or blouse should be left behind for this or that adjustment, a tuck here or there, a lowering of the hemline? And there was taking of new measurements for the clothes to be tailored that month, and heartfelt good-byes and messages of greetings to each other's families. But the best thing about getting to Baba Akinyi's stall was that as soon as they sat down he would send his young assistant to the nearby *Happiness Bar and Hotel* to buy his customers some tea and *Mandazi.* To young Wanjira this was a treat like no other, and it made her day. "What a pleasant man Baba Akinyi is," she would think.

After Baba Akinyi's, Wanjira and Njahira would go to another part of the market where her mother bought a month's supply of *Pishuri* rice, *Ndengu, Njahi* and any other type of bean that took her fancy. Sometimes it was the beautiful red type known as *Wairimu,* or the light whitish brown black-eyed *Njugu,* which grew in the dry, arid, lands of Ukambani. Although Wanjira's mother grew her own beans, she liked variety in the family meals, for beans were part of the daily diet. Luckily she did not have to buy maize, for the family grew more than enough to last the season. At Thika market Wanjira's mother bought a few other extra treats for the family: fancy brown bread from the bakery, and scones and cinnamon spiced *Mahamri* and dates from the Arab man's stall. Wanjira smiled at the thought of the excitement from the younger children when these treats reached home, and was very pleased with her mother for her taste in nice things the children could enjoy once a month.

These trips to Thika helped Wanjira realize the importance of choosing good and reliable providers of goods and services—The Indian man, Baba Akinyi, Mama Muiru, or the market women at Ngumo Market near the family home, where she and her younger sister went to buy fruits and vegetables every Tuesday and Saturday afternoons. In all the markets she had ever been to she had realized that buyer and seller shared an understanding, and that the sellers, especially, knew the value of attracting new customers, which made them use every possible method they knew of to bring in new business.

Now, years later, at City Market, she noticed how the sellers smiled, praised their products, and guaranteed satisfaction and happiness to their customers. It was hard to resist the sellers' entreaties, and a lot of wooing and resisting and still more wooing went on, with the overwhelmed and flattered customer finally giving in, to the consternation of the neighbor who had sold much to her just the other day. Wanjira smiled every time she witnessed the goings on at City Market. She loved the place—the fresh fruits and vegetables, the fish, chicken and other meats, and the multi-coloured baskets and other decorative crafts hanging in special sections of the market. She would buy a bunch of bananas and a few mangoes and oranges for her fruit bowl in the residence halls. It was all she needed since the residence hall cafeteria had as much food as anyone needed.

At lunch time most of the young women at the City Market ate generous helpings of mixed fruit salad made of pineapple, banana, papaw, and passion fruit. It was healthy to eat lots of fruit and to watch one's figure as well. On a few occasions Wanjira and Ng'endo, her former high school classmate, now an official at a bank in town, met at the market for a fruit lunch, something each enjoyed. There was no place to sit down but all the women gathered around the stalls that sold fruit salad appeared not to mind. They would finish their lunch and head out to window-shop, or buy a needed item, and then head back to their offices. Others, those with children and relatives to feed at home, finished their lunch and then visited various stalls, where they bought vegetables and fruit to take home later in the evening. They carried their purchases in plastic bags or in sturdy sisal bags, *ciondo*, which were perfect for holding many things a woman might need, or buy, in the course of an ordinary day.

On Kenyatta Avenue Wanjira imagined that the people she saw were on their way to hospital, or headed to Dagoretti, Ngong, and Kawangware areas. Older people especially had to be headed to Kenyatta Hospital, accompanied by a city-looking son or daughter. Most of the older people wore old clothes that often did not fit right. The clothes were either too tight, or were faded in parts, and had patches in several places. Some might be in brand new clothes, still stiff with yet-to-be washed out starch, which their children must have bought only recently, perhaps in preparation for this city trip. Children were hardly seen in this area. The city center belonged to the young hopeful or the successful middle-aged. Others were mere passersby. *Eehitukiri. Agendi.* Only if one walked into Uhuru Park did one see children in the afternoon, and these were *parking boys*, street children from Mathare and other growing Nairobi slums, young children who were out of school and out of luck. These children, some on the way to manhood already, could also be seen at night, and they were a special terror to university women, pelting them with stones and calling out, *Malaya*, Prostitutes, in loud voices.

Koinange. Biashara. Haile Selassie. Kenyatta Avenue. Each street had its own look and feel; its special character. Wanjira had come to love Biashara Street with its variety of dress making materials. Kenyatta Avenue was posh, out of reach for many. You needed money to enter those big-time Indian shops with their expensive things. Any newcomer to Nairobi immediately understood that certain places were out of bounds. No one would say to you, "Keep Off" or "Stay away," but the price tags on the clothes and shoes and other things one saw in certain places spoke louder than any harsh words. Wanjira felt she could not enter these shops for there was no point in longing for that which was impossible to attain. How could one possibly afford a watch that cost two thousand shillings? Or a tie that cost one thousand shillings? Or cuff links that went for five thousand shillings? These were ridiculous prices. One could pay for two years of secondary school in a high cost school for the price of these cuff links. Clearly there were people in this city with a lot of money, Wanjira thought. She felt a certain kind of awe mingled with disgust and envy. Who were these rich ones?

As she walked the streets Wanjira would try to imagine the many kinds of people who inhabited this city that had now become her home. She felt she was becoming a part of the city, but in her mind her home was Ngumo, where her parents and younger siblings lived. Ngumo was her real home, "Home

Home," or "Home Squared," as everyone she knew called his or her original birth place, or the birth place of his or her parents. Home squared. But Nairobi too had people who called it home, and they came from all over the country. Others came from India or England. She thought of the colonial days, and of the city's founding. She had read in history books that Nairobi evolved from a small stopping place during the building of the Kenya-Uganda railway before becoming this sprawling place that had now become an internationally known city with tall buildings and a population that was growing rapidly by the day. Nairobi: City in the Sun. Everyone knew about its founding all those years back, about its meaning: place of cool waters, in *Maa,* the language of the Maasai. In those long ago days Maasai and Gikuyu people had exclusive right of abode in the area, but after the arrival of *Euros,* as her Form Two History classmates called Europeans, and the horrible settlers who took all the land, that riff raff from England, losers and adventurers who longed to fashion themselves into aristocrats in East Africa, knowing full well no-one would mistake them of being *that* in their own country, the original owners could enter Nairobi only by permit. History. In her secondary school some of the girls had scratched Lord Delamare's eyes out of the page, leaving little holes, and had drawn moustaches on any European woman's mouth. This was after they learned of Lord Delamare's role in pushing settler rights and of his expansionist vision of a Kenya that was owned and ruled by Europeans. Imagine that! How could such people dare think they could own the land of Kenyans? The scratching and moustaching had begun with a few girls, but as soon as others learned about it, all the history books were brought out and the relevant eyes and mouths dealt with. Everyone had laughed, but they had had to make sure the nuns did not get wind of it. This was the girls' own little revenge. It would be discovered, for sure, but that would be later, and besides no-one would snitch. But the story of European settlement of Kenya, and the establishment of Kenya as Britain's prize colony, had all sounded remote, too far in the past. History. But now! Now she was living in Nairobi, and like her brother, Kairu, and her older cousins, would most likely settle in the city on completing university. She would join all the others. The future leaders had come to Nairobi.

It was common for women from the Box to visit the men's halls during the evening, to relax, and to get into friendly discussions, especially about the never-ending story of corruption in the country. Wanjira never stopped marveling at the new information she was learning about who owned what and where, and of the many deals being made all over the country to acquire land, buildings, and contracts of all kinds. These evenings left her wondering how it was possible for her to have known so little about these matters. She felt like a young child learning the ABCs of life in modern Kenya as lived by a select few. She was especially shocked to learn that the current coffee boom had so enriched some people, a good number of them parents of some of her classmates, that they were literally swimming in cash. That was how they could afford Range Rovers, Mercedes Benzes, and all other kinds of things. Some of these rich men and women could fly to London for a weekend, to shop, or to attend to some unnamed "business," their young girlfriends, their *tucau*, their little calves, in tow. They would leave on Thursday night, arrive in London on Friday morning, shop all day Saturday, go to a pub somewhere in London, feel very important as a result, and board a flight on Sunday evening that would return them to their wives, children, and offices on Monday morning. Some rich wives also went to London and returned with a lot of clothes and shoes, which they would sell from their own homes or in their boutiques in town.

One evening Wangu invited Wanjira to the home of one such rich woman where many other women had gathered to try on the "London Look" they were so fond of and eager to acquire. Wanjira was amused to hear the conversation between the older woman and some of her friends who had also been through "Hiithiru" Airport and spoke proudly of "Pikandiri" Square and other such places in London. They felt very important as they recalled their visits to the famous city, and Wanjira marveled at the competitiveness in their talk, and at the realization that these women had more money than she could have imagined possible. How can people own so much, she wondered. What will they do with all this money? Do they want to own the whole country, then? What about the rest of us? What will be left? She hoped she wasn't showing all the agitation she felt in her heart.

Sometimes the young men and women would walk down to Snow-Cream, treat themselves to ice cream, or go to town if they had money to go to the movies, or to a disco. Wanjira loved these evenings. For the first time in her life she was mingling with men other than her brothers, cousins, or their friends. These were her very own friends she met on campus, or in the residence halls. She liked being on neutral ground with them, not being anyone's girlfriend. And yet she was attracted to many of the young men she was meeting. What an exciting feeling! She liked everyone, but no-one in particular. Everyone had his strengths. *Ciumbe cia Ngai!* All these creations of the almighty are just too much! She would think to herself. There was Samuel, for starters. He was bright, articulate, and handsome. Her first friend on campus. Then there was Mungai, his friend, a student of commerce and a real heart throb, according to Wangu, who claimed to have a crush on him and so

Wanjira knew he was out of bounds. Even though Wangu was dating a man outside campus Wanjira still observed this important rule of friendship. In any case they soon learned he had a girlfriend working at a bank in town. And Fred Mambo. Heavens! Fred, whom everyone called by his two names, was some *mambo mazuri* indeed. What a name, Wanjira thought, when they first were introduced. She had laughed and said, "And what is this you have in store for us?" Let's hope its some *mambo mazuri!"* She'd felt brazen teasing a stranger, but he seemed to like it, and so did she. He had smiled, and said, "Are you going to tease me all evening then? I'll have to ask my old man to change this name…it causes me too much trouble everywhere I go." He sounded so calm, saying this, as if he'd said it many times before. But he sounded pleased.

Talking with her friends at the Box Wanjira learned that many women were actively "Husband-Hunting." It was said, however, that the men were only "Girlfriend Hunting." One evening, as Wanjira and three other women were visiting Wangu's room, Wangu declared, to much merriment by her listeners, that university men were just too young and too poor to think of marriage, so good riddance! A woman anxious for that ring had better look outside the university gates, like herself, who had what she called a "lively interest" in a man with a good position as a bank manager, who had graduated from the university four years earlier. "A man with good prospects, to sum it up, ladies," she told the now guffawing group. But marriage should also wait for a woman to finish university, she said, mincing no words about Jessie and others like her at the university, married, pregnant, or nursing babies while holding their books at the same time. "Fools," she called them. "Where's the rush, girls?" she asked the room, now full of laughter. "What about the pill? Available right here at the university—free of charge! Don't these women know anything?" Wanjira was impressed by just how much Wangu seemed to know. She longed to be as sophisticated.

CHAPTER SEVEN

One evening Wanjira accompanied Wangu and Sarah, a fellow hall mate, to the Serena Hotel, where Wangu's banker friend, Mwangi, treated them to a wonderful dinner. Wanjira was not used to eating out, and in such luxury, but Wangu and Sarah seemed all too used to this. They seemed to be in their element. Mwangi teased the women, calling them "schoolgirls," and everyone laughed, but soon he started making sly comments to Wanjira, the gist of which was that it was clear that she had not yet "matured," was still "green," and "needed to begin to taste of the fruit of life." Wanjira was astounded by the fact that Mwangi could feel so free to say such things after meeting her for the very first time only that very day, and retorted that she had enough teachers at the university and did not need an extra one. He laughed, dismissively, and said, "Just remember that they can't teach you everything on campus…you must learn from *dunia* as well," to which she replied, "Thanks but no thanks," to everyone's amusement. She felt a dislike for this man begin to grow in her, and was both embarrassed and irritated that her friends thought him funny. Imagine that! They were in cahoots with Mwangi. Wanjira was fuming inside.

Sarah and Wangu drank beer after beer, and as the evening progressed they appeared giddy, happy. They laughed easily, as did Mwangi. Wanjira longed to return to her room and at about ten O'clock she excused herself, thanked Mwangi for dinner, and walked quickly back to the Box, feeling lucky they had not gone to some far-out place, for surely she would have been stuck. There were many students walking up and down University Road, and she felt grateful for their presence. In her mind she made a note to avoid going out with Wangu and Sarah in the future.

It had not taken long for Wanjira, that first month of beginning university, to realize that many women at the Box drank beer and other alcoholic drinks. She had been surprised. "Another fact of *Chuo Kikuu*," she had thought. As the weeks progressed, and she met more and more people, she understood that some women at the Box drank alcohol to assert themselves, to say, "Here I am, and here's my Tusker. I like it. If you don't, you know where to go." These women enjoyed the challenge of partaking in a habit generally assumed to be out of bounds for women. Others, once used to it, simply loved beer, wine, or hard liquor, and slowly became addicted to these drinks. They loved the light-headedness of insobriety, the letting down of their guard, and the more they drank alcohol the more quickly their bodies learned to need it. When she had first seen Wangu having a beer in her room, one evening a few months earlier, Wanjira had expressed surprise, which was much laughed off by the other woman.

"Oh, Wanjira, come off it!" Wangu had a wide smile on her face. She had seen the look of surprise on Wanjira's face and was ready to tease her. "A girl can have a beer now and then, and that's alright, as long as she does her sit ups. No beer belly for me, my friend."

"How long have you been drinking?" Wanjira's voice felt shrill to her ears. In her mind only men should drink beer, and even then, only much older, men. She knew many young men who drank beer, including her older brothers and many of her cousins, and she disapproved of the habit. Too many families had been ruined by drink, she thought. But a woman drinking? Oh well, her grandmother occasionally drank some *Njohi,* on special occasions, but that was a different type of beer. Or was it? All she knew was that the older men and women she knew who drank *Njohi* seemed to mellow out, and almost all of them sang happy songs, either at the beer party, or on their way home. Those who drank Tusker and other modern drinks seemed to retreat inwards, become abusive, and, like her father, generally seemed displeased about something after taking these drinks. Or had she imagined these things?

But this Wangu also! Drinking, and so comfortably too? A strange feeling came over Wanjira as she observed the comfortable look on Wangu's face. She decided to hold her tongue, though, to say nothing, but in her mind a strong judgmental chorus was on: "Let her ruin herself if she wants to. What do I care?"

Wangu sipped once more into her Tusker Premium, and said, in a soft, almost dreamy tone, "Since Form Five. That's when I got to like beer—in the evening. You know, my own kind of a sundowner in boarding school. The *wazungu* didn't come up with that name for nothing, my friend. You sit down after classes, and relax with one. I mean a beer, or a real sundowner. I tell you, there's something very good about that. And the sun going down, the beautiful colors of the sun setting in the distance, the light in my room, and the books awaiting me in the evening. I loved it. It helped me relax. I learned to sneak some bottles into my cubicle every Saturday...a week's supply. And that was it. If anyone knew about it they didn't snitch...It could have been bad."

"They could have suspended you."

"I know. I was lucky. But you know Wanjira, some of these rules are nonsensical. What if I loved a beer or two? did that stop me from reading like crazy? I loved my books, and had some of the best results in my school, and now I'm here. *Chuo Kikuu!*"The young women laughed, loudly, but Wanjira felt uneasy. She just did not think one ought to risk so much—suspension, expulsion even, for a bottle of Tusker. A bad habit. A few girls in her school had been suspended for an entire term for sneaking in beer and a bottle of expensive whisky, gifts from a sugar daddy one of them was going out with at the time. What a scandal it had been!

"I just hate the smell. It doesn't sit well with me." Wanjira wanted to change the subject. She associated beer with everything bad she had experienced so far in life: her father's occasional bouts of drunkenness, the village drunks who stood outside the shops and shouted abuses at women passing by, the constant fear of being attacked on an evening as she hurried home from the bus stop, or from the shops, or from confession on Saturday evenings. A girl was not safe as long as drunks were about. How had Wangu escaped the fate that so haunted Wanjira's thoughts—the feeling that the world was not safe for a woman, and that therefore, a woman had to pay extra attention to her own behavior lest she invite untold problems into her life? Somehow Wangu gave the feeling of being in total command of herself, of whatever happened to her. Was it her upbringing in the city? Or what was it? Wanjira had found herself envying Wangu ever since they became friends—for her calmness, her sense of self, her apparent full satisfaction with her life, her daring ways. But drinking beer?

CHAPTER EIGHT

One evening in late September, two weeks since they had first met on their first day at university, Wanjira bumped into Samuel on his way to the tennis courts. She was on the way back to the Box after a long day on campus. They had spoken briefly and he had invited her to play tennis with him the following day. She had laughed and said, thanks, but tennis was a mystery to her and she had better not meddle in things that would only help waste his time.

"Come on, Wanjira, no-one is born with a racket in hand," Samuel said, his voice warm and encouraging. "I have a spare racket, and I want you to meet me at the courts at five tomorrow. I have reserved it and my buddy will not mind if you and I play for a while". She was about to say something but he said, "Now, now…don't let me down, Wanjira. You're booked for a lesson with me. Tomorrow. Five O'clock sharp!"

"I can see I've been ordered to court," Wanjira said, smiling, saluting

Samuel, and stamping her right foot hard on the ground. "Yes sir! I'll be there. Five O'clock!"

"You're funny," Samuel said, as he walked away. "See you tomorrow then."

She had felt embarrassed running back and forth that first lesson. She missed most of the balls Samuel sent her way, and felt rather foolish each time the ball whizzed past her. Samuel showed her once more how to hold her racket, and sent softer, shorter, balls her way. After about half an hour she felt herself enjoying the running back and forth, and she returned a few balls. She felt her confidence rising. When they stopped she marveled at how much she had sweated, and as she breathed hard she felt a strange elation come over her. It felt good to breathe this hard, to sweat, to work her muscles.

Wanjira now spent many early evenings at the tennis courts near the men's halls. She had become one of Samuel's tennis partners, and occasionally played with other students she had met at the courts. At first she had not taken up his invitation to play for fear she would be called, or considered, *Kahee* by the other players, who clearly had learned the game earlier, in their high schools, perhaps even in primary school. They would realize immediately that she was not in their league, she feared. A part of her felt that tennis, field hockey, rugby, badminton, and other such sports were for those who had gone to high cost schools all their lives, people who had learned *Wazungu* ways early in life, and not for the likes of her, girls from the village, *Ushaguu*. In her A-level program at the Advanced Preparatory she had known girls who routinely called others *Kahee* or *Ushaguu,* sometimes to their very faces without blinking an eye.

Wanjira thought to be called these names would be the ultimate insult, and yet she found herself intrigued by the fact that she was now conscious of labels that had previously only amused, rather than annoyed, her. In secondary school and during her A-level program she had been convinced that the arrogant girls from the city were foolish, especially those who were poor, or just average, students. In her school, brains mattered, and while it was true many town girls, the *Tauus*, were quite bright, so were the *Ushaguus,* and these daughters of village teachers, low-level government officers and peasant farmers often did the best in O and A level exams. It shows you that what counts is opportunity, Wanjira thought after her O-levels, because boarding school gave everyone an equal chance to study in well lit rooms, eat regular meals, sleep in clean beds, and bathe daily in clean, ever flowing water that did not have to be fetched from the river. But in spite of her confidence as a student, Wanjira—and many other girls from the villages and rural areas of Kenya—had an inferiority complex when it came to some *Tauu* ways such as playing tennis and other fancy sports.

One early evening in late October Wanjira and Samuel had a game that made her realize just how much she had come to enjoy tennis. She was sweating away, and feeling particularly competitive, wanting to beat her coach in at least one set, but to no avail. All the same she had a wonderful time, and before she knew it the sun began to set in the distance. Looking over, beyond the halls of residence to the small valley below the tennis courts, Wanjira realized how beautiful the evening was. A strong emotion came over her, perhaps from the excitement of physical exercise, the elation of playing with Samuel, and the wonder of it all that she, Wanjira, was getting to play tennis. Samuel had shown so much faith in her! Perhaps it was all this that sent her heart pounding. Everything seemed lovely, wondrous. A thought planted itself in her mind that she was a lucky woman, that hers was the very best place God ever created. To be a university woman, to be meeting so many new and bright people, to be one of the chosen few, for that was what being at the university really meant. To have all her expenses met, to have a safe, clean place to live in...all because she had been blessed with an ability to do her lessons well, because she had been born into a family that could send her to school, and ensure her continued success! Wanjira suddenly felt weak with emotion. A feeling of gratitude filled her heart. This, then, must be the moment her headmistress had once talked about. Sister Benedict had said that each of us will hear the voice of God in strange moments, when we least expect it. She had urged the girls to feel and experience the power of God in the trees, in the beautiful flowers resplendent in the midday sun, in the heady, excited moments of a netball game well played, in the voices of their sisters and brothers, in the daily rhythms of work in their homes. She had said this voice might come after a homework exercise done to the fullest of one's ability, in a quiet moment in the bathroom. "God speaks to us in different ways. Its up to the individual to allow the lesson of that moment to lodge in the heart. After that no-one can tell you what that lesson is. Only you will know it. You will be enlightened in a new way. You will feel the spirit, God's special gift. A reminder that he's always in your heart." These words had sent a chill down Wanjira's spine when she first heard them. In them she heard an invitation, an admonition, a call. But to what, and about what? She had had no idea then. But the words had spoken of freedom. Of revelling in one's thoughts, independence of mind and of interpretation of things read and heard. How joyful it was to learn that one had the right to interpret one's own feelings and reactions about things, to decide for oneself how to feel! There were so many people everywhere telling one how to act, to think, to do things. Parents, teachers, older men and women everywhere, who wielded authority on the roadways and byways of the villages. It was good to respect everyone, yes, but one could never utter a contrary thought without being jumped upon. And yet...these same authority figures expected one to take control of the home when they were not around, of other people's children when you were walking by, so that you had to conduct yourself in ways that brought honor and respect to yourself and your family, and in school you had to conduct yourself in ways that showed you were well brought up, and could respect teachers, prefects, the matron, the school secretary, the cooks, the gardeners. So many layers of authority. But Sister Benedict was saying: you were free. In what really mattered. Your mind. Your heart.

Wanjira learned to trust her instincts during her high school years. She felt happy and satisfied in a way she might find hard to describe to anyone. This feeling had helped her cope with the sadness caused in her home by her father's all-too frequent bouts of drunkenness. During such times Kamau, her father, would shout, belittle her mother, and create tension and anger in Kairu, her brother, herself, and the younger children. Njahira, their mother, would admonish him and strongly voice her anger that a grown man could deliberately cause his family so many problems simply because he could not control his drink. Wanjira hated these outbursts and would feel herself cringe, wanting to vanish into thin air, whenever these troubles arose, which was often during her teenage years. But one day she had felt herself come to a realization that helped her cope with her father's alcoholism. "He has chosen his ways," she found herself thinking one Saturday evening when she was in From Three, as she watched her father staggering into the house, and as she heard his litany of the angry words he spoke during his drunken states, "And I will choose mine. I will work hard in school and try to do better. I can do it."

From that day on Wanjira would look at her mother's sad and angry face whenever her father arrived home drunk, and think, "I will not live with a drunk when I'm out of this house!" I hope I meet a man who does not drink too much. I am his daughter, but I am also me." She would remember her favourite lines from the song *Desiderata* which often played on the radio, and from which many of her friends quoted in letters to friends and in autograph books at the end of their O and A levels:

You are a child of the universe
No less than the trees and the stars
You have a right to be here

The words had a strangely powerful effect on Wanjira and whenever she felt sad and frustrated by the condition in her home she would repeat in her head, over and over again, "You are a child of the universe." One day, thinking about her father and mother and how things had suddenly changed in her family when her father began drinking heavily it occurred to her that he too was a child of the universe. She sat, almost transfixed in her seat, and thought hard about something, only she was not quite sure about what this something was. When she finally rose from her seat she felt as if a heavy burden had been lifted from her. She felt light. Free. From that day onward Wanjira did not feel angry about her father. Instead she began to pity him. She wondered what frustrated him so much that it made him drink more than was respectable; for he was a respectable and respectful man, and therefore something really terrible must have happened to him to make him a drunk. Maybe it had something to do with that terrible war he had fought in. That experience might have something to do with her father's heavy drinking, or could it be something else? Kairu had told her that some people were just prone to addiction, no matter what. "Their bodies, Dada," he had said. "Once the fermented brew touches their lips they are gone." These thoughts and feelings about her father and his life before his children were born had seemed to intensify shortly before she entered university.

Now, as she gathered her things this early evening she felt simply wonderful, excited in a totally new way. She looked at Samuel, and a strong feeling toward him filled her heart, which now made a little jump, as though it had truly only just now seen him for the first time. "Thanks, Samuel," she said, shyly. "Thank you for everything." Samuel noted her somewhat subdued manner, and said, "Don't mention it, Wanji." He and a few others at the university called her by the shortened version of her name. "Wanji, You're good, you know that? See what I meant? There's an athlete inside of you waiting to be freed." They laughed, and Wanjira said, "How I wish!"

After a few weeks of practicing every other day Wanjira was confident enough to play a game with Samuel and two of his friends, and once she played with Josephine, a second year student of Medicine she met at the courts. She was a friend of Samuel and his tennis buddies. Josephine obviously knew the game, so hard and confidently did she return the balls. Wanjira found it exhilarating to play doubles, and she and Josephine agreed to play again. "I have so much to read sometimes I think I can't bear it, but tennis puts me in a totally different mood," Josephine said. I swim in the morning sometimes, but I also want to keep up with tennis. I'm glad you like the game, and yes, let's play again."

Wanjira immediately liked this woman. Besides Wahito and two of her medical school classmates she did not know many women from the Chiromo campus. It was good to make a new acquaintance from that campus.

One Wednesday evening Wanjira and Josephine played doubles with Samuel and his friend Bob. It was an enjoyable game and despite losing to the men Wanjira felt happy.

"You're quite the teacher, Samuel, do you know that? You should open a tennis coaching business. I'll recommend you highly." Wanjira and Josephine laughed loudly, as did Samuel.

"OK ladies. Send some clients my way, and Sam's Coaching Service is born! You'll be my partners."

They were now out of the courts. Josephine and Bob said good-bye and hurried off to complete their evening tasks. Josephine had a meeting to attend at Chiromo, and Bob had a meeting with a friend in town. Wanjira and

Samuel walked slowly, rackets in hand. Any observer would have noticed Wanjira's strong legs, and how especially beautiful she looked in her white shorts, which hugged and showed off the round hips her friends in secondary school claimed were just too sexy for words. The same observer would have noted the very well built man with her, also wearing white shorts, his strong back, legs, and carriage, all of which implied a self-possessed presence. Wanjira and Samuel made a handsome pair. Lately Samuel had begun to feel a strong liking for Wanjira, but he had decided to say nothing to her because it might ruin their otherwise developing friendship. And what could he have said to her, he wondered. "Wanji, I'm getting to like you a lot...would you like to go out sometime?" He had imagined taking her to a nice restaurant in town. They would have a fine meal and then go out to dance. But he had a girlfriend back in Mombasa, Rehema, a woman he had often fantasized getting married to. Things had changed fast since he came to university, however. All these beautiful women on campus were beginning to affect him, and he had found himself thinking of asking some of them to go out with him, alone, and not in the large groups he tended to go out places with. For example this Wanjira was something else altogether! He liked the way she laughed, the sound of her voice, so melodious, so interesting to listen to, and he liked what he realized was a basic honesty in her. He also admired the seriousness with which she took her studies, and noted the zest with which she had committed herself to learning to play tennis. She had laughed at herself, but he had seen that behind that laughter was true determination. He liked that in a woman. A sense of direction. He imagined her as a very successful woman down the line, and felt a longing to be her boyfriend. But what about Rehema! What a mess things could turn out to be! Rehema was a very special woman, and understood him completely. They were from the same world, the Coast, and that was important. *Tabu, Tabu*!

Samuel's thoughts were suddenly interrupted by a voice calling out, "Sam!' Hi Guys." They turned and Wanjira saw a young man who looked vaguely familiar come toward them, a big smile on his face.

"Luka!" Samuel was pleased to see the new arrival. His thoughts turned to the present, and he felt a certain gratefulness toward the young man striding toward him and Wanjira. This man, Luka, had saved him, in a way, by interrupting his impossible dreams in daylight, for now at least. He introduced Wanjira and Luka to each other, and they shook hands. "Wanjira Kamau. Luka Owuor, but call him Luka O. That's what everyone calls this fellow." The two men slapped each other on the back, and laughed.

"Pleased to meet you, Wanjira." They shook hands. "What a grip," Wanjira thought.

"Pleased to meet you, Luka. Oh, Luka O, I mustn't forget." Everyone laughed.

Samuel said, as if the situation needed explaining, "Wanjira is my tennis partner. Luka you should join us one of these days, man."

"Would love to. When do you play?"

"Mondays, Wednesdays and Fridays for me." Wanjira said. "I'm new to the game. How about you?" But before he answered Wanjira said, "Hey, were you at the podium the other day? At the Kamukunji on campus? One of the speakers?

Luka smiled. "Yes, I was. One of the troublemakers, as the guys in helmets call us." Another laugh from everyone.

"Well, its good to meet you, troublemaker," Wanjira said, a cheeky smile on her face. But don't mind those guys. We should make our views heard, right? At least you brave souls are saying things we all care about."

Thanks, Wanjira, thanks. We are just trying, just trying." Luka suddenly felt good. He liked what this woman had said. And it seemed she wanted to say more, for she had a frown on her face. She appeared to be thinking about something. He was about to speak when she said, "But really, Luka...do you think this Kamukunji idea works? I mean, is demonstrating about this thing going to accomplish anything?

"We think it will. We want the country to begin thinking about these things, and we campus people should be leading the discussion. J.M asked these questions and they killed him. We want to show them that he did not die in vain, and that we'll continue to condemn corruption in high places. Otherwise we are sunk as a nation. It must stop." Luka spoke in a clear, firm voice. He was used to explaining things to his friends, but this time he realized he wanted to create a good impression. He liked this woman's question, and the ease with which she had spoken. She interested him right away. Wanjira appeared to be pondering his statement, and Samuel also seemed lost in thought. He was the first one to speak.

"Man, these things are heavy. I think of them sometimes but I guess I'm not brave enough to join these demonstrations. I'll let you guys do it." Everyone smiled.

"We're just trying, Samuel." Wanjira noted that he had said this before, "We're just trying," He continued, "Its tough, as you say, but also interesting. Besides, we'll all have to do something, sooner or later, and everyone in this place will play a role in the second liberation struggle of Kenya. You can be sure of that." Wanjira thought he was kind. He could have challenged Samuel. The three were now at the Box, and as Wanjira said good-bye she wished she could have talked more with Luka, for he had piqued her interest.

"Bye for now," she said. "Thanks a lot Samuel, and I'm pleased to meet you, Luka O," she said, smiling. "See you around."

"Bye, Wanjira, see you soon." Both men spoke in unison. Wanjira smiled, feeling elated. What an afternoon.

The next day Wanjira was disappointed at a fine morning suddenly turned overcast. She looked out her window and noticed it had started drizzling, and felt disappointed. She had made plans to play tennis with Josephine at noon, following her morning lecture, and now feared it would be impossible to play. Just when she was getting into tennis! She had begun to really enjoy it, and did not want to interrupt the rhythm. Hoping the drizzle was a *Mahahura Iguuta*, The-lazy-bones-fright, as her mother and other women called this kind of rain, a passing shower that made lazy men and women quickly leave their weeding and hoeing and hurry home, only to be surprised by a lovely burst of sunshine five minutes later, she decided this was just a passing cloud which would soon be over, and set off for the courts. But the long rains had indeed come, a bit early, it would seem, and how! Suddenly the skies opened up, and as she hurried back towards the Box, disappointed that the rain wouldn't let up, and realizing that Josephine had not shown up, obviously being the wiser, she saw Luka hurrying towards her, a large black umbrella shielding him from the rain. She was glad to see him, and grateful for his umbrella for now the rain had begun to come down in torrents.

As they hurried to the residence hall Luka said, his voice a little loud, "Wanjira. I actually came to the courts to look for you. I first went to your room. I'd like to talk to you." He moved closer to Wanjira, making sure that she was fully covered by the umbrella, and placed his arm around her waist. Wanjira noted this, and immediately thought Luka was bold, but the rain was quite serious now, and she snuggled closer, making sure he too was under the umbrella.

"Why do you want to talk to me?" she asked him, her voice sounding much too loud to her ears. She tried to skirt a pool of water that had gathered near the entrance to the Box, and she could feel her canvas shoes getting all wet, and her bare hands as well. Luka tightened his hold on her waist, and a warm feeling coursed through her body, making her nervous all of a sudden. She did not even know this guy! Yes, she had met him the previous evening...But that was less than twenty four hours ago!

"I've thought a lot about you since yesterday," Luka said, "and I would like to get to know you better, if that's alright with you."

"Oh, really?" she did not know what else to say, and then added, quickly, for now they had reached the main door to the Box, "Why don't you come in and have some coffee? Or cocoa? At least get out of the rain." Months later he told her this was the happiest invitation he had ever had in his life.

He was a second year student of law. He was from western Kenya, near Kisumu town. Wanjira knew of Kisumu, of course, and her brother Kairu had attended Kisumu High School for his A-levels. She had not been to that part of the country yet, but would love to, someday. She told him of her family in Ngumo, and he of course had heard of the place because of the famous high school, to which, Wanjira informed him, her two older cousins had gone, and where a younger one was currently in third form. He also had not been to Ngumo, but some members of his family, his uncle and a few cousins, had attended the high school near Ngumo, and he had gone there once to visit one of the cousins. Wanjira and Luka laughed much at the discovery of all they had in common; both their mothers were primary school teachers, and their fathers were government administrators. His father had been posted to various places, including Mombasa, for five years, and that was why Luka had started primary school in Mombasa. Now his father was based in Kisumu. Her own father had had various posts, and was currently based in Kiambu Town. Each was from a large family. Luka was the fourth-born in a family of nine, and she was the second-born in a family of seven. They were both Catholics, and both had been active in the Young Christian Movement in secondary school. They went on talking and before long Wanjira and Luka felt they had known each other for ages. They did not go to supper, not wanting to leave each other's presence. He had a second cup of Nescafe, and so did she.

"Why do they call you Luka, and not Luke?" Her question was unexpected, and Luka laughed. "Oh, I like your name, I'm just curious." She then said, almost to herself, "Luka, Luka," seeming to massage the name with her mouth. "Luka," she said again. She remembered an old man from her grandparents' home in Matemo whose name was Luka. It was an old man's name, and yet she liked it on the young man next to her.

"It's what I've been called since I was little," Luka explained. My teachers would call me Luke but I insisted on Luka. It felt more natural to my ears. It's also my late paternal grandfather's name and I just like it." He had a smile as he spoke. "Of course I have another name: Owuor, but hardly anyone uses it."

"I like your name, Luka, its unusual…" Wanjira might have said more but Luka said, "What about you? How did you get your name, Wanjira?"

"Funny you should ask…actually my name should be Muthoni, my Aunt's name…I'm named after my father's sister…are you familiar with the Gikuyu naming system? Luka nodded. "I've an idea. The man's parents, then the woman's, in alternating sequence, yes."

"You're right. That's the pattern. But sometimes the names change…nicknames that stick, and of course these days many of us go by our so-called Christian names. But my name came from the circumstances of my birth…do you really want to know?

"Of course. What happened?"

Wanjira smiled. "I was born on the wayside. That's *Njira-ini*, in Gikuyu. That's why my name is Wa-Njira, She-of-the-wayside. You see?" Luka nodded.

"Mother was coming from the *shamba* one early evening. Didn't expect me to be born that day at all—suddenly her labor pains began, and as she puts it, before she could even gather her thoughts enough to sit down somewhere, there I was, being born, on some village road, under a tree, my mother surrounded by three kind women who rushed to her side when they saw her plight. Strange, eh? She claims the women right away called me Wanjira, and mother claims my dramatic arrival is responsible for my—in her opinion—a touch of strangeness in me. According to her my personality was affected and influenced by the conditions of my birth, and the name those women gave me. She smiled almost coyly. Don't ask me why, though. I feel totally unstrange." She rolled her eyes and let out a big laugh.

Luka, intrigued, wanted to hear more. "Tell me about it! I don't think you are strange but you are…let's see…strong, determined, have strong opinions, and very bright." She laughed, louder this time, and he thought it was the healthiest, most beautiful, most honest, laugh he had heard in a long time. Many women laughed shyly, like they were suppressing something, giving only a bit of themselves. But this woman laughed loudly, with confidence, and oh, what beauty! He wanted her to keep laughing but she stopped, and this time she looked a bit shy, and said, "Thanks, Luka. I would say the same about you…standing up there giving speeches, unafraid of the Riot Squad. What makes you so brave?"

She had steered the conversation away from herself, deftly, and how it was about him. He quickly understood this, and liked her even more. What an intelligent woman, he thought. And modest too. He just had to be with this Wanjira, she-of the-way-side, the unconventional one. No wonder he had thought of her all of last night.

"Hey, Wanjira…I like your name very much, and I like the way you entered this world…were you a bit dramatic, do you think?" They both laughed, and Wanjira rose to change the radio station. They had been listening to some music from the Voice of Kenya, and now she played some lingala music by Tabu Ley Rochereau, and they found themselves humming to the sounds of the beautiful music. She said to Luka, "I wish I knew the language, what he is singing about, though I can guess, I suppose."

It turned out that Luka, like Wanjira, was free that afternoon, and that is how come when the Tabu Ley song was over she played some songs by the Bee Gees, and both hummed to "*How deep is your love,*" and suddenly Wanjira felt self-conscious. Here she was, spending an afternoon with a man she barely knew. Was she behaving in an appropriate manner? Singing so comfortably in the presence of a guy she met only a day earlier? She suddenly looked agitated, but calmed down when she noticed that Luka was simply comfortable, sitting on her bed, back resting on the wall, eyes closed,

How deep is your love?
How deep is your love?
I really need to learn
'cause we're living in a world of fools
breaking us down
when they all should let us be
we belong to you and me

Luka was singing along with Barry Gibb. They looked at each other and he said, "Let's dance to this one," and she re-wound the tape and moved close to Luka and soon they were swaying to the song, and Luka held her by the waist and she held his waist and she closed her eyes and let Barry Gibb say to them both

You know the door to my very soul
You're the light in my deepest darkest hour
You're my saviour when I fall...
I believe in you

When the song ended she looked at him, overcome with shyness, and he also seemed shy, and his smile was sweet and gentle and he said to her "Wanjira...Thank you," and she smiled and said, "Thank you, Luka," and returned to her seat, asked if he would like another cup of Nescafe, and insisted he eat a banana, and she ate one herself, and she then showed him one of her photo albums. She felt trembly, and shy, all of a sudden, and for a moment did not allow herself to look at him.

"Look at that fine girl," he said, pointing her out in group photographs. He said nice things about her parents, and siblings. So polite, so good with words, Wanjira thought.

Afterwards she wondered if she had held him too tightly while they danced, wanting to know that she had, and whether she should have waited to get to know him better before hinting, and showing, how attracted she was to him, but thought there was no reason to do so. She asked herself if this was what a decent woman ought to do, thinking that of course it was, and what happened to all those lessons, all that instruction and the admonitions from everyone about not showing a man love at first sight, no matter how struck you were by his loveliness, his poise, his personality, his smile, the grip of his hand when he greeted you...about how a girl should wait and let him make the first move, but here she was, dancing and sending all kinds of signals. But of course it was what she had really, really, wanted to do! Why had she, for instance, shown him her photographs, something she did rarely? She often felt invaded when people asked to see her album, feeling she did not want strangers to see a very personal side of herself. With Luka, however, it had all seemed very easy, very natural. She had, in fact, offered to show him her pictures.

When he left her room, about four hours since the tennis court, Wanjira felt agitated. It was already past tea time, and soon it would be suppertime. She had reading assignments, and a paper to begin writing, but somehow she could not concentrate on anything. Luka's visit had left her flustered. She felt excited, agitated. She was breathing fast, and she paced up and down her room, and then the corridor. She went outside and walked up and down the short road between the Box and the YWCA, needing to be outside, to get some air!

The outdoors felt fresh and clean, cleared of dust by the heavy rainfall of the afternoon, and University Road was busy with people hurrying past her, some toward the Box and others toward town, anxious to reach home. Transportation was always difficult and messy after the rains, what with many wet and damp clothes in city *Matatu*, and muddy pathways in the many unpaved areas of the city. But Wanjira's mind was elsewhere. Her mind was racing. What had happened? She wished Luka had not left, that he had stayed with her for the rest of the afternoon and all evening. She remembered him saying he wanted to get to know her better, if that was alright with her. The very first thing he said to her as they walked in the rain. No one had ever put it that way to her. No-one had ever said: *I'd like to get to know you better.* Guys had often approached her in what seemed to her a brash, cocky, fashion that always seemed to turn her off. But Luka had said something that had immediately pleased, flattered, and shocked her at the same time. "*I would like to get to know you better if that's alright with you.*" He had held her waist as they walked in the rain, and it had felt good. Once in her room he had conducted himself in a very decent manner, and never once had he made any attempt to touch her in any unwanted way. Until the dance. Oh, how wonderful that had been, his arms around her waist, her arms around his neck. The feelings she had felt coursing throughout her body! And the way he had spoken to her about himself, and his family. He had spoken to her with an open heart. She had loved hearing about his family. He spoke about them with happiness, and something about this had stirred her heart. He seemed so well grounded in something strong. Did he think similar things about her, she wondered. She wanted him to.

He had asked, on his way out, if she would like to walk with him to the main campus the next morning, and she had quickly agreed. "Let's meet by the gate at nine o'clock. I have an 11:00 O'clock lecture," she had said. He had smiled broadly, saying, "Nine o'clock then. Goodnight Wanjira. I'm delighted to meet you."

Thus began what soon came to be known as one of the hottest and most controversial romances on campus. An encounter at the tennis court, a walk in the rain, a cup of Nescafe, a walk to campus. As if it was the most natural thing in the world Luka had reached for Wanjira's hand when they met by the gate at the Box, and the two had walked down past St. Andrews, onto the Highway, and onto the campus itself. By the time they got near the cafeteria, Wanjira's heart was just about ready to jump out of her chest, such was her excitement. Luka's heart too was racing, and he kept squeezing her hand, saying hello here and there to his friends, and Wanjira felt like an offering as they climbed the stairs to the cafeteria, selfconscious, all of a sudden, for there, right in front of her and Luka, was part of the group of women she had so often admired, the same women she had also so often envied. Two of them, Nancy and Marie, now quickly exchanged glances, and Nancy, who obviously knew Luka, came by to say hello. Wanjira guessed that Nancy had come to make sure her eyes had not deceived her. She gave Nancy a big smile, such was her heart's happiness, but the other woman returned a cool one.

"Hello Luka, how're things? Oh, hello….?" The frown on her face left no doubt in Wanjira that Nancy was displeased to meet her.

"Wanjira," Luka said, quickly. "Meet Nancy…Nancy, Wanjira"

"Hello, Wanjira." Nancy said, staring straight into Wanjira's eyes.

"Hello, Nancy," Wanjira answered, her voice and manner wanting Nancy to feel comfortable, and to know she meant her well.

"Luka, let's get together soon. Remember your promise." Her coy manner and the familiarity with which she held Luka's arm as she spoke to him were supposed to send some kind of message to Wanjira.

"Sure, Nancy. Let the others know. We've got to go now," and holding Wanjira's hand tightly, Luka led Wanjira up the stairs toward the cafeteria and away from Nancy, who looked at them and shook her head from side to side, marveling, and muttering to herself, "Luka O!"

Luka came to see Wanjira every evening. It became their routine. He would come after supper, and did not leave until around ten or ten thirty. They loved each other easily, and with such passion that Wanjira could not believe the powerful emotions that overtook her whenever they were together. Luka swore she was the most beautiful, the most attractive, the most intelligent, woman he had ever met. She assured him she knew it, and he would roar with laughter and call her a wild woman. On weekends they would go out to the movies, dancing with friends, and sometimes simply to kill an evening in a friend's room if the books allowed them a chance. In her dorm room, which was still hers seeing that she still had not been assigned a new roommate, they would work on their various reading and writing assignments, she sitting at her desk and he by her side, and this might go on for an hour or two. Their love for one another was obvious to anyone who observed them and to Wanjira Luka seemed her true other half, the mythical self one is meant to find in order to feel truly whole. Luka called her his love, his beloved, his very own *Nyar Ngumo*, daughter of Ngumo. He was her love, her *Mwendwa,* her *Mpenzi.*

As they read together, she would sometimes mention some of the ideas she was coming across in her lectures and tutorials, and he would talk to her about some of the legal concepts he was learning. She became especially interested in the ideas on family law that he was reading about one week, and Luka suggested that she attend some of the law lectures delivered in the large lecture theatre on campus by the distinguished Kamau wa Kuria, a lecturer who, Luka said, made legal ideas lively, credible, understandable, made students laugh, and who took obvious delight in his work. He helped students understand that the law was about human beings and their welfare, and that understanding, and ensuring that it was used appropriately, was crucial to the development of society. Wanjira shared her feelings and impressions of government systems in Africa, and encouraged him to read more African writers besides their very own Ngugi wa Thiong'o and Nigeria's Chinua Achebe, for there were Camara Laye, Ayi Kwei Armah, Ama Ata Aidoo, Flora Nwapa, Ousmane Sembene and many other West Africans. And there were the South Africans: Peter Abrahams, Alex La Guma, Ezekiel Mphahlehle, and the poet Dennis Brutus. She read to him "Stanley Meets Mutesa," a poem by David Rubadiri, one of her own lecturers, out loud, imitating his huge baritone voice and dramatic nuance:

"...For the country was not sure...
The gate of reed is flung open,
There is silence
But only a moment's silence—
A silence of assessment
The tall black king steps forward,
He towers over the thin bearded white man,
Then grabbing his lean white hand
Manages to whisper
"Mtu mweupe karibu"
White man you are welcome
The gate of polished reed closes behind them
And the West is let in."

"And the West is let in." Six words that summarized a quiet, unheard, unremarked, tremor deep in the belly of the earth: the beginnings of a permanent and irreversible shift in relations between the eastern African region and Europe. Could there be a better way to say it? Wanjira did not think so, as she and Luka re-read the entire poem. He said he would attend one of Rubadiri's lectures, for what was the point of having writers and poets right there on campus who only benefited the lucky few such as his Wanji? He claimed he was already jealous of her, what with all these talented people teaching and interacting with her daily? She also shared with Luka the poetry of Walt Whitman, the intriguing American poet of the nineteenth century she had learned about recently. Taking turns with each stanza they read the entire "Song of Myself," marveling at the beauty and sensuality of Whitman's poetry.

She told Luka that she had recently learned about what inspired the title of Ngugi's novel, *Weep Not, Child.* It was a poem by this same Whitman, and here it was, "On the Beach at Night," a poem about a child afraid of dark, gathering clouds, being comforted by her father, a poem with multiple meanings and possible interpretations:

She read,

"...From the beach, the child, holding the hand of her father,
Those burial clouds that lower, victorious, soon to devour all,
Watching, silently weeps.
Weep Not, Child
Weep Not, my darling

With these kisses let me remove your tears;
The ravening clouds shall not long be victorious
They shall not long possess the sky—shall devour the stars only in Apparition...

"Think of the poem's emotion, Luka, and of the novel itself. So much meaning, so many possible interpretations, and can you see how a poem from New York could speak to the heart of a young writer from Kenya!" Wanjira's voice was full of excitement. Luka could feel her love of poetry, the written word, and ideas. He thought it was akin to what he felt whenever he studied concepts, ideas and practices in the legal profession. He thanked her for all this new knowledge he was gaining from her, and she for what he was teaching her about the law. She asked him many questions about campus activism, laughing at what she considered her "ignorance about these matters."

"But you're not ignorant," he protested, holding her close. "On the contrary, Wanjira, you are a woman of great intelligence and have a lot of potential. You can do anything you want. And never forget that." Wanjira felt giddy with excitement. She was so flattered! But Luka himself was exactly that: a highly intelligent man with very high potential. He too could be anything he wanted to be! She felt alive, hopeful. So is this love, she thought. This near-obsession with thoughts of one special person *all* the time? For she thought of Luka all the time these days. During lectures. During tutorials. In bed. In the shower. She might be reading, or walking to the Box, or to town, but Luka was always on her mind. Other people seemed to have faded from her mind, and she actually did not give anyone else much thought, even though she remained friendly and courteous to all, as was her way. She still played tennis with Samuel and Josephine, and Luka joined them sometimes, but she played less than she had before she met Luka. She also had not visited her family in Ngumo for four weeks, for the weekends had simply flown by, so busy was she with Luka and her new life with him. Why does my heart love him so much? Questions, questions, and always, on her mind, one thought: Luka. Luka. Luka O.

They went to the Arboretum one Sunday afternoon. She had never been there, and was amazed by the many species of plants to be found there. Luka had bought *samosas* and bananas earlier, and she brought some water and juice drinks, and they sat under the shade of a large *Muhuti* tree, where they watched other picnickers, most of whom were Indians. There were grandparents, parents, teenage children, small children. Three family generations in different clusters in different parts of the Arboretum. Luka and Wanjira remarked on this, and on the culture and family structures that created this kind of family life. Wanjira thought it was admirable, and that it was much like the pre-colonial, and still quite present, family living arrangements that allowed the sons of each family to settle on their parent's land and thus take care of their elderly parents as time passed. But this was gradually disappearing, the two lovers agreed. There was too much pressure on the land for most families, and many people now lived in cities, away from their immediate families. They spoke of the value of grandparents in children's lives, and Wanjira told Luka of her earlier days and the many school holidays she spent at her grandparents' home in Matemo. "I'd love you to meet my *Cucu*—she's a wonderful woman, and tough too! I bet she'd have a name for you immediately after meeting you."

"Such as?"

"*Njong'i.* Ugly."

"What? Handsome me?"

They both burst into loud laughter.

"My *Cucu* is just like that. It's her way of telling you she likes you and finds you right—just maybe, for her granddaughter. She called my cousins' boyfriends many names when she first met them, but always with a hearty laugh."

Luka told Wanjira that his maternal grandparents both died while he was a very young child, and that he hardly remembered them, and that his father lost his mother shortly after his marriage, years before Luka was born. The only grandparent he had known in his life was his paternal grandfather, who had died two years earlier. "He died a month before I entered university. It was quite a blow to us because the old man was wonderful. The family took it hard, we really did." The memory made him sad, and he was quiet for a while, his eyes looking into a distant time and place Wanjira did not know. "As you might recall me telling you, his name was Luka Omondi, and I feel privileged to carry his name." He was quite a character."

Wanjira told Luka she felt lucky to have at least two grandparents, her mother's parents, for her father's parents had died years earlier. She had known her paternal grandfather but only for a brief while, for he had died when she was about eight.

Perhaps it was the talk of grandparents, or the sight of the beautiful children and their families picnicking at the Arboretum that made each one fall silent, lost in a far-away, private world of thought. Luka began to hum a song, quietly, eyes closed, and Wanjira listened, and for a while the only sound to be heard was Luka's humming, and the laughter of small children in the distance.

The trees around them swished and swayed in a gentle breeze, and the warm and sunny Sunday afternoon seemed a magical, rare, moment for Wanjira, who suddenly imagined herself far, far away, transported to a place in time she wanted to never leave. And then, just as gently as he had started humming Luka started to sing, and Wanjira recognized the melody, but not the words:

Wan wadhi ka yesu wan wadhi
Wan wadhi ka yesu wan wadhi
ka kongo odong kodi kanyo
wan wadhi
Wan wadhi ka yesu
Wan wadhi chamo ngima

She immediately recognized his language, and watched his face and mouth as he continued,

Wan wadhi ka Baba
Wan Wadhi…

She thought it was a hymn, from its sound, and from the mention of *Yesu* and *Baba.* Luka finished the song and said, "My favorite hymn, a song my mother loves a lot"

"I like it, Luka. Teach me the words. Tell me what they mean."

He spoke the words:

We are on our way to Jesus
We will enjoy ourselves there
We will leave you there drinking
So hold on to your booze if you choose
We're off to enjoy life in
Our father's house

"Now let me teach you something else…but first, a kiss." He reached out for her hands and held them. He had been lying on his belly but now sat upright, and so did she.

"Oh, you mean there's a price? you, you!"

"Ok, Wanji. Repeat after me…"*Aheri ahinya. Aheri nyakachieng.*"

Wanjira repeated the two sentences after him, her mouth full of laughter for she suspected a trick, and was about to say something when Luka, a soft look on his face, his hands holding on to Wanjira tighter, said, "Wanji, say it again. *Aheri Nyakachieng.*"

"But what is it that you're making me say? Translation, please. Don't let me incriminate myself!" She laughed, her hands returning Luka's tight grip, but felt shy and nervous all the same.

"Ok, Ok, I'll stop the short-wave. You've just made an important pledge, Wanji. I'll translate. You said, "*I love you very much. I will love you forever.* And you repeated, *I will love you forever.*" Luka's voice was warm, and he seemed vulnerable, his whole demeanor one of hope and longing.

"Oh, but Luka, that's not true!" Wanjira rolled her eyes but a big smile lit up her face. "Why would I lie?"

"Wanji, Wanji, it's true, isn't it?

"No."

"Yes, yes!" He held her closer. "Say it is. Say it."

"Alright, *alright*, rascal, you win this time…Yes!"

As they continued their Sunday rest Wanjira thought of the peacefulness all around, the fresh air, the beauty of a well kept Arboretum with trees marked and identified by both their indigenous and scientific names, mostly in Latin. Our fellow students should be coming here for visits. It is so close to the halls of residence, but very few ever do, she thought. I might never have come here if Luka hadn't suggested it and accompanied me, but maybe it is just habit. "Someday" she said out loud, "when we have a better transport system, people from the Eastlands will get a chance to enjoy this beautiful place." Luka agreed, adding that most people could not come to the Arboretum because it was much too out of bounds and out of the way of normal transport routes. "No *matatu* makes it this way, you see." After a long pause he said, "Someday, someday. It will happen."

On Sundays Wanjira and Luka went to St. Paul's, where they sat together, and hugged each other tightly during the passing of the peace prayer. And they went to the National Museum. She shrieked at the snake park, so frightened by the large reptiles. Luka laughed and laughed, and held her close. He said he was not afraid of snakes and she dared him to go closer to the cages, especially the one that held a large, angry, puffed-up-ready-to-strike Cobra. He would not go. They had tea at the Boulevard, by the pool, and did not leave until sunset. That afternoon they talked about their interests, and about the country. They talked of travelling to different parts of Kenya someday, "Just to see the many places I hear about—your very own Kisumu, Mombasa, Nyeri, Isiolo," Wanjira said, her voice full of longing.

"Let's take the train to Mombasa, Wanji," Luka said, excitedly. "I'd love to show you my old haunts, my primary school, and the big Indian Ocean! And Fort Jesus, of course." She felt elated by the prospect of travelling on the train to the coast, having only taken it in the opposite direction, to her A-Levels Preparatory School in Eldoret. Then she had enjoyed the slow climb up the Escarpment, even though it got colder and colder as the train moved toward Nakuru, where it deposited many school girls and boys headed to school in that town. As the train proceeded on its way to Eldoret, Wanjira never tired of the chug, chug sound of the wheels as the train moved, her mind captured by thoughts of the past and the present. She would remember her history lessons, thinking of the men who worked night and day to make this railroad, the workers brought all the way from India to supply the labor, and the lions at Tsavo that ate a lot of workers until the famous George Patterson shot them to death. That was the story as the books told it, but she also never forgot the other story told to her by her grandmother, and later by her mother, the story of the old seer, Mugo wa Kibiru, who had seen this very train long before it was ever built. It had appeared in his dreams as a long snake stretching all the way from the sea of salt, *Iria ria Cumbi*, the Indian Ocean, to the lands of the Agikuyu. The train had been accompanied by waves of white butterflies, and the old seer saw the butterflies perch all across the land, and felt his heart grow heavy and sad with the knowledge revealed to him: the snake and the butterflies would forever transform the lives of the people. The people would lose everything, and their suffering would be great. As a child she had felt tears start in her eyes when her grandmother told this story, and on the train to school she would muse at the prophecy, not sure what to think of the life that had befallen Kenya after the arrival of Europeans. She had studied History with an excellent teacher at the Preparatory, Miss Musomi, and had begun to ask many questions about the life of Kenya as a colony that her parents and just about every other older person she knew had refused to talk about when she was younger. If any of the children asked about life during the colonial days, and especially during the Emergency period that preceded Independence, the older people would say, "Ai, those were hard times! Ai, all the suffering!" But they would not say much more. It had been left to her older brother, Kairu, to sum it all up for her and her other siblings when they were much younger. "The people fought for the land. They fought the British, and won, but the British also won." This had sounded a bit confusing to her young self, but Kairu had then said, "The most important thing to know is what the people said:

Kuuma Ndemi na Mathaathi
Ithaka ciari ciitu
Na gutiri ungitutuunya"

From the days of Ndemi and Mathaathi
The very beginning of time
The Land belonged to us
And nobody can take it from us!

This had pleased Wanjira, and for days she and the younger children had marked time to the tune they made up with the words. They would march around the house, holding up sticks, pretending they were guns and *mapanga*, for Kairu had told them the people had used these weapons in their fight for the stolen *ithaka* of their families. They would emphasize the word "*Tuunya,*" stamping their feet in gestures of defiance and rage. Inserting some English words for added emphasis they would shout, "Nobody can Tuunya us!" "Nobody can take the land from us!" The adults nearby would smile, and sometimes emit short, bitter, laughs, sadly shaking their heads, but make no comments.

With Luka, however, Wanjira did not think of the prophecy, or of anything else in history: the idea of the two of them visiting Mombasa was simply wonderful. She would save some of her "Boom" for the ticket, and they would stay at his cousin's house. They thought they could visit for a week.

Wanjira and Luka recalled the Young Christian Student meetings they had attended, and realized they had been together at one such meeting when she was in Form Two, and he in Form Three. But they had been located in different dormitories at the teacher training college where the gathering was held, and in any event there were hundreds of students in attendance.

"I wish we'd met then, Luka. I'd have liked you even then," Wanjira said, earnestly. "But who knows? Maybe I wouldn't have. Maybe you wouldn't have liked me either…I guess things happen when they should and hey, we were supposed to meet here."

"Oh, Wanji, we'd have fallen for each other right then!"

"So you think, Son of Owuor!"

They imagined the many things they might have said to each other as teenagers. "One of them," Wanjira said, smiling, would have been "Buzz off, fellow!" I was very strict in those days. I feared my strong attraction to guys, and thought any interaction with them would interfere with my dream of going to university."

"Really?" Just talking? " He had a smile on his face and she could see he was getting ready to tease her. "I keep telling my younger sister not to be *sooooo* scared of guys, to tell them what's on her mind, but not to insult them. We have feelings too, you know."

"I know, I know, that," Wanjira said, passionately. "Of course I know that. But think about it: what would a girl do—at least in those days—if her passion got the better of her? The boys aren't encouraged to be careful about birth control, and the girls don't have proper information. The burden is wholly on the girl, and if she gets pregnant, too bad! Just too bad!"

Luka watched Wanjira's face as she spoke. He liked the way she moved her mouth, the way her words, now animated, tumbled out, and what about her eyes! They sparkled with emotion. He wanted her to keep talking, to hear this perspective on relationships, really on everything, from her. He had often talked these matters over with his older sister, and his cousins, and he was in full sympathy with the women's viewpoints. He had always thought that a guy with sisters—and that should be almost everyone in this country—ought to be completely sympathetic to women. They are our mothers! Our aunties! Our sisters! Our cousins! He loved the women in his family. He found them beautiful, powerful, and great company. And now here was Wanjira, beautiful, passionate, and she liked him! Great stirrings of emotion coursed through his body. He longed to hold her close, for them to make beautiful love together. He was absolutely wild about this woman and although he had not shared this with Wanjira, his friends teased him, calling him a bewitched man. Ben, his close friend, had called him "a doomed lad."

On a different Sunday at the Hotel Boulevard, as they whiled the late afternoon away, Wanjira and Luka's peaceful mood was suddenly interrupted by the arrival of two couples who sat close by. They immediately recognized one of the men, a well known member of parliament, best known for the rapid acquisition of wealth he had experienced since his election into the august body a decade earlier. He was known to university students as Octopus, for he reached far and wide all at the same time to amass a vast fortune that seemed to know no boundaries. Coffee farms, tea plantations, office buildings, rental units, factories, hotels, wayside kiosks, private schools, *mandazi* and chips joints, night clubs. He was everywhere, seemingly with no rhyme or reason, just eager to diversify and grab as many money-making schemes as possible.

"Thug," Luka said, under his breath.

"Criminal," Wanjira said, adding "But do you see what I see?"

"Yea," Luka said, "Only I can't believe it. Who would have thought it possible?"

Wanjira and Luka were astounded by the sight of Octopus and a young woman who could have passed for a high school student, only she wasn't. She was a first year student in Wanjira's hall, a quiet and pleasant person who always seemed quite shy whenever Wanjira had come across her in the bathrooms or anywhere else in the Box. What do you know, Wanjira was now thinking, for it seemed clear that the woman was quite comfortable with the MP, judging from the way he had placed his arm around her shoulders as she sat next to him. And that alone would have been enough to surprise the young lovers had they also not recognized the young man at the table next to them: Murema, the very same person known to one and all on campus as an important student leader! With them was a second woman unknown to either Wanjira or Luka, but the sight of Murema and Octopus together sat heavily on the two.

"Well, Luka," Wanjira said, after a while, "It seems we are lucky to witness a union between our very own buddy Murema and Octopus himself." She spoke is a slow, deliberate, voice. She sounded angry.

"Wanji, let's not jump to any conclusions. Maybe there's nothing to it. They could be relatives for all we know."

"Who knows? Maybe. All l know is that I have a bad feeling. It's something about a student of Murema's caliber and ideas sitting next to Octopus that worries me. And I don't care if he's his uncle. The man's a crook!"

"Wanji, Wanji," Let's give Murema the benefit of the doubt. We really don't know what's going on, but you're right: Octopus and his type are dangerous types for whom the law doesn't exist."

Wanjira sent a sharp glance in the direction of the people near them who had obviously been saying something amusing to one another because they were now convulsed in laughter, Octopus being the loudest of the lot.

"And certainly do not respect ideas." She was especially thinking of Murema, as she said this. He was a second-year student in her faculty she actually admired, but about whom she was now, quite rapidly, developing second thoughts as she observed him sitting with the well known crook. But maybe she wasn't being fair. Luka could be right. What if he was his uncle? Or family friend? People had no choice about their relatives, so maybe she should not judge Murema too harshly.

Wanjira however could not get rid of the hunch that had taken solid root in her mind the moment she saw Murema and Octopus together, and even as the two lovers agreed to focus on other matters, and to have a second cup of tea, Wanjira could not help returning to the subject.

"Luka, they are together for a reason, and we'll soon know about it. Mark my words. They're hatching a scheme, you can be sure...you know these people have no sense of values...unless we could call grabbing everything in sight a value"

"You're right, my dear. These buggers want everything. They feel protected, and will take everything. And see what's happening to the country. Schools are beginning to lack supplies, and we hear there's not enough money in the ministry. And it's the same story with the hospitals...But what is Murema doing with this fellow?"

"We'll soon find out, won't we?"

Wanjira told Luka she had not thought too clearly about these things—about leader-crooks such as Octopus, and about the rampant corruption in the country—until coming to the University. "I guess that's what I should do, right? Think about the present conditions and what gives rise to them. My A level English teacher talked about that a lot...for our general paper we had to discuss politics, ethics, social issues. I found it fascinating, but I didn't talk too much about it. I guess I just read and read."

"We all did, Wanjira. I don't know about you but I was dying to come to the university. I just knew I had to hit the books. I read as much as I could, late into the night, early in the morning. I just had to make it! I have wanted to be a lawyer since I was ten. I was inspired by a fellow from our area who became a lawyer in the 50s...what a fellow! He visited my father sometimes, and I could see the old man respected him a lot, and valued his visits. I thought...a lawyer!

They burst out laughing. From where they sat Octopus and his group observed the happy pair, and many thoughts went through the politician's mind. He was fully aware that Luka was the well-known student leader at the university, and from Murema he learned, this afternoon, that Wanjira was his girlfriend. He had not made any comment, but he had fully noted the situation.

Wanjira and Luka were laughing at the way Luka pronounced that word, "lawyer" He had lowered his voice two octaves, and pursed his lips, making himself a "lawyer." What an actor, she thought, and remembered the announcement she had seen two days earlier calling for a supporting cast at the National Theatre. She had planned to mention it to Luka. Perhaps they both could join the play, *The Trial of Dedan Kimathi*, co-authored by Ngugi wa Thiong'o and Micere Mugo, one of the few women professors at the university. It was Kenya's entry into the Pan African Festival, FESTAC, scheduled to be held in Nigeria later that year. They might stand a chance of joining the cast. She would mention it, but for now she reached for his hand across the table, and they looked at each other, smiles now fading, each looking very serious. It was Wanjira who spoke.

"Luka...Luka...do you think we stand a chance? I mean...I didn't really want to bring this up because its sounds so, so, bad, but...you know what people in this country think about unions such as ours, right? *Inter-ethnic unions*, to be exact." Wanjira said the words "Inter-ethnic unions" with a dramatic emphasis that made both burst into laughter. Wanjira and Luka's laughter did not mean, however, that each was not fully aware of the fact that their relationship had taken a first, important, step. By acknowledging the fact that being Kenyans of different ethnic backgrounds, and especially of Luo and Gikuyu origins, was considered by many to be a "No-Entry" zone for successful love relations, never mind marriage, the young lovers had reached an important milestone in their life as a couple.

Luka nodded, and reached out for Wanjira's hand. He held on tightly to her, his face all attention.

"And you've heard those women on campus. And I heard some bad talk coming my way the other day after my political science tutorial...From a guy I've never even spoken to before. Stupid talk."

Luka squeezed her hand. "Wanjira, let them talk. You know what the WaSwahili say: "*Watasema, watachoka.*" This country needs to grow up, for God's sake. You know people are afraid to change..." his voice trailed off, and he seemed to stare into space. Luka felt frustrated. For a while neither he nor Wanjira spoke.

"Wanji?" Luka sounded hurt, but his voice was strong and confident. "Wanji, we're Kenyans. He spoke with passion. "*We're Kenyans. We're Kenyans, not just Luo and Gikuyu or whatever else. Wanji, my darling, we're Kenyans, our country's present and future!*" The two lovers were quiet for a while, and then Luka spoke, continuing his thought. "It's just that people are afraid to think differently about long-held beliefs and prejudices. I too have seen and heard the women, and even a few guys, but I'm not worried. Are you?"

"Yes, and no, Luka." Wanjira moved closer to Luka. Looking at the two of them one might have thought they were two members of a tutorial group discussing a difficult idea, a hard to understand concept, which they nonetheless must understand in preparation for the next day's tutorial session with a hard task master of a graduate student. Wanjira spoke with a soft, yet strong, voice.

"Yes, because I don't like being anyone's target, especially because I've done nothing wrong, and no because I really, deep inside, don't care about these women, and anyone else. And no, because you aren't worried, and because it's about us, not them."

Wanjira had started off strongly, but somewhere in the midst of her sentence her voice had started to tremble. She felt upset by the thoughts that had given rise to this conversation, and the tears that came to her eyes threatened to come down fast, but somehow she got a grip on herself and continued, "Luka, I can only worry about my family, and I'm not worried because my mother will support me in anything I do. I'm sure about that."

"Mine too," Luka said, his voice sounding a bit brighter than before. "I have full faith in my mother."

Wanjira and Luka were quiet for a long time, lost in thought. Each thought of a somewhat tired, yet hopeful woman who understood, and loved, her children dearly. Wanjira recalled the conversation she had been a part of at Jessie's wedding the previous April. It seemed like an event from long ago, but the young girls' conversation came back to her clearly. Since she started dating Luka the thought of their presumed differences had come to her now and then, but she had been too busy enjoying getting to know and love him that she had hardly remembered to be afraid of any social disapproval that might come their way. It was as if her mind had totally shut down any of its ability to smell or see potential danger until she was good and ready to face whatever danger lay in her path. Had the time then arrived? It seemed so, for here she was, broaching the subject, and recalling some painful words and ugly looks she had endured because of the supposedly taboo nature of her relationship with Luka.

She now imagined that some of her relatives and neighbors would talk, and that each of their villages would be abuzz with condemnation, or by mere curiousity, should it be heard that the daughter of Kamau, the very same Wanjira they had all seen grow up and become a beautiful woman called to study at University, had now disgraced everybody by daring to bring home a man from the west, from *"Ruguru!* Can you believe it? The things these children can do! And to think we considered her intelligent! She really was a foolish girl all along; we just didn't know it. And Luka's own village would talk, expressing surprise, dismay, and utter stupefaction that such a son of the village, a brilliant one at that, could allow himself to be trapped by a woman from Gikuyu country! Didn't he know these were not women anyone in his right mind could bring home, or about whom a decent young man should bother his parents with careless words such as "I'm interested in this girl, and want to marry her"? Was he in his right mind? Of course not! The girl had bewitched him, for sure, so how could he be normal? Didn't he know the only women one should marry, and hope to live well with, were from amongst his own people? The words would fly, but Wanjira and Luka knew, deep inside, that their mothers would listen to their children, ask important questions, perhaps even cry with frustration, worry and disappointment, but ultimately support them, be a bridge to their fathers, and create a wall of love and support between them and any marauding tongue from amongst the relatives and others in their communities.

The sun was beginning to set, and the beautiful evening scene was reflected in the pool. The big palm tree to one side of where they sat swayed gently in the evening breeze. It would soon be time to return to the residence halls.

As a way of breaking the silence that had come upon them, Wanjira told Luka that she had been invited to attend yet another London Look event at yet another wealthy woman's home, this time in Kileleshwa. The event was to take place the following Saturday, and Wangu had invited her and a few other women. She wanted to know if Luka wanted to join them.

"Of course you are invited, Luka!" He had teased her, saying he would not feel safe in the company of such rich and beautiful women.

"So now I'm a rich woman, eh?" But that's wishing me well. I just might be rich someday."

"Of course you will, Wanji. I'll make sure that I earn enough to help make you a rich woman who can buy whatever clothes and anything else you wish. Mrs. Owuor will retain her classy look for sure." Wanjira smiled, and reached out for his hand.

"*Chiega biro bedo maber nyakachieng*," he said, a confident smile on his lips as he translated: "My wife will remain beautiful forever."

"What are you talking about LukaO?" She often called him so when he was teasing her, which was often. "Who is this Mrs. Owuor, this wife, you are talking about?"

"Ah, you mean you can't see her? That's because there's no mirror around, but look into the pool, my dear. See the reflection?"

Wanjira burst into loud laughter. "You are joking, Luka. That's no good, you know. You know you shouldn't joke about certain things."

"And why not, my dear, if I speak the truth?" Suddenly he was serious, the smile leaving his face. He held her hand and looked very serious, seemingly lost in thought for what seemed a long time.

Wanjira was beginning to feel a bit awkward, for she wondered about Luka's sudden change of mood, but before she could say anything he sat up very straight in his chair and now held both of Wanjira's hands in his and looking into her eyes, said, "Wanji, speaking of visits to other parts of Kenya...the most important visit you'll soon be making will be to the lake region, my dear, and soon, too."

"What?" She understood him right away.

"Yes, Wanji. I want you to meet my mother. I want her to meet you."

Wanjira's heart did two to four somersaults in just one second. She was breathing hard.

"Aren't we thinking too far ahead…aren't we, Luka? We have all the time in the world…Luka?" She sounded confused.

"Wanjira. I am absolutely sure I have met Mrs. Owuor".

"Stop saying that, Luka. Please stop!" They burst out laughing, and as he held her close to him Wanjira felt her heart responding to his words, and wanted to hear more. Her anxiety of the previous hour seemed to leave her, for now that Luka had his arms around her she felt warm, safe and secure, and nothing could touch her now. And yet she did not want to respond to his words! No, she did…how long does it take to know how much you love someone? She needed no more time. It was Luka! Or nobody! But she said nothing, and simply held him tight.

As they walked back to the halls, Wanjira and Luka felt lighter for having brought up the subject of their presumed differences, and their hopes. His invitation to Wanjira to visit his family had left her in a state of exhilaration mingled with fear and anxiety. What if they rejected her outright? What if they thought, like so many in the country, and at the university, seemed to, that inter-ethnic relationships were to be discouraged, or stopped altogether? She began to wonder if her parents would themselves accept Luka, suddenly developing doubt. She thought they would not. Not that she had ever consciously planned to become Lukas' wife, much as she loved him. But it was a thought she must have nurtured in the deepest recesses of her mind as her relationship with Luka deepened, never giving it conscious attention until now. But she was not going to worry about that at this time, for in spite of that tinge of anxiety she could sense within her being, she felt much too happy with Luka at this very moment to spoil her mood with worries. Their spirits felt connected.

A taxi driver outside the Norfolk watched Wanjira and Luka as they walked toward the campus gates, hand in hand, and he smiled, struck by the beauty and freshness of youth, and he suddenly felt envious of the two university students. "Lucky children," he thought. They were the chosen ones, the country's future leaders. Men like him could only hope that their children would also, one day, walk through those university gates into a more secure and successful future. He felt doomed by a fate that had denied him a chance to obtain an education, confining him to this position of waiting, waiting to ferry rich *wazungu* here and there as they toured his own city, his country. But it was a job, and a man must work for his family. He watched the happy pair disappear into the campus grounds, and then shifted around from where he sat on a short stone wall, and faced the hotel. A tourist couple was just then coming toward him and he quickly faced them, ready for their instructions. He forgot Wanjira and Luka, now on their way toward the Box. Each felt at peace with the other. Luka said he was the luckiest man alive, and Wanjira smiled, and said the luckiest man in the world had made her the happiest woman in the world.

A week later Wanjira and Luka were surprised by a rumour circulating all over campus that Murema and a few other student leaders had received a huge payment from certain special interests in the government to destabilize the university student movement. It was said that from now on these "bought" students would disrupt any progressive agenda by the student body, and that they would assist the special Riot Squad, albeit surreptitiously, in destroying student leaders' plans and ideas. The news shocked Wanjira and she felt both sad and frightened when Luka and a few other friends talked about this new development on campus. It was only to Luka, however, that she mentioned the Murema-Octopus sighting of the previous week.

"No wonder—that criminal is behind it," Wanjira spoke passionately. "Didn't we suspect it that very day we saw them? We must do something, Luka!"

"What do you suggest, Wanji? Confront Murema?"

"Something. Some action, something to let Murema and the others know we know what's going on."

"Let's wait a bit, Wanji. Let's keep an eye on these fellows. They aren't the first to do this sort of thing, you know. These thugs have their informers who work all the time on this campus. It's just that we hadn't known that some of our own friends would turn against us in this manner"

Wanjira was quiet for a moment and then said, "I guess you're right, but more importantly I hope you will be more careful. Mind who you spend time with, and be on the lookout."

"I will, my darling. Don't worry." He seemed very serious, and both were quiet for a while. It was Wanjira who broke the silence.

"I, too, must watch, out, Luka. Do you know that First Year we saw with Octopus and Murema the other day? Can you believe she's trying to befriend me? Just this morning she said a very pleasant good morning in the bathrooms, and I just don't know why, I think she followed me there. I just had this feeling. And can you believe that a person I have merely nodded to up to now had the guts to ask me what I am doing this coming weekend, that there's a friend's wedding she'd like to invite me to? That was really fishy, I tell you."

"How did it start?" Luka seemed intrigued. "I mean, how did she get to that kind of invitation? Did she come outright and say it?"

"Well, you see, I gave her a hearing. It's my fault, but I didn't want to seem rude, and so when she acted friendly I started to talk to her. She started by saying that she saw us the other day at the Boulevard but felt shy to speak to us."

"Well, Wanji, just follow that gut feeling. She's probably on a mission."

"Oh, sure. Some missionary indeed! Well, I am not a willing convert." They both burst out laughing, and then in a very serious voice Luka said, "Whatever you do, Wanji, please don't accept any invitation to go anywhere with that woman. I don't trust the company she keeps."

"Don't worry, Luka. She's not my type, anyway. She's way out of line in thinking I might accept her invitation."

Wanjira spoke firmly, but in her heart she felt a stirring of worry. Why in God's name should things turn so complicated, she thought, but did not give voice to her thoughts.

And not wanting to worry Luka further, Wanjira did not tell him that earlier that afternoon, Kimani, her cousin, had sought her out at the library to warn her that word was out that all well known student leaders were being watched, and that something might happen to them in late February. It was now mid-January. The idea was to stop any demonstrations on campus in honor of J. M Kariuki, on March Second, the anniversary of the popular politician's still unresolved murder. The previous year's turnout, and the manner in which University and high school students all over Kenya had marked the day with prayer and protest had disturbed many in the government. That was why Octopus had convinced some of his colleagues that a large payoff was in order, and had proved his conviction that a good number of the student leaders could be bought off for a "few shillings," and it had proved easier than thought. He had told them, "Don't you know what the Waswahili say, "*Mwana wa nyoka ni nyoka*"? A snake's child is always a snake?" His colleagues had burst into loud laughter at this, one of them affirming, "Yes, they really are our children, after all," and more beers and *nyama choma* had been passed around for the highly amused leaders of the nation. But there was one small thought that nagged Octopus, and that was that he had, quite unexpectedly, been within twenty feet of that notorious Luka Owuor, who was rapidly gaining a reputation as a talented and remarkable student leader at the university.

What had galled him even more was the sight of the beautiful Gikuyu woman sitting with the *munjaruo* fellow: Murema had told him she was the student leader's girlfriend and that she was known to be a quiet but highly intelligent woman in the Arts Faculty. "How dare he!" Octopus had said, but only to himself. "We shall see, we shall see." He had immediately hatched a plan, but had not said anything, nor shown any particular outward sign that the sight of Wanjira and Luka laughing and talking happily to one another near him and Gathira, his new girlfriend, had disturbed him in any way.

Wanjira was about twelve when a famous politician was murdered on a Nairobi street. Every day after that, the radio and newspapers said much about this man. On seeing his picture in the newspaper Wanjira could not stop marveling at his kind looking eyes. Many people said he was a very intelligent man, and that was why he was now dead. It made little sense to Wanjira that one's intelligence could be the cause of such a bad end at the hands of a gun man. This murder was a rare event, so rare, she learned, that few had ever thought one could come to this sort of end in independent Kenya. In the colonial days, yes, many died such deaths, but not in these days of peace and freedom under the wise and loving leadership of Mzee. The old man, Mzee, had suffered a lot under British colonial rule. He had been detained in a far away, horribly dusty place, kept away from his loving people who had fought hard, and waited. He triumphed in the end. Kenya became an independent nation. Mzee brought peace to the land, and all was well.

Wanjira and her classmates had sung songs in praise of these events, and had reminded the Old One, on many occasions when they danced for him at his home in Gatundu, of these sad happenings, thanking him profusely for his suffering that brought so much joy to the land. Pole, Pole Mzee, kwa kufungwa. Sorry Mzee, sorry for being detained, for all your troubles, they sang.

On the morning the handsome and famous man was shot dead in broad daylight, on a very ordinary street on which, to anyone's knowledge, no one had ever been shoved around, let alone murdered, Njahira, Wanjira's mother, woke up with a troubled look, and all that morning could not get the night visions out of her mind. She told anyone who would listen, for often her children did not like to hear of her visions, and therefore did not like to pay attention on the days she woke up speaking of night visits to strange and frightening places, that this had been a vivid, bloody scene in which she was eating a chicken's head, and that this chicken's head had human hair which reached down to what was clearly a man's temples. Eating meat in one's dreams was a bad omen; it could only portend death, and eating a chicken's head was unheard of, and so this night vision could only mean that an unheard of death would be heard of in the light of day. That morning Njahira, Wanjira's mother, recited two rosaries and many other prayers to the Blessed Virgin, and to all the saints of heaven, hoping to undo what could only be inevitable. Unfortunately the event seen in her mother's dream was reported in the noon-day news; this man, a famous man in the land, was dead. This was the man in her mother's vision, of course, except in that vision he had come as a chicken. Wanjira would look and look at pictures of the man's wife and children and a feeling of pain and sorrow would fill her heart. Imagine losing a father! It would be terrible. But the most terrible thing was that the death of this man caused a lot of fear everywhere. She could feel it around her. She noticed that people visiting her home referred to this murder in strange, awed tones. They did not say things directly so she could understand them completely, but she understood enough, and it was this: This man's death was only the beginning. The old man had decided to eliminate him. But no one actually said, "Mzee did this," at least not directly. They said things like, "When the Old One decides what can we do about it? We are far away from the seat of power. It's not up to us."

This kind of talk meant that one had to come to one's own conclusion, and Wanjira knew it: there would be trouble. You could feel trouble. A lot of it. There would be trouble. She was very frightened, expecting something, but not knowing what.

On her way from school a few days after the murder Wanjira learned what these veiled conversations meant. Nyathira, her friend, explained it all.

"They will come for us. They will kill us all."

"Who? Who will kill us?"

"You know who. His people. The murdered one's people. My father said this last night."

"Why us? We didn't do anything to him."

"Yes, if the old man did it, it means we did it."

"Why? I don't understand. If he did it, he did it! We didn't do anything. I didn't do anything!" Wanjira felt a rising panic.

"I didn't do anything!" she shouted, then closed her mouth tightly, fearing the words that might come out of her mouth. She stared into space, challenging something, someone. But Nyathira looked straight ahead, and said, "If the old man did it they will say we did it. That's all."

"They"?

"Yes, the dead man's people. The people of the lake."

This was something new for Wanjira, these words, "The people of the lake".

"But aren't they Kenyans too? They just live there, don't they? And we live here." Wanjira was confused. It was so confusing! What did all this mean?

Nyathira continued with her explanation.

"They are different. Not like us. They eat ***ugali****. And fish."*

"But so do we. We had ugali with ***terere*** *last night. And my father brought us fish from Nairobi a few months ago."*

"I don't mean that! I mean, they eat ***ugali*** *and fish everyday!"*

"Every day?"

"Yes, every day. They are not like us. We eat ***githeri*** *almost daily, so we are different."*

Wanjira kept quiet, and tried to think hard about what she had just learned. But nothing made sense. The two young girls continued walking, and anyone observing them might have assumed it was just another ordinary evening for two ordinary girls in the village on their way to a neighbor's home to fetch their families' evening milk. Girls and boys did this every evening. An ordinary evening chore. But the observer would not have been able to see the turmoil in the girls' minds, especially in the slightly shorter one, the one who wore a blue tunic and white blouse, the one whose brow was now creased into a frown, the one whose heart was going tum! tum! tum! This girl had just experienced a troubling moment, but she had no words to describe the turmoil caused by her companion's words. The words had turned the world upside down just a few minutes earlier. These words had spoken of trouble, of danger, or things out there the girls could do little about. The words had brought pain into her heart, and confusion. All of a sudden, and in a very brief period, her world had started to look different. Why should she fear people who ate ugali and fish daily? What did that have to do with anything? And yet Nyathira, her friend, was no fool. She was a bright girl, and her family was educated, and knew many things. What she said had to be true, but was it? For a brief moment Wanjira looked into the distance and saw the beautiful colours of the sunset. Everything looked beautiful, as it always did at this time of the evening. Wanjira loved stopping whatever she was doing to look at the sunset, and always loved the sudden change in the sky, the reddish yellow and orange sky which changed so fast, just when the mind was beginning to enjoy it and to long for it to last just a while longer. She loved the feeling in her body, and always anticipated the subtle shock the drop in temperature caused as twilight set in, and the almost sudden slip into darkness as the sun dipped into the horizon. But today Wanjira did not stop to watch the skies. Her mind was elsewhere.

"So that's why the dead man's people are different, and why they don't like us, and why we don't like them." Nyathira spoke firmly, and with authority. Suddenly Wanjira felt scared. Goose bumps appeared all over her body, and she felt chilly. The sun had gone down, and soon it would be dark, and she was not supposed to be out in the dark.

"Let's hurry, I have to get all the clothes from the line before it gets really dark," she told Nyathira. No-one said anything else about "them." That evening, as her family said their evening prayers, Wanjira, distracted, could think of nothing but ugali. Pots and pots of ugali appeared in her thoughts. Every day! That's strange. But I don't know them, she thought, furiously, and immediately felt guilty for having such thoughts at prayer time. She raised her voice, hoping to drive away her thoughts, only to hear her mother scold, "Be respectful when you pray."

The handsome man was buried, but not before a lot of trouble erupted in the city and in some other parts of the country. It was said that his people were so angry that they actually stoned the Old Man! Imagine that! They stoned him as he tried to visit the dead man's town following the funeral, crying, shouting many words. He had to turn back. Imagine that! Mzee himself! That meant, surely, that there was trouble in the land.

CHAPTER NINE

The weeks went by fast. Lectures, tutorials, term papers, and thesis writing continued to rule life on campus and in the halls of residence. It was the middle of Wanjira's second year at the university and everything seemed orderly, familiar, and comfortable. Like others in her class she had settled down to the routines of life as a university student, even as her social life had slowly but surely become entwined with, perhaps even submerged, into Luka's life. She still saw her friends, but it would be fair to say that she was now entering a world more defined by Luka's friends and his preoccupations. She attended rugby games with him in the university fields and in various clubs around Nairobi, and she now and then accompanied him when he visited some older cousins and other friends who lived in different parts of the Eastlands.

Two months after they first met Luka had invited Wanjira to visit the family of his uncle in Woodley. She had felt self-conscious during the visit, aware that she was being studied keenly, and had wondered what his aunt, especially, thought of her and Luka being together. But everyone had been polite, and very kind, and the uncle had shown much friendliness, especially when he learned that an old classmate of his at Ngumo High School was her Uncle Kariuki, her mother's youngest brother. After the visit, on their way to the bus stop, Luka had squeezed her hand and said, "Wanji, they liked you very much, I could tell." She had smiled, not wanting to let him know she had felt ill at ease, and a bit worried during most of the visit. But by now word was that Luka was head-over-heels over "That beautiful Gikuyu woman" and all his friends had come to realize that Wanjira was more than a mere passing cloud for their friend. They envied Luka, even as they privately feared that the pair might be headed for a catastrophe at some point in the not-too-distant future, for most of them fully understood society's demand that one should stick to one's kind when it came to seriously considering a future life partner. They thought the beautiful couple was living outside the rules everyone knew and understood, and Luka's close friends were worried for him. Some of Wanjira's friends were also worried, but no-one had as yet said anything, for they all secretly prayed that the couple would see the danger they were in once they were out of the crazy, mad love situation they obviously were in, but which, clearly, showed no signs of abating. Wanjira was privately surprised, but also grateful, that none of her friends had said anything—positive or negative—about her relationship with Luka. So far the only naysayers were people she did not know, or care about.

For Luka and Wanjira, the approaching end of the school year meant they each had to make some important decisions. For one thing, Wanjira needed to decide on her final course of study: should she focus entirely on the study of literature, or on both literature and politics? Either path was attractive, but she needed to think a bit more about things before making a final decision. She planned to discuss the matter with Akili, her tutor, and with Professor Mwangi, her political science lecturer. She had shared some of her thoughts with Luka, who had agreed with her that she could not go wrong with whatever decision she made because she planned to become a teacher, but more especially, to enter graduate school to earn a master's degree in Literature. They both favoured a third year concentration on Literature studies because it would give her an edge when considerations for admission and funding for graduate studies were made, and she would be even more prepared for graduate work.

Luka's plans seemed clearer, for after graduation from the Faculty of Law he would join his classmates at the School of Law, as was required of all who wanted to practice law in Kenya. He had expressed an interest in studying for a master's degree as he wanted to eventually become a law lecturer, and one evening suggested they both consider applying for graduate studies at the same time. "That way, Wanji, we will both be students and our house will have nothing but books and two hard-working occupants for about three to four years, before we think of another small someone joining us."

"What"? Wanjira had been somewhat shocked. "Luka, let's cross that bridge when we get to it, you fast thinking fellow!" But she had pondered the idea, knowing, but not quite knowing, what she felt about it.

About a week after Wanjira and Luka had spoken of their shared knowledge that some might not be too pleased to see the two of them together, and in love, and he had invited her to meet his mother, she found herself face to face with very strong disapproval of her relationship with Luka from none other than her feisty friend, Wangu.

It all started with Wangu teasing Wanjira about Samuel, suggesting that Wanjira was losing her heart to him. Wangu had joined Wanjira and Samuel for a game of tennis earlier, and after taking a shower the two women had gone to supper in the residence hall cafeteria together. They had not shared a meal in more than two weeks, and being together felt like a wonderful treat. Wangu had been spending a lot of time away from the Box lately, visiting her boyfriend, and whenever the two women bumped into each other on campus they exchanged happy greetings as each went to her respective lecture or tutorial group. They had not had time to sit down and talk, especially about Wanjira's news of her growing relationship with Luka.

Wangu thought that Wanjira and Samuel had something special going, and thought this evening gave her a good opportunity to inquire, and tease the necessary information out of Wanjira. She thought her friend was keeping too much from her, and now was the time.

"So, what's the news? Pray do tell about you and our tennis friend." Wangu's face was lit with a big smile. "Come on, Wanji, *toboa*!"

Wanjira burst into loud laughter. She could not believe her ears. Was it possible that Wangu had not heard anything about the gossip about her and Luka? It was already well over a month since she and Luka started seeing each other seriously.

"Where have you been my friend?" She had a big smile. "Don't tell me you haven't heard the news!"

"What news? Please share!

"Listen, Wangu. Samuel's not my boyfriend." Wangu appeared unconvinced. Her frown said it all as Wanjira continued, "You know he's a dear friend, but that's all." Wangu gave her a knowing look, and Wanjira suddenly felt defensive.

"Do you think a man and woman can only be friends with a quote?" She felt roused to a powerful emotion by Wangu's face which suggested Wanjira was withholding, or avoiding, some truth, some unacknowledged reality. Wanjira became determined to set the record straight: she felt she needed to.

Since they first met at university, and certainly before she met Luka, Wanjira and Wangu had had many discussions that revealed the different ways in which they viewed life, and Wanjira had marveled at their growing friendship even as she understood how different many of her ideas were from Wangu's. Wangu, for example, had what she considered "clear and consistent" views about men and women. She believed, so she had told Wanjira, that men were after only one thing in women: sleeping with them, marking them as "theirs" as wives, concubines, or girlfriends. Wangu expressed this view one

Friday evening when she and two other friends visited Wanjira's room. The women had gone on talking about a variety of topics late into the night.

Wangu said she believed women were naturally inclined to agree to these arrangements of "ownership" by men even when most of them knew deep in their hearts that they were being tied down, and often getting a raw deal. "The trouble is children. Procreation, my friends. Survival of the species. A primitive emotion, really, embedded in our genes. Nothing else." The room had burst into laughter and Wangu, warming to the topic, continued, "My darlings, women accept these indignities because they love children. They want to raise them in safe and reliable arrangements, so called "homes." Her index fingers created the necessary commas around the word home. "You know I'm right."

"You are, In some ways you are, but you're wrong to think that is all there is to men and women—trouble." Wanjira felt somewhat breathless as she responded to Wangu, who snorted, a big smile on her face. Wangu loved arguments, especially if she could ruffle some feathers.

"You're much too cynical, Wangu. Is this what being a sociologist is about?"

"Show me what else there is," Wangu spoke defiantly, though her voice was warm. "Show me a home where a woman is not sitting on thorns, as my mother would put it." Wangu knew she had a point.

"My dear," Wangu's friend Judy had entered the conversation. "I think you're right…in a way…there seems to be a lot of trouble in people's homes, and mine has its share…But…what about love? Women love men, and men love women. That's why they marry in the first place…its just that…its just that married life is endangered by…money troubles, and….

"And grown men who can't keep their zippers closed!" Wangu had interrupted, raising her voice, fire in her eyes. "Yes, men, sugar daddies, big bellied, smelly things that are willing to sleep with girls their teenage daughters' age. Disgusting!"

"Yea, disgusting," Wanjira answered. The young women then burst into loud laughter, which, if you listened closely, might also have been a sob, a wounded cry.

"As for Samuel, Wanjira said, after a brief pause, and then sipping from her cup of tea. "He's become a good friend, but that's all. He's not attracted to me in a romantic way, and neither am I. He's my friend, and yes, I like him—a lot. He is very handsome, yes, but…"

"Hmm, yes. A good friend. But what a handsome one!" Wangu laughed loudly. "Some of us have eyes, but apparently we can't see."

"Oh, come off it, Wangu. You are insulting my intelligence."

"Our people, come hear this beautiful girl talk," Wangu was clapping her hands together dramatically. Women from the table next to them glanced in their direction. "My dear," Wangu continued, "you are oblivious to it, and Samuel is a proud guy who does not want a rejection, but I can see it. I've got good eyes. Very good eyes. And they've been seeing things."

"Well, ask your eyes to please stop seeing what doesn't exist," Wanjira retorted. She gave her friend a big smile, and as an afterthought asked, slyly, "And what makes you think he would get a rejection?" and they both burst out laughing, and would have gone on laughing for a while had Wanjira not said, in a soft voice, "The love of my life is Luka. You know him...second year law student. The student leader. I'm surprised you don't know it already since we've been together over a month now, and many seem to know about us. But I forget you hardly live around here, Wangu. He is the one. I know it." She seemed to be speaking to herself, staring into space, and therefore did not immediately see the shocked expression on her friend's face.

"Luka? Luka O?"

"The very same. Wanjira's raised eyebrows spoke volumes for she had heard Wangu's tone and the urgency in her voice. Seeming really shocked, Wangu fixed her gaze on her friend, and then, her voice stern and admonishing, just like a headmistress of old, said, "These things aren't done, my dear." She fixed a stern look on Wanjira, who stared back straight into her eyes.

"Let it be, Wanji," Wangu said, her voice firm. "Find someone else. Be realistic! Luka O? Are you crazy?"

"He loves me. I love him"

Wanjira heard Wangu's words, strong, yet kind, as if from a long distance. "Wanjira, find someone else. Look at all these guys on campus, dying for you! Give them a chance. Wanjira you're so desirable! You have a certain something men like...Wanjira, you are intelligent, down to earth, sexy, and yet you don't even know it! This is what all these guys keep telling me, but you only seem to want to make friends, to pair up with no one. Of course Samuel likes you a whole lot, and so does Kariuki P, Munene, Muriithi, and...I could go on. These guys have bright futures ahead of them! OK, if you want to wait a bit, don't pair up with anyone yet, but *please* don't pair up with Luka...It will ruin everything! Luka is wonderful, and bright, but he's not right for you. My dear, be realistic. These things aren't done. Maybe our children will be able to do them, but not us. Forget that Luka."

Just what Wanjira had feared. She was stunned by Wangu's words, even though she had expected some kind of disapproval, some words about being careful, perhaps some admonishment. She had actually hoped Wangu would surprise her by at least being curious about her and Luka. But no! She had gone straight to the point. She was quite sure of her feelings about this matter—had a ready-made response. She absolutely, positively, disapproved of inter-ethnic relationships. No way should they take place! Wanjira supposed many felt the same, like the male student who had, just a week earlier, called her *muka wa kihii*—wife of an uncircumcised man—so full of venom, someone she did not even know. But he had taken it upon himself to publicly insult her for a wrong he perceived to have been made against him by Luka's entire ethnic group that did not practice male circumcision as a rite of passage, unlike his own, which did, and which he must have assumed was superior to Luka's people. What nonsense! She wondered if others felt quite that strongly about couples like herself and Luka.

To Wangu now she said, in a sad, soft voice, a whisper, really, "Luka and I have so much in common. We really do! Why don't you ask me about it? You are jumping to conclusions, Wangu. You don't even know anything else about him. All you know is that he is from Western Kenya, but you don't know anything else! He is wonderful! He has a kind heart. He has very good ideas, and he loves me!" She was passionate, all heated up. "But in this Kenya of ours we are supposed to have nothing in common! Because of what? Because I was born in Central, and he was born in Western, Province. I am a Gikuyu woman, and he is a Luo man. That is all! You and I know this is *ukabila*. Tribalism. Luka and I should never cross this *ukabila* divide. Then Kenya would be safe. Uncomplicated. Free of strife. We should have known it: it should have been hello and good bye...for Kenya's future leaders."

Wanjira sounded bitter as her voice trailed off, but she suddenly seemed animated, nostrils flared, and she was breathing fast, "But it's all nonsense! Wangu, its all rubbish! That's all. It is nonsense.!"

Wangu knew she should say no more, unless she wanted a scene. She had never seen Wanjira this agitated, and she could tell she was very angry. In any case Wanjira suddenly stopped, as if her strength had left her, and she looked so miserable Wangu did not dare say anything more. To herself she thought, "I had to speak my mind. I had to speak directly, without mincing any words. Someone had to do it" She felt she had done her duty, even though she might have said something she might come to regret. She did not know what to do now that the words had been uttered.

The two women picked up their trays, and without another word walked out of the dining room and back to their rooms. At her door Wangu said, with a soft smile, "No hard feelings, eh?" and Wanjira said, quietly, sadly, "No hard feelings. Goodnight Wangu. See you tomorrow."

As soon as her door was closed behind her Wanjira threw herself onto her bed, beating her pillow, and grabbing whatever she could to stifle the loud sounds that were coming out of her mouth. She sobbed uncontrollably for a long time. Wangu's disapproval had hurt badly, and Wanjira felt terribly disappointed. Wangu was, after all, her daring, outgoing, and carefree friend. How could she be so conservative, so concerned with tired, old ideas about fellow Kenyans? What did it all mean? Could she, Wanjira, be totally out of step with the prevailing mood and attitude of everyone else around her? But that could not be, for that meant that Luka too was out of step. And there had to be others in the country who felt exactly what she felt: that there was no reason to close the heart against what it saw clearly and with no prejudice. She had learned to ignore the strange looks some of the women on campus and in the halls of residence gave whenever she and Luka walked by. She had decided to ignore their unspoken rage and condemnation. But Wangu was her friend. How could her friend be so biased, so close-minded, so insensitive? How could she dismiss her love for Luka in such a manner?

Wanjira felt defiant. Her heart knew what it felt, after all, and wasn't this exactly what her mother had once told her? *Ngoro iriaga kiria ikwenda*, The heart eats what it wants. Her heart loved Luka, and that was that. He was her *Mpenzi*, her *Mwendwa,* her true *Jahera*. Every thought led to this: he was her beloved. Those who wanted to talk could keep talking. They would soon get tired. *Watasema watachoka*

I'll never forget. How could I ever forget that terrible evening? The men and women who frightened me so, the missing tooth in the leader's mouth, his sharp, intense, eyes, the words that came out of that mouth! The women, their faraway, distant, distracted, look. They knew all of us but didn't show any recognition as we were brought in. Their leader was Wacuka, our neighbor, who sometimes visited our home. Many times she had helped mother in the planting and harvesting, but there she was, that evening, a leader of a night-time group, a woman of power and authority. She asked us to undress, and asked if any girl was seeing the moon, and if so, would the girl let her know immediately, for it would be taboo to be in that state on this special day. The fear, the shame of hearing that body process spoken about in this manner! I hadn't had a period yet, and had to answer "no," to Wacuka, for she interrogated each girl after her general announcement. She did not show any recognition of me, or of Wanjiku, my neighbor and best friend. The two of us had joined a group of nearly twenty girls from our school, walking in silence all the way. A beautiful sunset gave a soft look to the land, the maize plants in the fields swayed gently in the evening breeze, and one could hear the mooing of cows as they were milked, and bleats of goats as they were shooed into their pens for the night, and the smell of smoke filled the air. Mothers were making the evening meal, assisted by their children, but here we were, headed somewhere, led by a force greater than ourselves. An invisible force at school had organized our group, a force that operated through rumour, warnings, predictions of doom, and outright accusations. "If you don't go, they'll come for your family. They'll get your brothers. They'll take your cows and goats. They'll burn your home. They'll then do things." Who were "they"? We didn't know. But all over the place people had been going to this place to drink "Chai". There was no choice: you had to drink "Chai." The forces out there said you must. The girls who had already gone had smug, superior faces, and seemed determined to make everyone go. But they didn't use words. They didn't say, "You must go." And yet all the other girls felt their power, their unspoken orders. But these girls were also frightened. You could see it in their faces. When we asked, "What happens at the Chai?" they said, impassively, "You have to see it for yourself."

A small kerosene lamp in the front of the round hut into which we've been shepherded reveals a man, clothed in an animal skin. The man is telling us that we have lots of enemies. They want to harm us. They will harm us. We must not let them. They are evil. We are good. We are the chosen ones. Our house must remain intact, protected. We are the protectors. We must keep all interlopers and evildoers out. The evildoers do not speak our language. They eat fish. They have different habits. These habits are bad. They are dirty. We are clean. We are right. We are the rulers. No-one else must rule us. Our house has the right to rule. The house of Mumbi. We will protect it from harm. We will take up arms if called to do so. We will not speak of these things, or else harm will come upon us. We must keep this secret.

The House of Mumbi. Nyumba ya Mumbi. I have always loved hearing of this House. In stories, in songs. It reminds me of my great-great-grandfather, Gakinya. He is the farthest my brother can reach when he asks me to recite:

What is your name?
Wiitagwo atia?
Wanjira
Whose daughter are you?
Wanjira wau?
Wanjira wa Kamau
Kamau wau?
Kamau wa Kairu
Kairu wau?
Kairu wa Mugo
Mugo wau?
Mugo wa Gakinya

After this we have no more names, but everything is clear. The ancestors, through my great-great-grandfather, Gakinya, who was a Muceera, are with us. They look after us, in addition to God, of course. But this God who takes care of us is the Christian God, God the father, the Almighty. He is not really different from Murungu, Ngai, Mwene Nyaga, he-who-sits-on-Kirinyaga, Mount Kenya. He-who-sits-on-Mount Kenya is also Murungu, but somehow, along the way, he has been replaced by God-the-father. In any event, these powers are great. My grandmother says: when you trip, be sure to recognize the ancestors. You call on them, "Nduuri ici!! Even though some people think saying that is naughty, it really isn't," my grandmother told me, years ago. "It is a call to the ancestors: All you living beings!" The ancestors, beginning with Gikuyu, the original man, and Mumbi, the creator, the first woman, created the House of Mumbi. I have always liked knowing that it was HER house. The first woman, Mumbi, set up the great House to which I belong. But now

This HOUSE.
This House is saying something.
Something I don't like
This man is saying that IT
Wants me to fear someone
Someone I don't know
Someone who lives far, far away
Someone I don't know
Someone who might,
Will, do me harm

The man's assistants emerge from the shadows and give us some strips of goat meat. I start to gag, but we must eat it. Then they pass along a calabash of with some drink. Something I've never tasted before. It is awful. I want to throw up and hope I won't. At school they said a boy fainted at "Chai" and they revived him with water, and had him re-do the whole thing. We repeat things the man says we must. "If I ever reveal this secret, may this meat and this drink do me in. May I forever be cursed." I repeat this after the man. I do not really know what it is I must not reveal.

Afterwards Wacuka orders us to dress, and to walk home quickly. As we leave the hut another group of people is ushered in, but I can't make out any face. Its now pitch dark. We walk home in silence. I feel defiled, sickened. I pray I won't throw up, in case some of the older girls take me back. I find my father in the house, but I don't say anything, and he doesn't ask any questions. My older brother also does not ask anything either. Mother is away, and I am glad, for she has said publicly that she, a Christian, would have nothing to do with "Chai." She is away in Uganda with others who went to witness the Pope's first ever visit to Africa. So much holiness, so much unholiness everywhere!

When Mother returns I tell her that I had to go to "Chai" and she twists up her face disapprovingly and says, "The fools, what do they expect to gain?" and I feel somewhat vindicated. No-one ever mentions "Chai" in our home ever again, and at school all is mum. From now on when I make tea for the family I do not mention it by name. I simply say, when it is ready, "It is ready." I cannot bring myself to ever utter the word "Chai." I do not tell mother that I threw my beautiful yellow petticoat with white lace into the latrine, even though I think she would approve. This beautiful garment had been bought at Deacons by my older brother. A special treat. One of the most beautiful pieces of clothing I've ever had, but I could never ever wear it after that evening because the day after "Chai" I find a big fat louse in a fold of the petticoat as I wash it, hoping to take away the horror of the evening, praying that this will wash everything away. It is the first louse I've ever seen in my clothes, though I have seen lice on some children at school. When I throw it into the latrine I watch the hole keenly, wanting to make sure that the petticoat is gone, gone, gone, gone forever.

So, dear journal, I should not love Luka. His people eat fish.

CHAPTER TEN

Wanjira felt sad and bewildered after her conversation with Wangu, and in the following days spent a lot of time in her room or at the library, trying to read, writing in her journal, trying to understand the unhappiness that had entered her soul with such force. She avoided Wangu, not wanting to revisit their conversation. She had realized, that evening in the dining hall, that Wangu was set in her ideas, and that to argue with her would not help matters. What had hurt the most, however, was Wangu's dismissal of Luka…as if he was not a person, a very intelligent and good one at that, but *just a Luo*. She wondered if anyone encouraging Luka to look elsewhere would dismiss her in similar fashion: she's *just a Gikuyu woman*. That reduced people, their real selves, to nothing, really. If someone could ignore the love and affection she and Luka shared, their ideas about Kenya, and the world, the feelings she had whenever she was with him…and he with her…if all that was nothing, and was easily replaceable by a person considered "right" by virtue of the fact that they were born in western or central Kenya, then what was the point? What was the point of living, going to school, meeting people from different parts of Kenya, learning new information and ideas, hoping to live in a Kenya without *ukabila*? "*Hatutaki ukabila, Kenya yetu ni Kenya mpya,*" the song went. *We do not want tribalism, ours is a new Kenya*. And there were many other good things people spoke about, especially about being Christians. Was *ukabila* consistent with Christianity? What really, did it mean to be a Christian? People walked around calling themselves Christians, and yet…they really did not believe in the teachings of their own faith. They picked and chose what to believe in. They did not believe in love or the power of spirit. She admired Luka for his generousity of spirit, his concern for the welfare of others in the university and in the country. She felt that this spirit matched with her own, which she had sought to develop since secondary school. Then she had been inspired by her readings and discussions at Young Christian Student meetings, and when she found out that Luka had been a part of these discussions she had felt a great surge of hope and a great energy had filled her heart as their relationship continued to develop. She felt, as time went on, that Luka was an integral part of her soul, and that nothing could change her mind about this. Something deep inside her felt fulfilled by his smile, his handshake, his laugh, his ideas about things. She would look at him sometimes as they walked to campus, sat on the grass at the great court, in the library, or as they went to the movies, and feel that this was the man she had waited for all this time. It was very clear to her. With him, and together, she hoped to become something greater than that which she was or she had come from. Was that not what education was all about? It was about moving beyond one's limitations; it was about expanding one's horizons. She had come to this conclusion when studying for her A-levels. All the writers she admired urged their readers to look beyond the obvious, to look into a characters' circumstances, to see the soul, to examine that private reality that made them act in a certain way. Her relationship with Luka had happened naturally, with no-one forcing anything. She felt it was the right thing, and had wanted her friend to affirm her choice. She actually had longed to hear Wangu say, "It might be hard, but we must forge a new path to the future" But that had not happened. Wangu's was a knee jerk reaction, and Wanjira was upset because the world she thought university men and women could create seemed too far off into the future. "To hell with Wangu," she thought. "And others like her. What do they know about me and Luka? Nothing, nothing." She underlined words in her journal, and then quickly erased them, hoping to undo some act, some thought, but many other thoughts came flooding back. She was amazed at how hurt she felt, at how Wangu's words and attitude had stabbed into some part of her, of the sharp pain she felt; the constriction in her throat, the actual, physical, pain in her chest and head whenever she remembered their recent conversation.

Luka noticed her low mood when he came to visit her just before supper. It was three days since Wangu's and Wanjira's distressing conversation. When he asked what was wrong she told him that too many thoughts were crowding her mind, and she needed time to think them through. He did not pry, something Wanjira appreciated. He asked if she would like to see a movie in town, or take a walk, or go to Snow Cream, and she said yes to the ice cream place.

Wanjira took delight in the delicious banana float which Luka insisted she have because he feared she had had no food that day, which was true, saying the banana would help. She smiled, and called him her protector, and he smiled, happy that her mood was changing.

"So what's the matter, my love?" He held her hand and tried to look into her eyes. She wanted to tell him about her conversation with Wangu but did not really know where to begin, and she did not want to say anything against

Wangu, but there was no way of telling him about her problems without making someone look bad.

"Its nothing, and its everything...Luka, its just complicated."

"Maybe I can understand some of it. Just tell me what's wrong." He looked worried, and she felt such a flooding in her heart, and wanted to protect him from all this nonsense, all this history others had created long before either of them was born.

"It's...it's just that some people I know don't think you and I should be together. They think we should be *kaput*, out, looking for others...It's so silly, Luka!"

"Oh...Well...I should have guessed, Wanjira. I actually wondered if that was the trouble...but what has happened? Who has said anything?"

"Oh, you know...a friend...some friend, I suppose. She thinks we're unrealistic, dreamers. She thinks I should be dating someone else, and you should date someone else..."

Luka sighed, and a tired look came over his face, but he also smiled as he said, "My love, what does this friend of yours mean? Does she know what she is saying?" He squeezed her hand, and with the other raised his coffee cup to his lips, and then, as if speaking to himself, said, "You know, my love, I've been given similar advice by some of the fellows who realize I'm serious about you, people who've known me before, and after, we met. They know we have something good going, and are worried that we might be pushing it a little...our luck. But I've told them I'm the luckiest man I know," he smiled, and squeezed her hand, "and that you and I love and trust each other...we do, don't we, Wanji?"

"Of course, Luka, Of course." I guess it's just hard for people to see things as they are, and not as they should be. They disbelieve what we feel is real for us, what we know to be real. Instead they go by what they've learned *should* be real, what others have decided is real. I suppose that's tradition...you follow a path others have laid out before you."

"Yes, yes, And yet we all know that culture, and traditions, evolve daily. People make culture. Yes, Wanjira, you and I will make a new culture. In years to come, Kenyans will find it silly that people of different ethnic groups were discouraged, or prevented from, loving one another. That new culture will be informed by belief in love, new attitudes, knowledge about ourselves, our families, our interests in life..." He smiled, and she smiled back, feeling encouraged, uplifted, really. For a while Wanjira and Luka were silent, each lost in the wonder of it all. They would change things. They were not afraid to do so!

"Just imagine, Luka, all those naysayers, and their prescriptions for love. It must be a Gikuyu man for me, and of course one with a bright future. And you must befriend only a Luo woman, one with a bright future. It hurts so much to know that first and foremost a friend of mine distrusts my choice of boyfriend, and thinks she knows what's best for me."

Luka was about to respond but just then a fellow from his faculty walked into the café and joined them, and the conversation turned to other matters. After another half hour or so Wanjira and Luka excused themselves and walked back to the residence halls. It was a dark night, but the lights on University Way were on, and it was still early in the residence halls, so the place was well lit. Wanjira did not like walking in the dark, and often said there was no need to tempt fate by walking into potential attacks by criminal elements from Uhuru Park and nearby areas. However, such attacks, if any, were rare. In any case she was with Luka, and a woman walking with a man was ten times safer than ten women walking together, as some women in the Box liked to say. But this evening she felt safe with Luka, and she felt light, and so did he, and they held hands in their usual fashion. At the entrance to the box they kissed and said goodnight. Each had a lot of reading and writing assignments, and they promised to meet at their usual place in the morning.

Wanjira was happy as she entered the Box. She and Luka were of the same mind, and that was all that mattered. The rest can go hang, she thought, as she picked up her toiletries and headed to the shower room. She wanted to wash and condition her hair because Sue, one of her hall mates, had promised to braid it the following evening.

Just as she was leaving her room she heard a shriek, a loud wail, and the sound of running feet. A lot of noise suddenly filled the corridor, and Wanjira saw a group of people coming toward her: Wangu, Mercy, a friend who lived down the hall, and behind them three guys she did not know. Wangu was screaming, over and over, "My, God, no!! no!! Its not true, its not true, Oh, God!, Jehovah! Jehovah! *Ngai witu, Ngai! Ngai*! O God!" Tears ran down her face, and on Mercy's as well. The guys all looked solemn, and suddenly the whole corridor was full of people come to see what was the matter, and doors were opening all along the floor.

"What's wrong? What? What?" Wanjira, said, and suddenly very fearful, rushed to Wangu's side. She noticed that Wangu had a sling on one arm, and there was a bandage sticker on her forehead.

"Wanji," Mercy said, sadly, "Its Wahito. There's been a terrible accident."

"What? Where? What? Wahito? What happened?" Wanjira felt goose bumps all over her body. Her hair seemed to shoot up straight from her head. "What accident?"

One of the guys said, "It happened around seven PM, near the Nairobi West roundabout. Wahito, Wangu, and three friends were on their way to Nairobi West, and somehow there was an accident, and we have bad news

"About Wahito?" She felt herself suddenly tremble. Her toilet bag fell to the floor. "Is she alright? Where is she?"

"I'm afraid it isn't good news, Wanji," Mercy said, her voice hoarse from crying. "She's gone. Gone, Wanji." They couldn't save her. No-one could."

Afterwards Wanjira could recall the minute details of that evening. Her toilet bag in her hand. Her key. She was about to lock her door. She was on her way to the shower room. She remembered the motion of her head as she turned to the wailing that came from far off in the corridor, her gown, and the sudden chill that came over her body when she heard Wangu's shrieks; the way her hair seemed to stand up at attention, the men she had not seen before, the calm manner in which Mercy had said, "I'm afraid it isn't good news, Wanji." But she could not remember how she got to her bed, and how come Luka was there when next she looked up. He told her afterwards that someone had come knocking on his door and said he must hurry to the Box, that Wanjira needed him. He had stayed in Wanjira's room, keeping a careful eye on her, and Mercy had stayed with Wangu, as had two other friends who arranged with Wangu's roommate to keep vigil on the bereaved friend, who felt responsible for her friend's death.

"You know Wahito, and you know me," she repeated to her friends. "You know she was not into dancing, but I persuaded her. I insisted. I said, "You must come with us. It's a house party, not a club. I know you don't like clubs. Get away from your medical books for a while." I led her to her death. I did. I did." Her friends shushed her. They told her she was not to blame, that she had no control over Wahito's fate. They found solace in speaking about God's plans. They said he has a plan for each of us, and that we have no control over our deaths. "I know I was there. In the same car. And all I suffered was a broken arm. I invited her to the party. I led her to her death," Wangu repeated, like a record, saying the same thing over and over again. Her friends wondered if she should not have been kept in the hospital overnight, for clearly she was in shock. She had been dismissed after her arm was put in a sling, and after some medication, but her friends were worried, and took turns in staying with her over the next few days. Everyone feared she might do something dangerous to herself, and Wanjira and Luka tried to comfort her the best they could. Wanjira said over and over again, as if to comfort herself, "Her lung was punctured. She seemed alright at first, but when they reached the hospital, only about ten minutes later, she was dying. Dying! It was her lung, punctured!"

Later, Wanjira thought of the irony of it all: Wahito, the woman who loved medicine, who loved to explain the workings of the human body, the woman who pored over huge textbooks everyday, who spoke of her love of her chosen field. What a loss to her family!! to Kenya! God, it should have been me, she thought at times, but then quickly felt repentant, remembering her lessons of many years: God's plans should not be questioned. But why? Why? She wept so much she felt she could weep no more.

She had telephoned Mwangi at his bank the morning after the accident and he came to visit, and a day later invited everyone to have a drink at the Serena. He drove Wangu, Wanjira, and two other women to the funeral in Kiambu a few days later. Luka and many other guys from campus came by bus, and for days afterwards people spoke of nothing but the freak accident that took one of the university's best and brightest women, leaving her friends to marvel that only Wangu had suffered a broken arm and a mere scratch on the face, and to ponder about their companions, who had suffered only the jolt in their hearts from the accident. Wahito's family was devastated, and her mother's, sister's and many relatives' tears had caused many an eye to fill up, but there was also much love expressed at the funeral, and different groups of friends had laid beautiful wreaths on Wahito's grave: her friends from primary school, secondary school, A-levels, and her university friends. The church choir had sung beautifully, and the reverend had invited everyone to thank God for such a beautiful life, for the beauty with brains Wahito had been in this life. He had reminded everyone present to remember that cars must be driven with care, and that they owed it to each other to take the utmost care while operating a vehicle. Everything else was in God's hands, he said, and Wahito's life had come to the conclusion God had planned, long before he had bequeathed her life to her family's safe keeping. They had done well, he told her parents. They had done everything parents should do for their children. It was now God's turn to take back this beautiful woman back to her true home, and therefore everything should be accepted as HIS plan. Wanjira thought to herself: yes, what had happened is truly *Shauri ya Mungu*, inexplicable, hard to take, a matter to ponder for days, months, and to recall for years afterwards. For weeks afterwards Wanjira and her companions at the university walked around feeling as if something had hit them hard on the head. Sadness became their daily companion, an unwelcome *mgeni* who planted himself in their hearts with no visible signs of leaving. They tried to read, went to the movies for a temporary distraction, and gathered in each other's rooms at various times during the day, but especially in the evening, to listen to music or try to talk, something to soothe their heavy hearts. Tears would fill their eyes throughout the day—as they walked to lectures, tried to read in the library, or during lectures when their minds wandered far off, and their late friend appeared so close, so real, so alive. In the privacy of her room Wanjira would cry, covering her face with the pillow, not wanting to announce her seemingly permanent sorrow. She was sure she would never feel right, not ever again.

It never rains but it pours, dear journal, and I'll tell you why. Wangu is in a deep depression and all our friends are really sad. We don't know what to do. She drinks and smokes almost non-stop, and not even Mwangi seems able to help her. I personally went to his bank to inform him that Wangu was in a drunken stupor when I came upon her in a terrible state in her room last week. It was not a pretty sight to see her all broken up, crying about Wahito. She kept repeating, over and over, that Wahito understood people, making me and two of our friends who were present start crying. I actually came to admire Mwangi when I saw how gentle he was with Wangu. I think he loves her a lot, and seems to know how to calm her down. Now it is up to the medical authorities because her family had her check into Nairobi Hospital last week. She will miss the end of year examinations but still has another chance with the supplementaries. I assume she will manage with this second chance at passing the year, but if she does not they will discontinue her studies at the university.

She surprised me the other day when I went to visit her. Looking so much better, though very weak, she said there was something she wanted to tell me. "On the day before she died Wahito actually mentioned Luka. She did not say anything about you two directly but said we might soon hear surprising news about him and one of our friends. I was so caught up in my own thoughts, Wanji, I never asked who the friend was. All I said was,' leave those people alone.'"

Wangu paused, then said, "Wanji—I'm sorry. I am such an ignorant person, I now know." I did not say anything, and she continued, as if she were now speaking to herself, "We were both silent for a while, and Wahito, who had definitely got the meaning of my dismissive comment, looked at me and said, 'Wangu, You know what? There's no difference between a Luo and Gikuyu and Maasai and Luyha cadaver. As a current student of physiology and anatomy I can tell you there's no difference.' She said no more, and I now wish I'd been more responsive. I knew what she was telling me but at that time I didn't really want to know, so I simply shrugged my shoulders.

I told Wangu not to worry about it and thanked her for this piece of information from our late friend. I had no idea Wahito had come to know about me and Luka, and wished I had had a chance to tell her about him. I felt her approval in Wangu's words, and was encouraged. It is as if she had sent me a message from the dead. She's been visiting me in my dreams lately but they are peaceful visits and I wake up with a sense of longing and sadness, and I do not feel as overwhelmed as I did a few weeks ago. I do, however, miss her laughter and quiet, wise, presence.

But something else has thrown us off really badly. Its terrible, and in a different way. They have arrested Ngugi!! It happened when we were on Christmas break. We learned they went for him at night and now he is in detention! Without trial! The campus is bewildered. We are paralyzed. It seems no-one knows what to do. We hear the authorities have no response to the family's requests for information about his whereabouts. We hear that his detention was ordered by higher-ups and that there's little we can do. I am so frightened. I fear for his life. What will happen to him? To his family? People are now walking about campus without any joy. The other day a few students gathered for a Kamukunji to talk about him but it was unlike other Kamukunjis at the Great Court. I stood by the sidelines, terrified as hell, fearing for Luka, who was one of the speakers. He and five others demanded Ngugi's release. They condemned detention without trial. They compared the regime to a fascist dictatorship. They called for the rule of law in Kenya. It was frightening and exhilarating at the same time. At one point I shook like a leaf because Simon G, my classmate, who was standing next to me, pointed out a fellow in dark glasses who he said was a member of the Special Branch. I realized we were all being watched. I wondered what the lecturers in our department were feeling. Where were they? A few had spoken out courageously about Ngugi's arrest and detention. One of them was Beauty. But others have been dead silent, journal. One wrote a piece about the writer that read like an obituary. It was published in one of the papers. Maybe there's nothing to be done. I am terrified. Things have taken a terrible turn. I fear for Ngugi. And for Luka. After the Kamukunji Luka and I talked about our fears and agreed we cannot be cowed into silence. I feel like an onlooker, waiting, waiting. I admire Luka for his courage but also wonder if he is doing the right thing. Above all I am dissatisfied with my own behavior and lack of meaningful action. Why should I be just an onlooker when terrible things have happened in my country? They have taken away our writer, our teacher! A man who has made us proud. I was supposed to be taking his class this term, but God only knows if Ngugi is alive! Journal, what should I do? I must do something!

CHAPTER ELEVEN

The new term started with uncertainty and general lack of comfort in the student body. The calm and carefree days of first year seemed no more; the leisurely evenings in different dorm rooms fewer and far between. A combination of things had led to this state of affairs: Ngugi's arrest during the previous Christmas holiday, and the lack of information about his whereabouts, had made Wanjira and many in her department fearful and angry. Many were depressed. Five student leaders, Luka among them, had been picked up and detained for three days soon after classes started, and word was out that well known student leaders and their friends were being watched by members of the secret police, who were said to be present in lecture halls throughout the university. Students seemed jittery, worried, and conversations tended to come to a quick halt whenever a new person came by a group of friends talking on the Great Court, or in the lounges. Even the hustle and bustle in the main campus cafeteria seemed somewhat muted, subdued, and people no longer lingered to talk and exchange ideas noisily and animatedly as they had done in the past. It was as if the curtain had suddenly dropped on the stage that was campus life, and now it was on to a new act, one that seemed *ad hoc,* haphazard, unrehearsed.

But life went on despite the general gloom. Final year exams were just around the corner, and students had much on their plate. They had to do a lot of revision of material already covered, and new information to take in, for lectures and tutorials would not end until early May, after which exams would start, and Wanjira's second year would be over. Luka's time at the university was coming to an end with the upcoming June graduation, and then it would be off to the School of Law for a year's training. Wanjira found herself concentrating a lot on her studies, suddenly feeling that this year called for a different focus, major preparation, as it were. She was now concentrating on the study of African, Caribbean, and American literature, having completed most requirements for oral literature, literary theory and the study of European literature. Now she was encountering writers from the African diaspora, voices that intrigued and challenged her by their amazing stories of characters confronting the legacies of slavery, colonization, and dislocations of all kinds. It seemed she was expected to read more than her eyes or head could handle. She was also preparing to write a thesis, and had chosen as her topic the study of children's literature in primary schools.

She had held discussions with both her adviser and Akili, who had continued to be her tutor. Both encouraged her in her proposed study. She had always been interested in studying the earliest influences of reading on the minds and attitudes of young children, and her earlier studies on the African oral tradition had led to many questions in her mind. She remembered her early love of reading, her enjoyment of stories told at home or at her grandparents' home, and wanted to study these early influences on children in primary schools. Her teachers had made suggestions on how to go about the study, most of which would happen in the following school year. For now all she needed to do was put her thoughts on paper in the form of a proposal which, if accepted, she would develop into a thesis during the following academic year, her final one at *Chuo kikuu.*

Wanjira now had a roommate, Binti, a third year student of design. The two women got on quite well, perhaps because both were very busy at this time of their college career. Binti spent most of her time on "Golan Heights," the popular name for the School of Design, where students literary spent most nights of the week, working away on their drafting boards, planning future housing developments and other structures that needed careful mathematical computations. Binti was preparing for a career in fashion design, but had told Wanjira that her true love was in fabric design. She prayed that she would find a job with Maridadi Fabrics or any of the other few firms in the country that made clothes for *wananchi.* "I want to design beautiful *lesos* and dress material made of cotton. None of these polyesters we see all over the place. They are disrespectful of the human body, you know. The body breathes, and it needs natural fabric to breathe into." Wanjira loved Binti's passion and the two women had found a common area of interest in their love of African fabric and style. Binti was delighted when Wanjira agreed to be her model for one of her final exams. She would wear a dress made of fabric that Binti had designed in her second year and which she would actually make herself. Binti would photograph Wanjira in various poses and then make a calendar of her own design with Wanjira as her special model. Despite an initial anxious moment Wanjira quickly agreed to Binti's plan.

Luka and Wanjira remained inseparable during their free moments, which, though still very important to each of them, were becoming rarer as they coped with the increased work load and academic year-end demands. In spite of his academic workload, Luka continued to be heavily involved in student affairs. Since the beginning of the term the student government leaders had called a number of Kamukunjis at the Great Court, demanding the release of Ngugi and other political prisoners. They demanded official word on the writer's whereabouts. The students called for the abolition of detention without trial in Kenya, calling it a fundamental violation of human rights. Wanjira attended the Kamukunjis and as usual stayed on the fringes, her interest high but her heart racing fast. By now everyone knew that these gatherings were well attended by members of the Special Branch, and many students stayed away from the main campus, deliberately, not wanting to be involved in whatever skirmishes and attacks on students that might happen. After all, most had heard of the stories of what had happened a few years before their time when students were badly beaten, many of them maimed, and the leaders expelled from the university. That was after the murder of J.M Kariuki, an explosive period in the country's history.

No beatings had taken place yet, but it was at the back of each person's mind that the students' challenge to the government on the Ngugi detention might not go down well with the powers that be. Everyone knew of the three-day detention of Luka and other leaders, when they had been roughed up and verbally abused and threatened by security officers, but it was also clear that the really active students could not be cowed by rumours and threats of violence, harassment, and detention. Wanjira listened as speaker after speaker made courageous remarks with conviction. As one of the main leaders Luka spoke at each Kamukunji, and she would feel her heart swell with pride and love for him. "He is so brave, so articulate," she would think, "and so well built!" She thought he was the most handsome speaker at the podium, the one with the best facility for words. And she feared for him. On this particular day she wondered if he had crossed the line when he reeled off the names of the victims of detention without trial in Kenya: Wesonga Sijeyo, Simba Ogongi Were, Thairu wa Muthiga, Hadji Mahart Kuno Roble, L.B. Mwanzia, Adam Ahmed Matheenge, Martin Shikuku, and many others. She trembled with rage that so many were languishing in detention without trial. Why? Why?, she would think to herself. Why were people subjected to this treatment in a free country? Had we not fought the British? Is this not our very own government? What was all that protracted and horrific fight against the colonialists about if we have no freedom to write or think what we want? What was the reason for removing grown men from their families and locking them up because of their ideas? Speaker after speaker affirmed her thoughts, in words.

One Thursday evening Luka and Wanjira walked back to the halls of residence together and had supper at the Box. They had not shared a meal on campus in a long time. It was a pleasure to sit together and chat, joined by Wangu and a few other friends at their table. Wangu was doing so much better these days, and seemed back on the road to full recovery of her physical and mental health. Wanjira and other friends had remained connected since their friend's nervous breakdown, and Wangu, after her initial disapproval of Luka, now considered him one of the best "catches" on campus and often told Wanjira that she was lucky to have such a handsome and caring guy, and to be sure to hold on to him no matter what naysayers like her original self might say.

Later, after supper, Luka told Wanjira he had plans for the next evening, and so their movie date was off. It had been awhile since they had gone to the movies and she had been looking forward to it. Wanjira was somewhat taken aback and asked, rather sharply, why their plans had to change suddenly.

"Where will you go tomorrow?"

"I have a meeting, Wanji, but that's all I can say for now."

"What do you mean, its all you can say for now? What kind of meeting?

"Wanji, I can't tell you—much as I'd like to. Perhaps another day. Not now." He was matter-of-fact, and spoke distractedly, quickly, and Wanjira didn't like the sound of it.

"Luka, is anything going on? Is there something I should know?" She felt nervous; that familiar feeling from the Great Court was back. Since his recent three-day detention Wanjira had come to fear for Lukas's life.

"No, I can't, my darling. If I could, I would."

When Wanjira and Luka first started going out steadily he had once raised the subject of his interest in politics, and of his campus activism. Wanjira was aware of the serious nature of some of the meetings held on campus, and often worried about Luka. However, it was not until Ngugi's arrest that she had started to think that, indeed, Luka and others on student government might land themselves in hot soup because of the questions they were raising. When they had spoken, many months earlier, he had told her, "Wanji, remember if there's a fracas you've got to clear off—fast. Don't worry about me—we'll come through, but don't let them get you. And remember if they are keeping an eye on us they know who we are dating. Remember that." Wanjira had felt fear grip her heart but had told Luka she did not care about crooks and corrupt government officials and that she, too, in her own right, needed to oppose them and he need not worry about her. But now the secret nature of this meeting Luka was planning to go to did not please her.

"Luka, just don't do anything silly, alright?" They did not say any more. Wanjira however felt angry—at Luka, at the government, and at those who made decisions to hurt others. "Just don't give them a chance to get you by doing something foolish, Luka! Remember you have to finish your program! Don't let anyone stop you from doing that."

"Don't worry, Wanji. Don't worry," was all he said, but she had started to worry, and that evening proved hard for her. Once in her room she found herself unable to concentrate on her work.

The next evening Wanjira decided to play a game of tennis with Josephine, her friend from the Chiromo campus, now in her third year of medical training. They had not played at all that term and were delighted to play for an hour. After the game, Josephine invited Wanjira over to her room to have a cup of tea and some snack from her fruit bowl. The two women listened to music, and found themselves relaxed and happy on this Friday evening, when, as they put it, the books had "no power"over them, and they had a chance to sit back and get to know each other a little better.

It was almost eleven O'clock when Wanjira got up to leave, and Josephine decided to accompany her for the short walk between their two halls. They had hardly walked ten steps before they heard the screams. It was a woman's voice, coming from one of the men's halls of residence.

"Help me, uuuuuuu! help! *nisaidieni*, uuui!"

The two women stopped, and their hearts seemed to stand still when, just as they had figured out the direction from which the cry came, they heard a man's voice, and then another, and another, shouting, "Colleeeeeection! Collection! Collleeeeection!" and the woman's cry once more, ""uuuuuuu! *Nisaidieni jameni.*" Somebody help me! And then silence.

Afterwards Wanjira would tell her friends gathered in her room to hear the story told and re-told that she had no recollection of the specific events that led her and Josephine into the heart of the crowd gathered in the hallway of the men's dorm, or how the two of them managed to grab the woman, who was almost naked, from the clutches of her tormentors. Wanjira and Josephine would learn, later, that they had arrived in the nick of time for once the cry, "collection!" was given, there was always a willing male student, or groups of students, ready to participate in the rape of a woman unlucky enough to have accompanied a certain type of man to the university residence halls on a Friday or Saturday night.

"Brutes! brutes!" Wanjira remembered shouting as she pushed her way through the crowd with Josephine right alongside her. The two women might themselves have been attacked had a few decent fellows not emerged from their rooms. Determined to do something to help the unlucky woman, and discovering there were now three potential rape victims, they had used all their strength to shove off those who considered women mere things to be used and abused.

It later turned out that one of the men who helped the women was Mugo, who was in Wanjira's department, and a member of her tutorial group. Mugo was a poet and writer liked and admired by Wanjira and others in her class. The other guy was Shiundu, a third year student of veterinary medicine Wanjira had not met before, but who knew Josephine as both were from the Chiromo campus. Afterwards she was to reflect on the men's action, and their heartfelt expressions of sadness and apologies on behalf of their unruly and dangerous hall mates. "These fellows have no shame, or common sense," Wanjira remembered Mugo saying, a shamed look on his face. "They really don't respect women, or themselves, for that matter." But these conversations came later, when things had quieted down, and Mugo, Shiundu, two other guys, and the women, were safe, sipping cups of tea in Wanjira's room.

Lucy, for that was the woman who had been attacked by a would-be boyfriend, was invited to stay until morning, and Wanjira gave her one of her dresses to wear, for Lucy's red blouse had been torn, and all the buttons ripped off by the vicious hands of her attackers. She told them of how she had met George, the man who later attacked her, at Furaha nightclub earlier in the evening. They had shared drinks, danced, spent a good evening together, and she had agreed to accompany him to the halls of residence. She did not know his last name, or anything else about him. "And then he completely turned against me, just when I thought we were getting to know one another, and started calling me *Malaya,* and saying I was useless and to get out of his room. I told him I would leave, and I don't know why he became violent and started to hit me in the face. It was then that he opened the window and started shouting, 'Collection!' I did not know what that meant, but sensed it was something against me, and I started to scream. We were by the window, and I noticed that a few windows to my right and left were opening, and men were putting out their heads and beginning to shout, 'Collection!' George then opened the door, and I fought him hard, not wanting to get near that door because I realized he was ready to allow other men in, and thank God you and the others came to my help because, I believe I would be dead by now."

Lucy started to cry, silently, her shoulders heaving. Josephine put her arms around her and told her to take comfort. "Thank God you are safe," she said, over and over again. "You are now safe, don't worry." The men looked on, and you could see the shame, pain and frustration on their faces. Josephine decided to spend the night in Wanjira's room, too rattled to return to her own room despite offers of being escorted back by Mugo, Shiundu, and the other guys. No-one wanted to sleep, anyway. At about two in the morning the guys returned to their rooms, and the three women started to doze off. Josephine and Wanjira shared a bed, and luckily for Lucy, Binti was out visiting her sister in Buruburu so the unhappy and traumatized woman at least had a bed to herself. Wanjira used her spare bed sheets to make a fresh bed for Lucy, sure that Binti would not mind the use of her bed.

CHAPTER TWELVE

Things moved quickly after the memorable Friday night Wanjira and Josephine rescued Lucy from the unruly mob at the men's halls of residence. In the days that followed Wanjira went through a complex mixture of emotions—sadness, anger, and sheer stupefaction. How could university men engage in rape? Were some of these would-be rapists in her lectures and tutorials? Who were the individuals involved in so-called *Collections*? She had heard stories of such events taking place in the male halls of residence, but considered them hearsay; she had not had any way to personally witness the horror she and Josephine had come upon the previous Friday. She had also not heard of anyone known to her circle of friends who had experienced the horror and trauma of a *Collection.*

What about poor Lucy, the woman who was nearly mauled by these crazy men? Where were these men's hearts? And why was this a silent problem at the university, never spoken about, except in whispers and warnings to Boxers by their male friends, relatives, and a few kind and just men in the know? Wanjira's mind was astir with all kinds of emotions, and not even the joy of her strong and loving relationship with Luka or her friends could lessen the rage and sense of let-down she felt from the experience of the previous weekend. Everything had changed on that Friday. She knew it, and wondered how life could possibly go on as usual on campus if the horrifying and bestial practice of *Collections* was not dealt with, and stamped out altogether. She could not get this thought out of her mind.

On the surface one might not have noticed any change in Wanjira even as her insides continued to stir with an urgent, unfamiliar, restlessness. Sleep failed her, and each morning she woke up feeling quite unlike herself, as if something totally new and unsettling had been born inside of her. She was like a snake that had shed its old skin and was now getting used to the new feeling of the sun, wind and rain on a fresh and renewed self.

The following Sunday, she was surprised to hear the sermon at St. Paul's: the chaplain had picked Friday's event as the theme for the day. As she listened to the priest she wondered how he knew the details. He told the congregation about the two courageous university women students who came to the aid of a fellow woman in the true spirit of Christian fellowship. "They did not stop to worry about the danger they themselves faced from the unruly mob; they did not care that the woman was not from the university. No, my friends, they forged ahead with courage born of outrage. They challenged the would-be rapists and defilers of womanhood; they called for help; they rescued the woman from the very jaws of her attackers. They challenged the ungodly, inhumane, practice of rape on this campus that must come to an end."

Wanjira trembled as she listened to the priest. She had not thought of what she and Josephine did as an act of courage, or as a daring act. She wondered if Josephine thought of it as anything other than an automatic response to someone in danger. And what of Mugo, Shiundu, and the other men who had helped? They too were courageous, and acted on their own beliefs and conviction that women should not be defiled and forced into sexual acts against their will. They too heard that cry, the sound of a woman in distress, and took action. It was what had made the two women rush to the scene, not some pre-meditated act of courage. But the priest was right in one thing: the hurtful and dangerous practice of *Collections* on campus had to end, and the male students had to be challenged to help put a stop to it. As she continued to listen to the sermon, Wanjira felt goose-bumps crawl all over her arms and legs. Tears stood in her eyes. Luka, who was sitting next to her, squeezed her hand. He had said similar things to her the previous day, and was in full agreement with the priest.

"We must do something, Luka, and soon!" Wanjira and Luka had accompanied a few friends into town after mass. They had all gone to Snow Cream to enjoy an ice cream cone or soft drinks.

"Yes, let's work on something. A formal something." It was Wangu speaking. "And it must involve the university authorities."

"What do you have in mind?" Luka asked

"You know, some guidelines. Some rules. Repercussions for this sort of savagery, written down, known by all. And enforced. " Wangu spoke fast, and turning to Luka, his friend Ben and a few others with them said, "You're the lawyers, guys. You know what I mean."

"I agree," Wanjira said. "Luka, it's time your people did something. After all, this is crucial. It has to stop. Luka, let's say something at Thursday's Kamukunji..."

She had not quite finished her sentence before Luka said, "No, Wanji. Perhaps not right now. Things are a bit hectic—I mean there's an agenda in place for Thursday and Student Government is moving certain issues right now. Perhaps next time."

"Yeah, yeah, blah, blah, blah!" This came from Wangu, who continued, "Men! You guys are too funny, really. I can't believe Luka said that." She was facing Wanjira as she spoke, perhaps because she had noticed Wanjira's frown when Luka responded to her. But she need not have worried about it because soon enough a passionate argument was upon the group, led by Wanjira. The gist of the argument was that rape and harassment of women was as critical an issue as the fight for the release of political prisoners and the fight for human rights of all Kenyans.

"Tell me of a worse violation of a woman's human rights than rape" Wanjira's question was addressed directly to Luka. "*Ehe*, tell me!"

"Look here Wanji," Luka sounded a bit defensive. "I don't mean to suggest it's not an important topic. All I said, but I guess I didn't put it too well, was that our group has a specific agenda in place, and we need to get that out of the way first."

"Yes, yes, yes," Wangu said, rolling her eyes. "Come back tomorrow, ladies, not today."

"Wangu, let's not put it that way," It was Mugo speaking. He had joined them shortly after they started the conversation. Since Friday he had done a lot of thinking, sparked by the courage he had witnessed in Wanjira and Josephine, and the conversation that followed in Wanjira's room later that evening. Now he continued, "Wangu, I think you know what Luka means. I think many guys would like to fight this C*ollection* business and I for one just hate it. But let's make a plan."

When they left Snow Cream the group had agreed to disagree about the priorities the student leaders ought to have. Wanjira felt miffed at Luka, and he could tell. Later, they spoke about it.

"Wanjira," he seemed nervous. "I see your point, really. I want to support you in planning something but you know…" his voice trailed off, and he suddenly felt stupid, his sense of confidence suddenly shaken when she said, " It's not just about supporting me, Luka. It's more about your not seeing the value of this issue. That's what I think."

"You're wrong, Wanji. I think it's a very serious matter. I only talked of the timing, so let's talk about the best time to address the issue in a Kamukunji." He came towards her, and held her by the waist. "We're not quarreling, are we? Tell me we aren't."

"No, love, we are talking. Simply talking. Nothing wrong with that, OK?" But Wanjira was irritated, and Luka noted it. He decided to let things cool down a bit.

By evening, things were back to normal for everyone, or so it seemed. People made last-minute visits to friends' rooms to braid hair, to "shorten" the night a little bit, or to make plans for the coming week's tutorials and study sessions. Wanjira visited Wangu and they were joined by a few other women, and inevitably the discussion returned to Friday's events and the conversation in Snow Cream earlier that morning.

"We need to do something ourselves, as women. Why not?" Wanjira spoke with confidence. "Let's accept our responsibilities as women and fight this *Collection* nonsense. You know, some things need no negotiation."

"Hear, hear!" Wangu said, adding, "It's all common sense. Why should guys fight this one for us? Maybe they don't want to ruffle any feathers with their mates. And besides, they do all the work at the Kamukunjis. See how little women do on this campus? As if we have no minds, or mouths, for that matter."

Everyone offered an opinion, and the conversation went on well past midnight, so animated were the women. They covered a wide range of topics: women's groups in *Home Squared*, the courage of their mothers, their *cucus* and aunts, and the confusion they felt in their own lives. They wondered if they had not surrendered a lot of their lives to their boyfriends, and if the women, like Jessie, who had already married, had not done so to avoid being independent, or for fear of taking care of themselves, even though some thought it was to simply take advantage of the good relationships they had developed with their older, better established, spouses; but there was general agreement that university women were, for some reason, selling themselves short and not taking full advantage of the privileged positions they found themselves in as members of a select few.

Afterwards Wanjira found herself thinking of her own life with Luka, and a nagging feeling began to make her wonder if she was making a mistake in being so involved with him, dating him exclusively, and leaving no room for anyone else in her life. How different was she from Jessie, and the others? Was she trying to escape something? If so, what was it? She could be sure of nothing this evening, except that she was feeling troubled. Jessie's daughter was now almost a year old, and Wanjira thought her a pretty little thing who was growing well under the care of her *ayah* and the doting parents. Jessie had successfully cleared her first year exams, and was busy, like everyone else, waiting to finish second year in a short while. Wanjira wondered if Jessie was not luckier than most: she had her daughter and a loving husband, and a career in the works. Wanjira thought she was revising her earlier ideas and feelings about Jessie's marriage. It seemed that most people, herself included, wanted just those very things Jessie had so clearly articulated nearly a year ago. But the one thing that would not leave her was the thought of what she and her friends must do to help improve the quality of life for women at the university. The fight against *Collections* on campus was a problem that could not be solved by thinking of what others might, would, or should, do. It called for action that could not wait for any hemming and hawing or any kind of excuse, however clever or well-intentioned.

CHAPTER THIRTEEN

What a hectic week it's been, dear journal! I can hardly believe the things that have happened in just a few days! First of all, a group of us women caused quite a stir at last week's Kamukunji. There we were, as usual, listening to the list of problems that must be dealt with. All very important things. We stood by the sidelines, as usual, but this time not merely listening. We were waiting our turn.

Wanjira's journal writing was interrupted by a knock on the door. Wangu, a big smile on her face, dramatically held out a bottle of champagne in her right hand.

"Wanji! a present from Mwangi. He says we must celebrate. Quick, some glasses. The others are coming, and we have more coming."

Wanjira put out some glasses, and soon the party was in full swing. The women gathered in her room had not felt such joy in recent months, and what had happened only two days earlier was still fresh on their minds. All of them: Wanjira, Wangu, Akoth and Josephine felt a strong camaraderie and sense of kinship that seemed firm, old, ancient. They could not help marveling at all that had happened in the last two days, and needed to recount to one another the specific experiences each had gone through. Wanjira was not able to resume her journal writing until the following day.

She could see the whole event in her mind's eye as she began writing:

Wangu was the first to speak and you should have seen the shock on many guys' faces! From where he stood, near the front, Luka looked at me and winked, and I winked back. He knew we had decided to take action but I hadn't given him any details. Wangu began by introducing herself and immediately launched into her point.

*"Everyone here knows about **Collections** on campus. It's a horrible practice and a terrible violation of women's human rights. How can we blame the government for denying Kenyans their basic human rights when our very own community at this university keeps quiet about the rights of women who are raped by our very own fellow students? All our lives we have been called the future leaders. How can we, who will become Kenya's doctors, lawyers, teachers, businessmen and scientists engage in rape and such gross violation of the fundamental rights of women? **Collections** must stop immediately!"*

Cries of "hear, hear!" could be heard from many corners, but some students chose to boo and shout, "Women go home!" We did not care, and now it was Akoth Onyango's turn. She was one of the fairly quiet women in my hall in the Box and was a student of Commerce. Wangu had introduced her to our group and we had all admired her apparent sense of focus and confidence. When she rose to speak her voice was loud and clear:

"Our women's group has decided that Collections on campus must end. As our colleague Wangu Kamau has said, we are determined to bring them to an end. We have made plans to work with the university administration to make sure that anyone who attacks a woman on campus—whether she is a student, or a visitor—will be severely punished. We are calling for expulsions" Akoth was interrupted by loud cries of "Go home! Go Home!" at the mention of the word "Expulsion"—a dreaded word on campus. But our group had decided that a rapist was dangerous to all women and had to be forced out of the university if found guilty. Akoth spoke clearly, and allowed the shouts and boos to die down before she ended, "We shall be posting information on our meetings with student deans and other university officials as soon as they are finalized, and shall also liaise with the student government. Any student who wishes to join us is most welcome."

I spoke after Akoth but I'm afraid I was less interesting and less articulate, even though Luka and everyone else said I was very good. I began by stating that rape was anathema in all civilized society and could not be tolerated in our university community. I recounted the previous Friday's event, something the women in our group had thought important for me and Josephine to do. I thanked the men who had come to our assistance, and there was much clapping, even though one could still hear some booing and shouts that I should "Go home."

Josephine spoke after me and added her perspective on rape from a medical point of view. She told the assembled students that rape causes serious physical and emotional trauma in women, and said some of the most difficult things she and her fellow medical students were having to learn included how to deal with traumatized and badly injured girls and women who were victims of rape. "We must do everything in our power to stop the rape of women in Kenya, and the first place to start is right here, at the University of Nairobi." She received loud applause and the expected boos from the by-now obvious heckler's corner. Luka, Mugo, Shiundu and all our friends had come out to support us, and they applauded all the speakers and shouted loudly, hoping to drown the boos, many of which were clearly also directed against them by those in the crowd who cared little about women's views, and who obviously saw no problem in the practice of ***Collections*** *on campus and elsewhere in the land.*

I can't tell you just how energized we felt after that Kamukunji. The university paper later wrote that the women stole the show, and mentioned us one by one under the headline, "Future Leaders to watch." We have decided to maintain the spirit born on the night of the would-be collection of Lucy, a woman we must thank for helping us come to our senses and to realize that we university women have a job to do besides reading books and preparing for our examinations and good jobs upon graduation. We have an appointment with Dr. Mkala, Dean of Student Affairs at the university. She was very positive when we approached her on the day of the Kamukunji and commended us on our good efforts. She also had a few kind words for Josephine and me, and said the Vice Chancellor of the university would like to meet with us sometime next week. So much activity. I feel good, though. It's as if something I've been preparing for all this time has happened, only I can't quite name what it is, but I feel a level of confidence I haven't felt in a long time. Luka has told me that I am looking even more beautiful and self-assured than before, and for once I have not been bashful to hear his compliments.

A lot is happening in my life these days, dear Journal! More than I think I can deal with. Take me and Luka, for instance. Our relationship is once more under attack, from none other than my very own dear family. My brother Kairu has openly expressed his disapproval of my being with Luka, and has tried to influence our mother, Njahira wa Kamau herself! But I'm going too fast. Let me tell you what has happened.

After the Kamukunji a lot of people got to know about our women's group, and of the role Josephine and I had played in the events that led to the Kamukunji. The event was reported in the two main dailies, and our picture was in the paper. I was quoted, as were all the others who spoke. Well, my brother Kairu read the reports, and as it turned out so did my parents, on the very same day, for an excited neighbor brought them the newspapers on his way from his job in town.

Well, three days later my mother came to see me at the Box, accompanied by Kairu, who went straight to what must have been his real reason to visit me. In an unusually harsh and aggressive manner he started by telling me that he had heard one or two things about me from some of his friends on campus but had figured that my "Munjaruo man was mere experimentation." His exact words. I nearly died hearing him speak of Luka like that. He thought it was time I "came to my senses," for, after all, the end of second year was upon me, and it was time to start thinking seriously about my future, and looking around and dating sensibly, like a well-brought up woman.

"It's time to come down to earth, Wanjira. Find a real boyfriend, and forget this man who, it is very clear, is responsible for putting wild ideas into your head. Whoever heard of a woman addressing

a Kamukunji? Have you not heard of the one before your time, a big-time Kamukunji speaker, now a nobody? And she could have been great but for that mouth."

I let Kairu speak, but my heart was about ready to jump out of my chest. Imagine! All this time I had held my brother to a high standard of thought and behaviour, and had not fought with him, really. I never thought he had such backward ideas about things. What a chauvinist! I simply glared at him, fearful that if I opened my mouth I would utter words I might come to regret. He is my older brother, after all.

Mother said nothing all this time, but when a reasonable pause had come and gone, she began by saying that she is a Christian, a Roman Catholic, and holds no grudge against anyone on account of his or her ethnic background. "We are all God's children, and he put us in various parts of the world to do his work. Why should we all be the same? Even the country's climate is different wherever you go, and people are diffeerent for a reason. Only God knows what the reason is. So I will not say anything about this friend of yours because of where he was born. I am sure he is a good man because you otherwise would not find him worthy of your time." How I love mother! She is so intelligent, and very wise.

"But," she continued, "This man is in ***Uteti,*** *and that's what worries me. I'm told he's a big university politician, and now I see you are joining him. And I agree with what you and your friends have said about women's safety here—I had no idea these things happened here and I'm very happy Wanjira that you helped that woman even though you and your friends were in danger. But I came here today to ask you to please not let the mad people in government interfere with your education. You have come this far, Wanjira; don't let them stop you! Don't let them come for you. Please, Wanjira, keep away from this man—that is all I wanted to say to you today."*

My mother spoke fast, in a manner that betrayed her worry. Normally so calm and even-tempered, she looked ruffled and spoke uncharacteristically fast. Her beautiful face looked dark and somber, as if the blood within her had refused to move as it should. I felt sorry for her, especially because of what I knew I would soon be telling her about Luka and me. And to think it was the first time she had visited me at Chuo Kikuu! I felt a bit sad about it but wasn't about to let Kairu get away with his ideas unchallenged. I almost told them right there and then that Luka wanted me to visit his family, and that I wanted my own family to meet him…

"Kairu," I glared at him. "First of all, you don't know Luka." Turning to my mother I said, "Mami, his name is Luka Owuor, and he is a very good person. You'll find out for yourself one of these days."

No-one spoke for a while, and I added, "Very soon, Mami!" I looked at Kairu, and with as steady a voice as I could manage, said, "Please don't dismiss Luka…He is a real boyfriend to me, and not an experiment, and, Kairu, you'll find out one day that he is a good man. You will, but first you have to stop this ***ukabila****!"*

*Mother knows her children, and I think that's why she raised her hand in a gesture of peace, and stopped whatever words Kairu had planned to send my way…"****Haidhuru****, Wanjira. You are the wise one in this matter." She addressed Kairu directly, "Let us not allow our mouths to utter words we'll come to regret," and turning to me she said, "I will inform your father of today's meeting, but now I must leave, for the sun must not set while I am still in Nairobi. Come see us soon, Wanjira."*

I escorted them to Kairu's car, which was parked right outside the box. We were all quiet as we walked to the car, and anyone looking at us might have wondered at the weight of our footsteps and the tension that must have been visible on our faces. Kairu planned to drive Mother home, and I was grateful he would do this for I hated the thought of her in a ***Matatu*** *in the evening, for* ***Matatu*** *drivers and their* ***manamba*** *tended to be reckless in their attempt to rush passengers to their destinations in order to make as many trips, and therefore as much money as possible, before retiring for the night. In the process they risked commuter's lives. I did not want my mother in an accident in one of these* ***Matatu.*** *Kairu's car was therefore a comfort on an otherwise uncomfortable evening for me.*

What is a young woman to do? All I know is that I won't listen to anyone who says I should give up Luka. That, dear Journal, I won't do!!

CHAPTER FOURTEEN

Final examinations for Wanjira's second year were announced, and now it was study period for everyone. Most students buckled down to their books and it was rare to see students who did not seem to have a strong sense of purpose as they walked between the halls of residence and the main campus. Wanjira was comfortable, if a bit anxious, about the coming examinations, although she saw no reason why she should fail. She had always passed her exams, and why should second year be different from the very difficult first year? Luka was also deeply immersed in his books. On many evenings he and Wanjira studied together either in the library or in her room, for Binti continued to spend most of her evenings on Golan Heights with her colleagues in Architecture and Design. To each the coming exams brought a tinge of sadness for they knew their days together on the same campus were numbered. Luka often referred to this fact, seeming sad, and Wanjira would assure him that they would continue to see one another as the School of Law was not too far away.

Two Sundays before examinations were due to begin Luka surprised Wanjira by showing up at St. Paul's Chapel in a white Datsun, a loan, he said, from one of his cousins. "I have a special date this afternoon, Wanji," he announced, eyes twinkling. "With my special girl."

"Who is she? tell me!"

"Wanji, listen. Can you spare two hours before getting back to your books? I have something to show you."

Wanjira said hurried good-byes to her friends and got into the Datsun. "Luka, when did you get a license? You never told me about it." She was impressed by Luka's careful driving as they wound their way past their well-loved Arboretum, past State House Road, and into Ngong Road.

"I started driving way back—my Woodley uncle gave me lessons when I was in A-levels."

"So where are we going, Luka?" They had reached Kenya Science Teachers College and taken a left on the roundabout. "Don't tell me you're taking me to Ngong!"

"I am, too, my dear. The very place."

"Wooi, someone help me!" Wanjira and Luka burst into loud laughter. Everyone knew that the word "Ngong" was now a code word for murder, after what happened to the well-known politician, J.M Kariuki. Only five years earlier his mutilated body was found in the Ngong Forest, not too far from where the two young people were now. But Ngong was also the site of one of the country's most beautiful spots: The Ngong Hills, a place rarely visited by many people because it was not on a regular bus route, but one that families and others with cars had started to discover as a beautiful place to spend a sunny afternoon, walking in fresh air along the sparsely populated route to the hills. Wanjira had once told Luka how much she had enjoyed climbing the Cherang'ani hills and walking in the Kerio Valley trails as a member of her A-level program's Presidential Award's Scheme Club, and of the club members' disappointment when their plan to climb Mount Kenya was abandoned because the teacher who sponsored the club left suddenly after he fell ill, and was flown back to his home in England. What she had loved most was the fresh air, the sunshine, the dawn, as she and her team woke up from their night in a tent on the Nandi Hills; the vast fields, and the landscape which had made her imagination roam. Luka's own school had climbed Mount Kenya, and he had told Wanjira he longed to climb Kilimanjaro someday.

In half an hour they parked the Datsun at the Ngong foothills and started their climb, hand in hand. They met a few women carrying firewood, the heavy loads on their backs making them bend nearly double.

"What misery," Wanjira said, after they had greeted the women. "I wish life wasn't so hard, every day, you know?" Luka nodded, adding that it was like this throughout the country. "I know, Luka, doesn't it make you wonder? This foraging for firewood everyday is really hard for women in this country. And for the whole family, really."

Wanjira's mood was somber as they continued walking. She was thinking of her mother and other women in Ngumo, her village, and all the work the women did every day, the unending work of fetching water from the river or the one well in the village, the daily search for firewood.

"Yes, Wanji, Luka said, continuing the conversation...Someday we on campus have a debt to repay our parents and all the producers of wealth in this country."

"We have to, Luka. We have no choice."

The two young people felt frustrated by the thoughts that had entered their heads, even as they continued their climb up the gently rising hills, pausing now and then to look back at how far they had come. The tall buildings of Nairobi were coming into view, and the two young people paused a while to admire the sight. A flock of birds flew by, and Wanjira and Luka watched the seemingly synchronized formation until the birds were out of sight, small specks in the distance. Continuing their climb the lovers met another group of women and teenage girls, and the older women smiled, perhaps remembering their own youth, and wished Luka and Wanjira a good day. After both parties had moved on, the teenage girls turned almost in unison to stare at the walking pair, perhaps wondering how on earth anyone had the time or leisure to walk up the hills for purposes other than the search for firewood, and secretly admiring Wanjira and Luka, who looked so very beautiful walking together. Wanjira remarked to Luka that it was strange to see women gathering firewood on a Sunday; in Ngumo it was uncommon, but then again maybe it was easier for the women in these hills to search for firewood on a Sunday morning. "What a life," she thought to herself. After about an hour of climbing the gently rising path the lovers stopped to admire the view and to rest awhile under the shade of a *Mukinduri* tree.

As he always did when they went out Luka had brought along some snacks, and fruit drinks. They enjoyed them as they sat; looking into the distance, listening to the various sounds of insects and the swaying of the wind in the short trees and bushes all around them.

"Wanji," Luka said, after a while. "Remember what I asked you the other day?"

"About"…She knew, but wasn't too sure how to respond.

"About you and me. Us. Our future together."

"Yes, Luka. I remember." She spoke quietly, deliberately, picking her words carefully.

"Wanji, I remain serious about it. He moved closer and held her, his hold around her waist becoming tighter. "Wanji, Please be my wife. Let's live together, work together. I love you, Wanji, and always will. My *Mpenzi*. You love me too, Wanji, right?" She nodded. "Please say yes." He spoke fast, and his voice was urgent.

Wanjira had a breathtaking feeling, a sudden desire to cry. Maybe it was the Ngong Hills, the beauty, the splendour, the quiet, busy, sounds of nature around them. She was falling in love with Luka all over again, and it was as if everything about them was totally brand new. Doubt and anxiety that had crept into her mind in recent weeks about any possible future they might have seemed to recede to the background, replaced by the reality of what she and Luka were at this very instant: A Luo man and a Gikuyu woman falling in love all over again, in Maasai country. She remembered what he had once said to her following their heartfelt conversation at the Boulevard a month or so earlier: *"We're Kenyans. We're Kenyans, not just Luo and Gikuyu or whatever else. Wanji, my darling, we're Kenyans, our country's present and future!"* The passion with which he had spoken then was once again evident, and a bright light shone in his eyes. His nostrils flared with passion, and she felt his heartbeat as he held her to him. She held on tight, longing, for what, she didn't know, and her own heart beat in rhythm with his, and their lips met and they blend into one, and it was a long time before she pulled away, gently, and sought his eyes. He had removed his glasses and placed them on the ground, and now she looked into his eyes. They seemed soft, liquid, and she was astounded to see tears beginning to come down his face. She wiped them off, gently, with her index finger, first one eye, then the other. She said, softly, "Darling Luka, my sweetheart, *Aheri nyakachieng*," kissing his face, like a mother cow and her calf, all over the face, while a warm and powerful feeling came over her.

She still had not answered him, but her heart was pounding hard. Her mind was saying, "*Leo ni leo*, this is the moment you have imagined. The moment you didn't think would come upon you so soon." But her mouth said nothing.

Luka spoke again, and his voice was strong despite his tears. "Wanji, please be with me forever. Let's get married, stay with me forever. You know I'm crazy about you. Wanjira, she of-the wayside, my darling!" He seemed to be in a trance.

Sweet, sweet words. And his voice, our people! She was melting inside, dying a little, then coming right back to life, and all the time she held on to him, and he held her tightly. A light breeze blew, and she looked over his shoulder to the hills in the distance, to the small specks, far away, that were Nairobi's tall buildings. The white clouds above, the vastness around them, and the silence, the absolute silence, made everything seem blessed, holy. The Maasai people called these hills E'Ngong, God's Eye, and now she knew why. In this place, a powerful presence, the Great Spirit she believed was God, reigned. She felt safe in Luka's embrace, and was convinced that she had been touched by grace. A strong awareness came to her that the present, and the future, would be rich with possibility, with love. How could loving Luka be wrong? How could what they felt make anyone unhappy? Suddenly she felt sad, yet elated, at the same time.

Wanjira felt her body tremble. Luka held her tighter, and he too was caught up in the emotion going through Wanjira, for his own body felt taut, waiting, a bow ready for the hunter's command.

And then her mouth spoke. "Yes, Luka. Yes!" She spoke with passion, calling from some depth inside her a sense of power, a conviction. "Yes, Luka," And then, suddenly, she began to cry. Something was pouring out from her heart, something powerful, almost tangible, something bitter, yet sweet. She was emptying out something from her being, feelings she had no idea were locked in her heart. A surge of joy accompanied the tears, but what was that she was also feeling? Luka whooped with joy and lifted her way up, dancing around with her in his arms, shouting to the heavens and the trees and bushes around them "She said yes! she said yes!" and after what seemed a thousand more kisses he took out of his pocket a carefully wrapped package which he asked her to open, and to her astonishment a beautiful gold ring engraved with a beautiful ruby, her birthstone, stared at her. He placed it on her left middle finger and she experienced a mixture of pure happiness, and a fearful hope. She felt a strong sense of something overwhelming and difficult lying in wait, in her path, and Luka's as well. Even as she understood the depth of her conviction that she would be with him forever, she also understood that by saying "yes" to being Luka's wife and life's companion, she had entered a battle—with friends and family members who thought Kenya's different ethnic groups should work together, make polite conversation, perhaps even visit each other's homes now and then, but, *never, ever, intermarry.*

CHAPTER FIFTEEN

And then Mzee died. Just like that, the old man died. One early August morning he died while on a visit to the coast, a place he loved. He was an old man whose time for the inevitable and unavoidable event had come. Had he not been the man he was the fact of his dying should have been accepted without the shock, sadness, and fear that gripped the land. If you asked most people about it they might have said they wanted the President to go on living because as long as he was alive the world had a certain predictability to it, a safety net that allowed the nation's affairs to continue in a seamless and untroubled state. Mzee's continued breathing placed a firm lid on dangerous emotions, words, and actions that might jeopardize the nation's peace. Many, Wanjira and all her classmates included, had taken his continued living for granted, even as they grumbled about the many not-so-nice things that had come to be associated with the old man's rule.

Not that nature and all her creation had not announced Mzee's death all that week. Those with eyes to see and ears to hear had not missed it, as Wanjira was to learn, weeks later. The sun, the wind, the rain. They had all spoken! Who had not wondered at the strange brilliance of the dawn on that August morning, and the unusually striking colours of the sunset of the previous evening? The women of Ngumo had witnessed it, and old Mama Ciru had seen it all in her dreams. Njahira, Wanjira's mother, whose dreams were known to foretell important events, had also been sent the message of Mzee's death. And who had not noticed the unusually dramatic flight and singing of the birds of the air, especially the ominous owl, *Ndundu*, that well-known harbinger of death? *Ndundu* had hooted in every corner of the land, accompanied by his wife and children, sent everywhere to announce the death of the great one. *Thonjo,* weaver bird, and his entire family in every tree in the land had kept their incessant chatter, wondering why everyone was not paying attention! Even the cows, goats, and sheep had spoken. In their moos and bleats they keened at the news to come. And what about the chickens in people's coops, and Rooster, announcing the day with an unusual, yet unmistakable, sob in his voice?

Wanjira was to reflect, later, on the fact that her father and people in her age group were the only people in Ngumo to whom these things had not been revealed. It was not surprising, for as was well known, anyone who enjoyed *kanywaji* before bed, like Kamau, her father, did, lost the ability to understand dreams and other night-time visits from the world beyond. Many young people had not fully developed these gifts, but Wanjira noticed something herself, although she did not mention it to anyone. She did not want to sound as superstitious as she thought many in her village sounded, but on that fateful morning she was awakened by the howls of dogs in Harambee estate, where she was staying at Kairu's house. She was on her long holiday from University, having been fortunate enough to secure a clerical position at the Ministry of Education. She had thought to herself that Like *Ndundu,* howling dogs were ominous. They too were messengers of death.

On the fateful August morning Wanjira woke up with a strong desire to see Luka, who was living in Buruburu with two other roommates. One of them, his cousin, owned the house. She could not explain this urgent need to see him as they had been together the previous evening until about nine o'clock. Luka had successfully finished his law studies and was now awaiting entry into the School of Law in September. Unfortunately there was no telephone in his house although Wanjira was lucky enough to have access to a phone in Kairu's house. Harambee Estate had had a head start on luxuries such as telephones, amenities that the more recently constructed Buruburu Estate Phase Two did not enjoy.

Mzee was dead, and things got into a turmoil after the announcement that he was no more. Wanjira's first thought was of Luka, and he was to tell her later that he took the first bus to Harambee Estate the moment he learned the news, for he had gone into town for an appointment earlier that morning. All the while he prayed Wanjira was at Kairu's. He also prayed that no-one in his family was en-route anywhere into Nairobi or any of the major towns. He needed to reach his father and hoped it would be possible to use a telephone once he reached Buruburu Center. He had made a quick decision not to wait by the city post office telephone booths once he saw the long lines of people waiting, obviously as anxious as he was to reach and pass on messages to loved ones in far corners of the country.

By the time he reached Wanjira, who luckily had just heard the news and was frantically trying to reach Wangu, or any other friend by telephone, Luka's heart was beating unnaturally fast. He held Wanjira in a tight hug, saying over and over again that he was just happy to know she was well, and thank God she had not been at work that day, and did she have any news of anyone in her family? She informed him Kairu had telephoned to report that their father thought everything would be alright, and was, as they spoke, driving to Ngumo to be with the other members of the family, and that he had instructed Wanjira and Kairu stay put in the house. Wanjira told Luka that Kairu had asked about him, and had told her he hoped that she and Luka would stay safe, and away from any crowds. In the last few weeks he seemed to have come around to seeing that Luka was indeed a fine person, and although he had not said so in words, he seemed less disturbed by her relationship with Luka than he had been in the past.

"Let's just stay home and listen to the news, Luka." Wanjira had already decided she would not leave the estate that day. "We'll see what happens later on."

"You're right, Wanji. Let's stay here. By the way may I use the telephone?"

"Of course! Have you reached your old man? Please try to reach him. No, Luka, we don't care about the trunk call charges, just call him. This is an emergency!"

Luka was fortunate to reach his father, who had just been off the phone with his brother, Luka's Woodley uncle, and was very happy to hear from his son, whom he had been terribly worried about.

"Now, young man, listen to me. No town gatherings until we know what's what. My information is that things will be fine, but we can't be too sure. I'd like to know you are safe, and in Buruburu. No meetings today, son. Let's wait this thing out."

"OK, Baba. No meetings, no town. I will ring tomorrow, and please tell Mama not to worry."

"*Erokamano*, son. She will be happy to hear your news. Now be sure to take good care of that special girl of yours."

"I will, Baba. Good bye, and greet everyone."

Luka had a big smile after the call, and Wanjira wanted to know why he was smiling on such a dismal day. "It's my old man, Wanji. He told me to take good care of you."

"He did?"

"Yes, Wanji. You see everyone in my life loves you?"

"I know, Luka, I know. Thank you."

The two lovers sat side by side, hands held, eyes glued to the television, which was now showing footage of Mzee's biography. Classical music played in the background, and occasionally there was a presentation by the Kenya Police Band and others playing the national anthem and other tunes familiar to the nation. "*Kenya, Kenya, Kenya Taifa Letu,*" and others. The still photographs on television showed the late leader in various places and situations: there he was, at the famous Kapenguria trial. There he was with the delegation that had visited him in detention in Lodwar. Most of those in the photograph had gone on to become who-was-who in Kenya. Some were now dead, and others had been relegated to the background after Independence and in the ensuing years. Among those standing with him in the pictures was the vice president, Daniel arap Moi, a gentleman, a man who had always "been there, but not there." Few knew anything about him except that he was a dutiful and quiet Minister of Home Affairs, and then Mzee's vice president. *A good and decent man!* And there was Mzee with traditional dancers, his famous fly whisk up in the air, his sandaled feet keeping time with his favorite *nyakinyua* women's group. Mzee and the lovely Mama Ngina and their children; Mzee with his other wives, Mzee with his children from his different marriages, Mzee with his ministers, Mzee with other African Founding Fathers, Kwame Nkrumah, Leopold Sedar Senghor, Houphouet Boigny, Sekou Toure, Kenneth Kaunda, Hastings Kamuzu Banda, Julius Nyerere, Milton Obote, and with the late Emperor of Ethiopia, Haile Selassie, in Addis Ababa, on the one and only foreign visit he made as president of Kenya. He had left other trips to his deputies, and his vice president. Mzee with foreign dignitaries, Mzee, Beloved Father of the Nation, *Rais Mtukufu*, *Mheshimiwa Mzee*, *Mpendwa wetu*, Commander of the Armed Forces, Mzee, *Mzaliwa wa karne iliyopita*, Kenya's Beloved President dead, gone to join his ancestors.

As if acting on cue, people in the nation's towns flocked to the bus stations with as many belongings as they could tuck into hastily packed bags. It was "*O kaihu na kwao,*" as many were to remark, later. "Every squirrel into its own hole." Buses to every point in the country quickly filled up, and *Matatu* changed, or adjusted, their routes to accommodate the human flight. The normally rowdy and noisy *manamba* and bus conductors were somber, quiet, and, in an unusual show of politeness, quickly and efficiently led the slightly panicked, though composed passengers into their vehicles. It was an eerie sight, this urgent and unnaturally quiet human activity at the bus station, normally a deafening and unsightly center of bravado, rudeness, and noise. The old man's death had led to this, and the nation moved fast toward the supposedly safe zones of the country, holding its breath. Waiting.

The telephone kept ringing. Wangu called from Kileleshwa, where she was staying during the holiday. All was well from her end. Her aunt had been to town at three, coming home from the airport, where she worked. According to her there were hardly any cars in town, and it felt quite odd and almost frightening. However, no sign of chaos could be seen anywhere. Almost every shop along her route was closed. Wanjira and Luka called other friends, who reported similar things from various parts of the city, and by four o'clock it seemed safe to assume that the country was not tearing apart at the seams, as had been predicted long ago. No-one was throwing stones, or setting anything on fire. The radio continued to play sad songs and classical music. On television still photographs, now and then punctuated by footage from many of Mzee's speeches, continued to be shown. O that voice! No-one in public life had such a vibrant, powerful, well modulated, voice, and that command of language!

No official of the government was seen or heard on radio or television all day, but the most trusted voice on national radio continued to offer condolences to the family and nation of Mzee, and to ask for the nation's prayers at this time of national grief: Leonard Mambo Mbotela became Wanjira and Luka's hero that day. His soothing voice and his masterful command of language became, in their minds, the famous balm of Gilead, which would "make the wounded whole, and heal the sin-sick soul." On this day the nation's soul was wounded, and quite sickened by fear of the unknown.

Wanjira and Luka's now calm afternoon was interrupted by a knock on the door. It was Ben, his friend and roommate, who had driven over with a cousin to see if Luka and Wanjira were up to going into town, "Just to see. Let's see what's happening."

Wanjira surprised even herself by immediately jumping into the idea, despite her earlier decision not to leave the house.

"Yes, Luka, let's all go explore. Let's see how the city is taking the news."

Luka surprised them all by his hesitancy. He suddenly thought it unwise to go into town with Wanjira, whom he thought he should protect from all possible harm, but didn't want to voice his fears. "Guys, let's wait a bit. Let's watch it from here, perhaps tomorrow."

"Come on, Luka, don't tell me you're that scared, after all! Come on!" Wanjira, challenging him, was all ready to leave. "Besides, everyone has told us things are calm."

"Remember, guys, we don't know who is in town, and where. We must assume that a lot of people with guns are everywhere, but hey, I won't ruin the party!"

Off they went, Ben at the wheel. The estates were quiet, the usual bustle and noise of children at play missing. All the children must have been called indoors, Wanjira thought. They were surprised to see the municipal buses running, keeping to their schedules. They noticed that a few passengers waited by the regular stops, perhaps curious minds like themselves, or maybe they were just workers from the factories in industrial area for whom life, and the machines they operated for a living, hummed on as usual even on this remarkable day.

By the time they reached the city the four young people in the blue Datsun were convinced that Nairobi had become a ghost town. Few people moved about, and parking spots were available wherever one looked. They parked near the Hilton, and decided to walk toward Nairobi Cinema and surrounding Streets. Hardly anyone was around. They thought of going towards Parliament but decided against the idea. "Some well armed ones might be there, let's not push our luck," Luka said, and the group agreed. All shops were closed, and it was only about a half an hour later, after the quartet had by then explored the entire city center and assured themselves all was indeed well, that they entered the Hilton, where they ordered tea, and were served by a seemingly worried waiter, who greeted them warmly, serving them faster than students and most locals were ever served in this place whose focus seemed to be only foreign patrons. Today the waiter smiled, and made small talk, and the four young people returned his warmth and friendship, feeling, as everyone did today, that life without Mzee called for a re-negotiation of the old order, a new skin to live in, so to speak.

Wanjira and Luka returned to Harambee Estate almost three hours later to find Kairu and his fiancée, Wagio, at home, glued to the television.

"Quick, people," Kairu called out, excitedly, "They are about to make a special announcement!"

"O God!" Wanjira prayed. "Let it be good news. We want no coup! Please don't let us be another Uganda!"

The national anthem was played for probably the fiftieth time that day, and soon the nation was taken to the Attorney General's chambers, where every member of the cabinet was present. In less than fifteen minutes, the transition to a new government, as required, and guaranteed, by the constitution was conducted in full view of any *mwananchi* who had a working television, or a working radio, or who could gather at any public place to view, and listen to the Chief Justice of the country conduct the solemn ceremony of pronouncing the gentle and mild-mannered Daniel arap Moi, Mzee's vice president, the new president of the Republic of Kenya. The new president held the Bible firmly and promised to execute his duties faithfully, so help him God, and tears flowed freely from his and many other eyes in the special chamber.

Years later Wanjira was to reflect on this evening, and smile painfully at the memory of these tears, which everyone later said could only have been tears of joy and anticipation by the new president as he envisioned the vast personal fortune and unlimited power that awaited him as Mzee's successor.

CHAPTER SIXTEEN

A week after Mzee died Wanjira went home to Ngumo purposely to inform her parents that she and Luka had decided to get married, and that he planned to visit them formally, accompanied by his people. She had been anxious to know what her parents, her mother, especially, felt about her relationship with Luka. Now that she had agreed to marry him she wondered if she had not moved too fast, and without first introducing him to her parents.

But with Mzee's death something in the country had shifted, and everyone was worried about the future in spite of the formal, peaceful, transition to new leadership. A part of Wanjira's mind wondered if the political changes would affect anything between her and Luka. But why should they? What did the two of them have to do with the changes? But even as she pondered these thoughts she knew that Mzee's death would mean something to their two families, and maybe to other families throughout the land. But what were w*ananchi* to do, except watch events, talk about them, try to come to terms with the present, and an uncertain, future? No-one could tell. Would the new leader, a man from a small ethnic group, be fair to those who came from larger groups? And what did it matter that he was from a smaller group? Were his people also not her people? Were all Kenyans not one people? She believed, very strongly, that all Kenyans were one people, and had kept in a special part of her heart the beautiful words Luka had said to her at the Hotel Boulevard on the afternoon they first broached the subject of their presumed differences: *"We are Kenyans,"* he had said. *"We're Kenyans, not just Luo and Gikuyu or whatever else. Wanji, my darling, we're Kenyans, our country's present and future!"* Did it matter that the new leader was not from Wanjira's, or Luka's, "people"? The questions floated about the air and people could not stop talking, even if it was in hushed, awed, voices. Those who felt they had something to lose under a new political climate felt sad and disturbed, their thoughts and dreams troubled. Those with nothing to lose, or gain, felt uneasy all the same, even without knowing exactly why they felt this way. It was as if they felt complicit, coerced, really, into believing that they were guilty of *something,* for which they would be punished under the new dispensation, but were not quite sure what that *something* was. The bars had opened, even though patrons had not returned in their usual numbers, many preferring to do the very unusual thing of buying their daily ration of Tusker or Pilsner and drinking at home, away from their evening companions in their special, regular, bars. Suddenly wives and husbands found themselves at home at the same time in the evening, and there was much tension, each wondering what to say to the other. They had long lost the practice of speaking to one another in the evening, and even the children noticed the new, uneasy, arrangements brought about by the death of the old president.

Njahira did not miss the ring on her daughter's finger, and mentioned it quickly, shortly after Wanjira finished the cup of tea her mother had offered her when she arrived home. Wanjira was actually relieved by the question for it saved her from the slight anxiety she had begun to feel as she wondered how best to break the news of her engagement to her mother.

"Yes, mother, it's a special *Mbete."* She paused, and then said, "I have a lot to tell you today, Mami."

"*Hii,* give us the news then, Wanjira." Njahira smiled warmly as she spoke, but Wanjira was not fooled: she saw the anxiety on her mother's face, and heard it in her voice.

"It's from Luka, Mami. I've said yes to his marriage proposal. You remember Kairu talking about him that day? He wants to marry me."

Njahira looked at her daughter, and a welter of emotions filled her body and soul. So, this was it. She was quiet for a while, and then asked, "And you? Do you want to marry him?"

"Very much, Mami. He is wonderful!"

Njahira smiled, remembering her own feelings when Kamau proposed to her, years earlier. It all comes to this, in the end, doesn't it? You raise them, you love them as much as possible, you long to have them always with you, but it is not possible. And it's also true what our people say, *"Airitu ni mbariki,"* Young women are *Mbariki,* the beautiful and wild bean that bursts out of its shell dramatically, and is dispersed far and wide, to all corners of the land. Her very own *Mbariki,* Wanjira, she-of-the wayside, was affirming all this right here, in front of her eyes. She wished she did not have to hear what Wanjira was saying, but it could not be avoided. She was not happy at Wanjira's news but thought it best not to show it. She had had a strong feeling after her visit to Wanjira at the university nearly two months earlier that the young woman was totally smitten by Luka, this man from the west. On her way home she had become convinced her daughter was serious, following a few questions she had asked Kairu. She reflected, for days afterwards, on Wanjira's reaction to Kairu's disparaging remarks about Luka. Njahira had, in a way, been preparing herself for Wanjira's news, wishing it was not to be, but thinking there was little she could do about it if her daughter was convinced Luka was the man for her.

Njahira did not ask more questions, for she needed time to think. This was not a simple matter, and it needed to be handled carefully. She thought it best to wait until later to say more about it, and therefore got busy with the evening meal's preparation, all the while thinking of how best to respond to Wanjira. All she said to her, for now, was, "Alright, Wanjira, I have heard your news. Your father will also need to hear the news this evening," but in her mind a quiet, intense, conversation with herself was going on: Why can't these children find husbands we can speak with in our own tongues? How can we talk to his people? Yes, we can do so in Kiswahili and English, but is that good enough? These languages are clumsy on our tongues! How will they raise their children? What will they eat? Where will they live? Those people of the lake will kill my daughter! Njahira went on thinking such terrible thoughts, and felt even more anxious. This beautiful child of mine, why is she doing this? Why couldn't she find a good Mugikuyu man to marry, to have a good future with? All the way to the lake? How does one get there? Oh my God, so someone did place the *Githemengu* on her, after all! And to think of how hard I tried to fight it off!

Njahira's thoughts were furious, and she felt some bitterness begin to plant itself in her even as she tried to fight it off. She was a Christian woman, after all, a Catholic, and the teachings she had valued all her life were about love, and acceptance of all God's people. We are his people, all of us. All the world's people are the same, she had learned, many years earlier. That was why she had not encouraged her children to talk ill about people who were different from them, in Ngumo, or wherever they were. She had scolded Kairu as he drove her home only two months earlier, telling him she had been disappointed at the way he had spoken of his sister's friend. "We are all children of God," she had told him, amidst his protestations that his sister was making a big mistake in becoming attached to a MjaLuo fellow, and one with Luka's political ideas. "Mami, just watch. One of these days your daughter will be picked up by the secret police, and all because of that man. Just wait. Keep on encouraging her, and you'll see." She had protested, discouraging him from saying more about Luka, and said she would support Wanjira's choice of boyfriend because that was the correct thing to do. Words, words, ideas, ideas. She was to blame. She should have taught her children to be more careful, to love wisely, to be daring, but not *this* daring! Now she was eating her own words, and the worst had happened. Her first daughter! This is what happens when you raise an independent daughter; when they enter university. You can't control them, but what would be the point, anyway? Wanjira has to make her own decisions, because I made mine about her father, and it is not as if some of my brothers did not think he was wrong for me because he was poor, and his family had very little land, but aren't we alright today? We have enough food and school fees for the children, and haven't two of them already gone to university? And the five younger ones, aren't they doing well in school? So let Wanjira make her own decisions, but the west! the land of the people of the lake*! ruguru*!

Njahira's thoughts were interrupted by a commotion outside. A loud and piercing cry reached her ears, and there was no mistaking its source: Waithira. She was the baby of the family and for some reason found much to disagree with her brother, Karangu, who was ten. Feisty Waithira was eight going on eighteen, and Njahira often smiled whenever she looked at these two, who actually really liked each other and found much to laugh about when they were not fighting. All she could make out was the young girl's loud voice saying, "You will know my name is Waithira today!" and her brother's retort: "But isn't your name Mercy? Mercy, Mercy, have Mercy on me!" He always made fun of his sister's Christian name, which always provoked her ire. Njahira smiled. No major crisis out there, she decided.

Njahira continued to churn her earlier thoughts in her mind, but a sense of shame was gradually replacing the gall and rage of the previous hour. She suddenly remembered that Wanjira was with her, and looked around her like one who had just awoken from a an unexpected mid-day nap and was feeling a bit disoriented. Wanjira was not in the room. She had stepped out once she realized her mother was lost in the world of her own thoughts, not wanting to disturb her. Wanjira felt nervous as she went outside, feeling guilty for having obviously shocked her mother with her news.

In the kitchen Njahira brought her mind back to reality. She began a silent self-reprimand. Ah, these thoughts! These were bad thoughts for a woman who considered herself open to the world her children lived in. For it was different for her and Kamau. The world of Nairobi, university, friends from all over Kenya, was an alien world to her, but she had always taken pleasure in listening to Kairu and Wanjira talk about the many things they had learned in boarding school, their impressions of their classmates, and their teachers. Was it not Kairu himself who had first helped their family know something about the lake region? By attending school in Kisumu he had brought new stories and new ideas to the family. She remembered him telling them about some of his classmates, and of his growing friendships with some of them. She had met some of his friends from A-levels, two young men from Kisumu, who had visited Kairu during a trip they had made to Nairobi during the holidays. Of course Wanjira had been exposed to these new ideas by her own brother, and by the general attitude she, Njahira, and her husband Kamau had toward people in general. For Kamau too had an open mind, and had often said there was little difference between people, for he had seen a lot in the War. He had once remarked to his Njahira that differences came about when people had either too much, or too little, money. That is why, he had continued, all children should acquire a decent education so they could all find a way to earn a decent living. Without exaggerated economic differences between the villages and the cities people could live decently, doing whatever they valued and enjoyed to do—be it farming, or working in offices in town. She had agreed with him, marveling at his way of thinking.

Njahira had enjoyed her children's stories from school, and of their many different friends. Kairu and Wanjira had given her a glimpse of their world, which she herself had entered during her own school days, but in the old days women like her could reach only so far, and she had been contented to obtain an education that allowed her to earn a living as a teacher, and to be open to the possibility that her children could go to great lengths with their own education. Njahira's joy had been great when Kairu, and then Wanjira, entered university, and her thoughts had taken her into the future, where her daughter commanded a good salary and therefore lived a decent and dignified life. A life that did not require a man to either make, or unmake, her, for the world had many cruelties in wait for a woman without her own way of making a living. That was why she, and many other women of her generation, wanted their daughters to obtain a certificate in one profession or another. It did not matter what the profession was as long as it provided the young women an opportunity to earn their own salaries.

But Njahira was a fair woman, and towards evening she had come to the conclusion that her main problem with the news Wanjira had given her was not simply about Luka's ethnic background, even though that was an important consideration. The more she thought about it, the more convinced she became that her real problem was with the young people's timing. She did not think her daughter was old enough to be taking this important life step, marriage, and even this Luka himself, what was the rush? Could they not wait a bit more so they could be sure they were making the right decision? But how could she think so when she herself had married at eighteen, three years younger than Wanjira was now? She knew she could not convince her daughter to wait on these grounds, but then didn't everyone know that women in her day were ready for marriage by the time they were sixteen? There was not much education to be had in her day, much less preparation for paid employment, and today there was. Wanjira was getting ready to tie herself down as a wife and mother when she was far too young! She should be thinking of graduating, earning her money, spending it as she wished, saving some of it, and doing whatever further training she needed! Why not wait another two or three years? She could then marry as a more mature woman ready to take on the many and difficult duties of marriage. And did she know how complicated it could be to be married into these families from *ruguru*? His people would move in immediately! She would be cooking day in day out, and she would have no support if she complained. And she would have to start paying school fees for his entire clan! At least in our part of the country we have done away with most of these responsibilities even though some still remain. These thoughts went around and around Njahira's mind, and she felt a new surge of pain and fury envelop her being, making her feel that her normally calm demeanor was leaving her. She took a deep breath, and, looking down into the *gitaruru* on her lap, picked up a handful of baby potatoes in her left hand, ready to continue the peeling she and her daughter had started working on a few minutes earlier in preparation for the evening meal. She remained quiet for a long time, even as part of her mind paid attention to the cat, which had smelled the meat in the cupboard and was waiting to do its well-practiced jump so steal a piece the moment one opened the cupboard.

"And you think this man really loves you?" Her question came out strongly, almost harshly. Wanjira, who had joined her mother in the quiet intensity of the last half hour, had concentrated on the task in front of her, her own hands working methodically on the potatoes, and she was taken aback by her mother's abrupt question.

"Mami, yes. He does."

"Good. Because he must have very strong love for you if you are to survive marriage in his culture."

Wanjira sat back in her chair, her hands quickly dropping the knife and potatoes into the *gitaruru,* and looked directly at her mother. Of course Luka loved her intensely, and she loved him back with equal intensity, but what did her mother mean? Luka was the first man she had ever felt this way about, her very first boyfriend. Could it be possible that she did not fully know what her mother meant? Was what she felt for Luka, and what he felt for her, not the required recipe for, the essence of, a loving marriage? It seemed that she had had this conviction ever since she met him, and especially since their engagement. But her mother had said something important, and she wanted to ask for an elaboration, but before she could say anything Njahira, as if she had read her daughter's mind, said, almost as if speaking to herself, "I mean, he has to be fully convinced that you are the right wife for him because he will probably be disapproved of by his people. But if he loves you fully, then that's good, because he will resist attempts by those who will insist that he marries a "proper" wife one of these days."

"Mami!' Wanjira's heart was pounding. "Why do you say that?" She was beginning to tremble.

"Oh, don't you know that a lot of people believe that a wife or husband from outside their own *kabila* is not a "proper" spouse?"

"Mami! Those are old ideas. People have changed, after all. We are the future generation, Mami. Many of us don't think like that these days."

"Hmm," Njahira said, and then she shrugged her shoulders in a gesture that said, "I hope you are right," and was quiet for a while, as was Wanjira. Finally, as if she had reached some conclusion, the older woman said, with what seemed a lighter heart, "*Haidhuru*, Wanjira. If this is the man for you then he is the one, and nothing I say will change it."

A sense of sadness filled Wanjira's heart. She had wanted her mother to be happy for her, to tease her happily about Luka, but obviously it was not to be. She held the last two potatoes in her left hand and with her right continued to peel them, ever so slowly, thinking things over, wondering why her love for Luka had to come at such a high price.

After a while she said to her mother, who was now washing a *sufuria* ready to begin sautéing red onions and garlic in vegetable oil, the first step in the preparation of her special dish of meat, beans, maize and potatoes "Mami, he is the one for me, really, and it's just like you once told me, that when I met the right man I wouldn't need anyone to point him out, and when we met, over a year ago, I knew it that very day. And do you know that he told me the same? He knew it too!"

As she spoke Wanjira was peeling a large red onion, and using the cutting board on the kitchen table, started cutting it up. It would soon be ready to accompany the meat Njahira had already prepared. The older woman turned to her daughter and smiling, asked, "You both did, and on the first day?"

"I'm telling you, Mami. The very day. I thought I was having a heart attack. When it hit me that he was *The One* I almost stopped breathing."

Njahira now let out a loud laugh and said, "Wanjira, that is really good. It makes me remember some things..." Her voice trailed off, and Wanjira looked at her mother, whose face had turned soft as she looked into something in her own past life, something Wanjira did not know about. She wanted to ask her mother something but did not, thinking it best to leave her to her special thoughts, thinking that her mother might say something about it, and if not now, at some future point. Suddenly Wanjira started to sniff, and to wipe her eyes, and for a while she could not be sure if all the tears came from the onion she was chopping.

"One thing, though, Mami," Wanjira's voice was strong, and she had a smile on her face, and Njahira knew her daughter was alright, ready to tease her. "You haven't asked me about his family, although I know it is coming. You would like them."

She then told her what she knew of Luka's father's work, about Luka's mother and siblings. Njahira commented they were a big and very well educated family. Wanjira knew her mother was impressed. She loved well educated and accomplished people, she really did.

"But that's not all, Mami. They are Catholics."

Njahira heaved a sigh, and Wanjira wondered if it was a sigh of relief, or from the exertion of turning and stirring the food, which was now sizzling and letting off wonderful aromas throughout the kitchen. "Now that is very good, Wanjira. That is very good. Why didn't you tell me sooner?"

And as if a heavy load had lifted off her shoulders, Njahira smiled. Her step seemed lighter as she continued with the food preparation. Wanjira was astounded by her mother's change of mood, for she now seemed to be smiling to herself.

"Ah, Wanjira, if this man is this good, then marry him. You know that God makes the decisions for us, actually. We just fool ourselves when we think we do, but marriage, and children, are God's gifts. He decides for us."

Njahira was quiet for a while, and then, in an excited voice said, "Wanjira, do you know that one of Ngumo's most beautiful women married a man from Kisumu in the 1960s? You were a young girl then and would not remember the excitement. It was a big and lovely wedding, and you should have seen the bride and her bridesmaids! We had not seem such beauty before. People flocked to the church to see this man come to marry off their daughter, and even as they prayed they predicted, and expected, many bad things to happen to her. Her name is Wanjiru, and I have heard that she remains very happily married to this man, and they have eight children. They say she learned to speak *Dholuo* and has managed very well out there in the land of the lake. She has a big farm and her children are all doing very well. The man was a teacher at Ngumo High School and he loved her so much he was willing to change his religion and agree to let their children grow up Catholic. Can you imagine that? Now that is love!" Njahira's face was animated as she recounted this tale, and Wanjira found herself getting into the excitement of this marriage from long gone days.

Wanjira was about to say something when Njahira said, in a strong voice, "And do you think some of our so-called good Gikuyu men might agree to do the same?" She paused before answering herself, "I think not. I suspect most wouldn't!" and added, her voice getting stronger with conviction, a complaint, really, "They might even be eager to beat a well educated woman, *ati* to teach her a lesson. So marry Luka, Wanjira, and don't listen to whoever says anything about it. I am just very glad that he's Catholic because that is our faith, and when I come to visit you there will be no problem because the mass and the rosary are the same in *Dholuo* or *Gikuyu*. It's the same thing."

Wanjira laughed. Her mother could always spring a surprise when least expected to. "Mami, you are something else! You are too funny!"

"Not funny, Wanjira. Just happy that you share your faith with Luka. That is all I prayed for, and my prayers have been answered."

"Except not exactly, Mami." Wanjira had a teasing smile, and her usually good mood had returned. "They tell us that God always answers our prayers, but not in exactly the way we had imagined."

"That is only partly true, Wanjira. I have always prayed that God should send you a good man, and man who would respect, and not be afraid of your intelligence, and I now believe he has."

"Thank you, Mami. I knew you'd like knowing that we both go to St. Paul's." How to explain this joy? Wanjira thought to herself. If Mami agrees nothing else matters! She approved of Luka.

"That is good, Wanjira. That is good."

Mother and daughter, their short but intense struggle now under control, then spoke about the next step, and Njahira assured her daughter that she would talk to her father, and they would send word to their people about the first visit by Lukas' people. Once a date was set Wanjira would let Luka know, and he in turn would let his father know, and they would make their own arrangement about the first, introductory, visit.

"But first things first, Wanjira. Luka must visit us and tell your father of his intentions. In his own words. When his people make the request, it will be a formality, of course, but your father must first hear it from Luka himself."

"Gosh," Wanjira sighed. "How complicated!"

"Yes, Wanjira. But if it must be done right. I am sure Luka's own family would want it done right. They can't be different from most other families in this country. And it is also your insurance, don't forget."

"What do you mean?"

"These marriage negotiations are done patiently, according to a set of rules. They are the steps families make as they join each other in marriage. Remember now: once you are Luka's wife you will belong to his people, and he will belong to us. When it's done right, its your certificate, witnessed by hundreds of people. Later on, after all the negotiations are complete, you will, of course, have a wedding and a formal, legal, certificate of marriage. But this kind of open discussion about marriage is your really true certificate. A certificate for life, witnessed by all members of your two families."

"Oh God! How boring!" Wanjira laughed, a cynical, yet excited, laugh."Wanjira!, "It's not boring, you'll see. Really. A marriage is like giving birth to a new son or daughter, and it takes a while, you know. Those nine months a man and woman get are important: they help them prepare themselves for the new visitor from the other world. The months of marriage negotiations serve a similar purpose. Preparation." Njahira was quiet for a while and then, almost as if she was speaking to herself, continued, "Yes, it will need time, and in the meantime you both will have a chance to be sure you want to go through with it or not."

"Fear not, Mrs. Kamau! I will not change my mind." Wanjira was animated. "Not at all!"

"He might." Njahira had a broad smile.

"Oh, no, no! Don't even think about it, Mami. He won't."

Wanjira's mind had begun to turn around and around, and she was back in Kahoti, at Jessie's wedding. "Oh God, so many things must happen before that day! I have to think of so very many things!" "That is why this engagement year will be good for you. For one thing you'd be better off if you first completed your degree. And from what you tell me, Luka will then, at least, be done with the School of Law. It will take at least a year to do all the negotiations, Wanjira, so you'll have enough time to finish university, and to think of your dress and all the other things that come with a wedding."

Njahira's advice was what Wanjira needed. She had not thought of such practical details and she appreciated her mother's common sense and practical mind.

"And of course," Njahira said, by way of conclusion, "Nothing can even be done before Mzee is buried. Once he is laid to rest we will begin to talk about these matters."

Njahira fixed a direct look on Wanjira and for a while said nothing. Then, in a clear, strong voice, said, "One last thing, Wanjira. I like the fact that Luka will qualify as a lawyer. I think he will be a respectable and honourable man. That is very good."

"Ehe," Wanjira said, her face serious. "I hope we'll make a good home together, Mami, both of us."

"Wanjira, I am happy to know that Luka is a good man, and I pray that he remains a good man. But the day will come when you will both disagree, and I hope you will both manage to use words carefully as you settle your differences. You know what our people say, '*Mathanwa meeri kiondo kimwe matiagaga gukong'orania.*' Two axes in the same *Kiondo* are bound to knock against each other at some point. But let me tell you this: if on any day he ever hits you, you must gather all the strength within you and hit him back *very* hard. A woman who lets a man hit her without hitting back can be sure of one thing: her problems have just begun."

The day after Wanjira returned to Nairobi, it was announced on radio and in all newspapers that Mzee's funeral would take place in a week. He would be buried on Parliament grounds, and representatives of many governments were expected in Nairobi. In the meantime, *Wananchi* were free to pay their respects to Mzee, who now lay in state at State House, his former official residence.

People flocked by the thousands to line up at State House for a last glimpse at the Old Man. Wanjira and Luka took the bus into town and, alighting at the Serena Bus Stop, walked the half mile to State House, where, at ten O'clock, thousands were already in line, deadly quiet, waiting their turn to enter the great house. Wanjira noted the beautiful gardens everywhere, the robust and lovely colours of hibiscus, bougainvillea, and the well cut and maintained lawns. *Kumbe* this is State House!

The young lovers took their place in the line. It was a beautiful, sunny morning, and the air felt light and comforting. Looking about them they noticed the various people waiting to pay their respects: Africans, Indians, Europeans, and from all walks of life as well, judging from their clothes. Rich and poor stood side by side, united in grief at the parting of the grand old man, but also in the relief everyone felt because the country did not rip apart when he died, as had been feared. Now people could shed tears of sorrow, and even if they nursed some private worry that things *could* go wrong, they need not have feared that such a calamity would happen right away. All over town one felt that things were contained, and that the new president could be trusted to walk a path not so different from that of his predecessor. The future leaders could take comfort in knowing that the paths they had prepared for in all their years of schooling remained open, waiting for them, the ground already trodden firm by the steps of an earlier generation. They felt grateful to Mzee, who, while he lived, had taken measures whose effects could be felt everywhere now that he was gone: the country was stable, and life marched on without him. He had ensured that the succession would not be traumatic for the nation. As Luka and Wanjira inched closer to the where the Great One lay in state, they felt with everyone around them that they were witnessing a powerful moment in the history of their country, and of the large, misunderstood, exploited, yet mighty African continent that was their home.

CHAPTER SEVENTEEN

The best laid out plans have a way of going awry, and that is what happened to Wanjira's and Luka's marriage plans. A few days after Mzee's burial, Luka learned that he and two other student leaders were barred from entering the School of Law. The news reached them just when everyone was starting to feel settled into the new regime, when the cities had sprung back to life and were now filled with the normal hustle and bustle of daily activities. No explanation was given to Luka and the others; indeed there was no official word that they could not enter the school, only that there was a problem with their applications, and could they immediately report to the school to clarify a few matters?

Luka's heart beat hard when he read the letter from his law faculty dean advising him to report to his office immediately. He sweated profusely, his mind as agile as that of an animal hemmed into a corner, instinctively smelling danger. A few hours later he learned that Kariuki, A.K and Amos, P., his two classmates and fellow members of the Student Union, were also in the same situation, and immediately smelled a rat.

The following weeks were very difficult for Luka, Wanjira, their families and friends. The irony of it all was that the news of their "missing" applications, for that is what the problem turned out to be, reached them two days before the new president pardoned most political prisoners, Ngugi the writer included. Luka and Wanjira were heavy-hearted even as they celebrated the writers' return to life after detention without trial, and the tears each shed upon seeing the former detainee, looking as calm and collected as they remembered him, and strong of spirit as he addressed the throng at the university grounds, come to celebrate his return, were a combination of joy, sadness, rage, and fear for the future. For why would the new government give with one hand, and take with the other? Or were they merely sending out a warning to any suspected "dissidents"? For that's what it seemed to those familiar with Luka and his two friends' campus activism. But who was behind it all? Who had singled them out for punishment, and in such a sneaky way, too?

Thoughts of marriage were cast aside as Luka fought to regain his place at the institution that would qualify him to practice law in Kenya. He could not imagine being denied the right to complete a study program he had so enjoyed, and which he planned to make his professional life's work. His father arrived in Nairobi the day after he learned the news, and sought interviews with various people he knew, and others to whom he had been introduced in an attempt to advocate for his son, but it seemed that no-one knew anything about Luka and the others' applications. The main reason for their not receiving letters of admission into the school was simply that *their applications were missing,* and no-one could tell why only these three applications had disappeared from the lot of the other applicants, who now happily waited to enter the school of law in only a month. The "missing" applications could apparently not be replaced by new ones because the application period had passed, and it would be illegal to allow new applications past the official deadline. The three young men found themselves truly caught between the proverbial rock and a hard place.

Wanjira returned to her final year disappointed and distressed. She tried her best to get into the rhythm of her classes, and more importantly to complete her thesis proposal, which was due two weeks after the term started. She worked hard despite her sadness, staying late into the night to write, re-write, and write some more. The words took a while to say exactly what she wanted them to say, and it was a challenge that she found herself beginning to enjoy despite the struggle. Reading and writing with a specific end in sight helped her cope with the anxiety of what had happened to Luka, and the many questions this raised for their plans. She would do her best to focus on her work, but there were moments when she broke down and tears ran down her cheeks. She would wipe them away, wash her face, and resume her studies. Luka encouraged her to keep going, to remain focused, and to aim for the top marks he knew she could earn from her thesis. He also urged her to stop worrying about him whenever she brought up the topic of his future.

A month after Luka's bad news he and Wanjira had tea at the Serena Hotel. It was a lovely afternoon, but the two young people hardly noticed the beautifully manicured lawn and the lovely flowers all around them. Their hearts were heavy with the knowledge that nothing about Luka's case had been resolved. Luka was the first to speak what was on their minds.

"I have a feeling things will work out, Wanji. Many people are trying to help."

"Oh, Luka, what if…?"

Luka was quiet for a while, wondering if it was the right time to share the thought with Wanjira. After a while he looked at her, and holding her hands in his, said, "If things don't work out, Wanji, I may have to leave the country. That's my plan B."

Wanjira groaned, and began to weep. Tears ran down her face. She did not even try to stop them. He had given her a big shock.

"Where? When?" Her voice was weak, and she was blowing her nose noisily, unable to stop the tears.

"We don't know yet, but maybe the States. I would go into graduate school, and at least continue academic law…I do want to teach someday, and it may not be too bad, Wanji, if I could secure a place. Uncle O has got the process started, as has my dean, and we have a few possible options."

"Would these fellows here stop you from going?"

"We aren't sure, but must make plans all the same."

Wanjira went on crying for a while, holding on to Luka, who also had tears in his eyes. For a long time the two lovers held each other, wondering if all their hopes and dreams were being dashed right in front of their eyes, fully conscious of the bad fortune that had hit them just when they felt their lives were going as each had hoped, and prayed, for. Wanjira had not even had a chance to tell Luka of her happiness that her mother had asked her to bring him home sometime in late September, and she had not heard from him that his parents wanted him to take her to visit them. Wanjira and Luka had not had a chance to share information on how their parents had reacted to their news, even though they might not have shared *everything* that had been said. There had been a fierce struggle, even on Luka's side, particularly with his mother, who had even wept upon learning he wanted to marry "outside." It had taken Luka's father's good-natured and strong personality to convince his wife that they could not judge this girl from afar, and that it was important to believe their son when he said Wanjira was a good girl, fit to be his wife. "Let us trust him, for he tends to make good decisions," he had said, adding he did not see why Luka would suddenly turn out to have made a wrong one when it was his own future wife he was making the decision about.

But as he now struggled with his son's problems Mr. Owuor privately wondered if his son had been too hasty in considering marriage, an intercultural one at that, and so soon, even before he had started earning a salary. What could have made Luka so anxious? Was it a fear of losing this beautiful young woman he obviously loved so much, or was it something else, some inner knowledge, that his life was about to be disrupted, and therefore he should hurry up and grab the chance of a lifetime? For Mr. Owuor believed that love, true love, was not easy to come by, and had actually been the one to persuade his wife that maybe this was really what Luka had found in Wanjira, and that they should support and give him their blessing. He had reminded her of his determination to marry her when her own parents had considered her much too young, and him too poor to marry. Priscilla had smiled, and later laughed out loudly at the memory. He wished only the best for this bright and courageous son of his, and it was no use clinging to the idea so many seemed to have: that happiness could only be found within one's own ethnic group. In his dealings with all kinds of people during his postings to the Coast, Central, and now Western Province, he had come to the conclusion that men and women really wanted only one thing in life: to be loved and appreciated, and to have a decent way to earn a living. The rest was *bakshish,* really, a gift from God. If one could find all these things in the very place he or she was born, why, then, that was simply God's special, extra, gift to the person, and nothing to hold up to the world as a personal achievement. Let Luka and Wanjira tie the knot in a proper, traditional way, according to the ways of his, and her, people, and also in a Catholic church, just like he and Priscilla had done some thirty years earlier. When he learned that Wanjira's and his family shared the same faith, he had, like Njahira, and later, Kamau, felt his heart settle even more, especially when he noticed Priscilla's positive reaction to this information, a radical change from her initial reaction. In his heart Mr. Owuor welcomed this daughter of Gikuyu country into his home, and prayed her parents had no difficulties with his son becoming their son-in-law, for, like any adult Kenyan, Mr. Owuor knew that people's positive reactions to matters such as ethnic mixing in marriage could not be taken for granted.

But other, also seriously important, things had changed in the last two weeks. Mr. Owuor's main concern now was with the urgent matter of what Luka would do if he was denied the chance to become a practicing lawyer in Kenya, and thus be forced to do other things he would rather not do. The thought of his son having to leave the country unexpectedly, and without having a real choice in the matter, galled him; he felt bitter at his country, at the people who had interfered with his son's long-held dream of becoming a lawyer, although there was no-one in particular to whom he could attach these feelings, seeing as there was no name but simply the "Application Procedure" and "The System." For now, the only thing that was absolutely clear to him was that any talk of his son's marriage to the young lady from Ngumo had to wait until some other time, when things were more settled.

Luka was denied entry into the school of law despite all entreaties by many different people. He, Kariuki and Amos, the other two students in the same boat, were advised to re-apply the following year, but also warned that no-one could guarantee anything, and that they could not assume acceptance into the school the following year. They were, indeed, being told to clear off, like three annoying flies at the feast table of those deemed worthy of entering the legal profession. Wanjira wept when Luka informed her of the new development as the two of them walked over to the Arboretum one afternoon, hoping to get away from the city and its annoyances, if only for a brief while. They sat quietly under their favorite *Muhuti* tree, lost in thought, until Luka said, "Wanji, I hope you won't give up on me."

"Never, Luka. Never!" She spoke with passion. "How can that be possible?" She held his hand tightly, and smiled, hoping to help lighten the burden in Luka's heart.

"You know, love, this is temporary. We will not be defeated. Not by these thugs, or anyone else." Luka spoke in a strong voice, staring straight ahead, as if he was addressing someone in the distance. "Our resolve can only be strengthened by such setbacks, Wanji. They are small, in the grand scheme of things."

Wanjira realized they had not mentioned the word *America* or *Europe* in the last week, ever since Luka first informed her that his family was looking into these two countries for a program he could get into. He had told her he favoured America, for he had learned it was easier to find a scholarship there. It was also because the dean of his faculty, incensed at what had happened to his three very promising students—the three students from the current graduating class he considered most likely to make a high impact on society as practicing lawyers—had called up a number of people and requested application materials for the "Trio" to seek entry in universities in the United States. Dean Muthama was bitter about the run-around everyone gave him as he tried to have his three students enrolled in the School of Law, all the while fully aware it might be a losing battle.

What the dean and many others did not know was that the decision to thwart the careers of the three students had been engineered by none other than Octopus. Octopus, whose corrupt and vicious ways had many supporters among politicians, wished to "teach a lesson" to the upstarts at the University who had dared put them to public shame and exposure in their rabble-rousing speeches in frequent Kamukunjis on campus. Since that one time he had seen Luka and Wanjira enjoying a beautiful late afternoon near the swimming pool at Hotel Boulevard, Octopus had played around with a few ideas in his head. This one had proved to be the perfect, untraceable, form of punishment for the brazen *Munjaruo* fellow and his proud *Gikuyu* girlfriend who obviously had no manners. Imagine going for such a fellow when all of us are around? It galled Octopus to remember the beautiful pair. And the other two good-for-nothings would have to pay for putting him and his friends to shame. Did they not know their exaggerated, untrue, claims that he, in particular, was a big grabber had reached his ears? And from the mouths of their own friends, too, for example the trustworthy Murema, a good young man related to him through marriage. *Wataona cha mtema kuni!* He would show them. Did they not know he had friends in all kinds of places? The young clerk at the relevant office had done what needed to be done, and now the three fellows' applications were nowhere to be seen, and no-one, *no-one*, was above the law! There could be no re-application. Let them eat dust!

The only thing Dean Muthama knew for sure was that the gate to the School of Law had been tightly shut against his three top students, and the alternative to go abroad was the best option to pursue. He was at least given word by a top Ministry of Education official that no obstacle would be placed in the way of the Trio's exit permit, and that they would therefore get the necessary clearances. The "Exit Clearance" was a control device only two years in existence, and one that the students at the University, the Trio among them, had fiercely opposed when it was first introduced as a pre-requisite for anyone leaving the country.

In the end, however, only Luka and Kariuki chose to try America, for Amos decided he would wait for the following year's application process, and hope for the best. In the meantime he would work with his father on their family farm in Kitale, where they grew maize and wheat. "I'll return to the land, man," he told Luka, smiling sadly. "Just like Mzee advised us often to *rudi mashambani.* Little did I know I'd be answering the call so soon after his death."

"All the best, man. Wish us luck, Amos. Maybe this is not the best thing, but it's all I can do for now."

It was now late August. Only a week earlier Luka had received word that he had been admitted into a well known University in Chicago, in the American mid-west, and that he would have all his tuition and living expenses paid under a special grant for promising law students "most likely to become legal scholars" from African countries. Kariuki also got a similar package to attend a university in the state of New York. Luka would specialize in human rights law, an area his dean had highly recommended, assuring Luka that the university needed someone with that specialization. "Don't you worry, young man. You will return with your credentials from a good university, and we will have a place for you right here. Mark my words."

Dean Muthama had called Luka and Kariuki into his office a few days after they received the good news from the United States, and given them a few words: "Now, young men, you have come of age. We have prepared you well in this faculty, and we had high hopes for you, but unfortunately you have come face to face with the worst abuse of power some in authority in this country are willing to undertake. But take heart. All is not lost. You are getting a second chance, and who knows, this just might be the fire you needed to strengthen the will and power within you. You will go out and do the best you can—and I have no fear about this—return to us with new insights and strategies for using the law in this country. Go well, and keep us posted. See you in two years!"

The dean then formally shook hands with Kariuki and Luka. Luka felt a lump in his throat when the older man was speaking to them, vowing to himself that he would do his best, and that he would return as soon as his studies were over. It was more than he could have hoped for, and when he got the visa for entry into the United States, without any problem, he and Wanjira, despite their misgivings at their changed plans, thought it worth celebrating. They called a few friends to Luka's cousin's place in Buruburu for a quickly arranged party.

That evening nearly fifty people, Kariuki and Amos among them, crammed themselves into the small space, not caring how tightly packed they were. They danced, sang loudly, and many drank wine or Tuskers to drown their sorrows and disappointment at life's vicissitudes. Laughter and tears were the order of the evening, especially when someone, moved beyond words, asked the DJ to stop the music so he or she could make a toast to Luka and Wanjira, or to Kariuki and Amos. Everyone wished Luka and Wanjira well, and spoke of love conquering all. Wanjira found herself weeping silently, sometimes alone, at other times in Luka's arms as they slow-danced to the Commodores or Franco, or Tabu Ley Rochereau. MBaraka Mwinshehe spoke their thoughts with his words:

Hakuna kitu kibaya humu duniani kama shida…
haijui…hata…wala—yoyote
Kila siku shida shida haishi
Mpaka siku ya mwisho…

Nothing is as terrible in this world as trouble
It knows no special person—
Every day its trouble, trouble
To the end of one's days...

Everyone had a kind word for Luka, and there was much comment that the thugs who had "tripped" them could go someplace hot if they so wished. Luka only smiled, not wanting to show the sadness he felt at having been so wickedly stopped from pursuing a long-held dream, and not wishing to show the ambivalence he felt at having to leave home and his beloved Wanjira and go to America, when that had been the furthest thought from his mind barely four months earlier.

The end of the year was soon upon Wanjira and her classmates. Last-minute preparations for end of year examinations were upon them. Wanjira and a few others in her faculty who had opted for the thesis option were busy with the typing and editing of their work, anxious beyond words as they feared missing submission deadlines. She had learned much from her study of children's literature, and as she compiled her results and attempted to understand the lessons she had learned from her research study, could not help feeling sad and dismayed at some of the findings. So many of the children interviewed had shown a total dismissal of stories set in Kenya and elsewhere in Africa. They had told her they loved the stories of children with long hair and fair skins. One brave little girl had explained, to the cheery agreement of her classmates: "Because these children are good."

Another child from a different school had said, "They wear nice clothes and speak English."

Here, then, Wanjira thought, was the work to be done: to help find reading materials for children that affirmed, and showed respect, to the very world the children lived in. Children are honest, she knew, and could not be made to think something was other than they saw and experienced it. The reality reflected in stories for children could only be honest. Reading material should not be distorted, or slanted, to make children think that there was nothing good about the way they looked, acted, or played. Or that these same experiences were more important and appealing when done by children from Europe and North America. But was it the writers' fault, or the perception of the children, itself shaped and nurtured by their families, their home and school environment, and by their teachers?

Wanjira's research experience had puzzled her at times, but she had also enjoyed her talks with the children and found much food for thought. She had discovered that many children, particularly those in the three rural schools she visited, loved to tell stories, sing songs, and tell riddles. They incorporated song and specific dance movements in their play outside the classroom, and they took great pride in mastering these forms of expression. They read little compared with the city children she met, for, unlike the latter group, their schools and families had very few books besides the required language study texts from the ministry. Wanjira had found herself wondering if these were not actually the luckier group of Kenyan children.

Luka wrote her every week, and she had come to love these messages from what she considered the big void, an unbearable and hopelessly faraway place. He sometimes referred to his new life as "Exile," but always, as was his way, managed to make her laugh in the details he gave of his new life. He had written of the long flight, first to New York City, and then to Chicago, his new "home," and of the jet-lag he had experienced, his night and days totally confused. "The sun does not shine in the normal way, Wanji, given our position here in the northern hemisphere, and the humidity is unbearable at times." This from a man who had spent his early years in Mombasa, and whose home was near the great lake, where, Wanjira had told him when she visited his home shortly before he left for America, it was much too hot. He had laughed and laughed at the time, calling her a true daughter of the highlands. "Nyarhighlands," he had teased her. Now he wrote that he missed her every day, but that he was also starting to enjoy his classes, and even the strange weather, which was beginning to cool down as the autumn progressed. Later he wrote of his new winter wardrobe, making her laugh as she read of all the things he had to wear before stepping out of his room. "Oh my God," she would think. "What kind of place is this Chicago?" She had read of winter, but how could anyone imagine such cold? The descriptions, vivid as they were, could not fully help her "feel," or begin to understand, this strange climate.

Her thesis was done, and submitted. Like everyone else in her class she began to think seriously about the next step, and a few days after submitting her thesis she made an appointment to speak to the head of her faculty. She wanted to know what her prospects for graduate study were, for she had always wanted to continue her studies. Luka had written to say it would be wonderful if she could join him in America, and that she stood a good chance of obtaining a scholarship to study for a master's degree in Literature or any other course of her choice." Believe it or not, Wanji, you could even enter an MBA program, or Law School, if you wished. You'd need to take specific exams, but you'd stand a good chance. That's how flexible this country is. Your first degree is a mere introduction, basic preparation, as it were." She marveled at all this, but America? It was not in her plans. Luka should simply hurry up, be done with his study program, and return home, were her thoughts.

In addition to looking into graduate study possibilities Wanjira also began actively seeking a job. A number of options presented themselves: advertising, reporting or editing for one of the dailies; administrative work at the Ministry of Education or Ministry of Information. Akili, her former tutorial fellow, now a newly hired lecturer in her department, suggested she look for a job where she could develop her writing skills in preparation for graduate school. Kairu supported the idea. She sensed, these days, that he was sorry about all that had happened to Luka, but the two of them had said very little about the matter. She wondered if he was secretly pleased that Luka was now out of the way, for even as he had warmed towards him she suspected he had not fully come to terms with the fact of her engagement and planned marriage to Luka.

Wanjira sent out some letters to the newspapers seeking an editorial training position. She waited for their response as she prepared for graduation, which was in three weeks. She would miss Luka on the big day, but she already had word that his mother and sisters Rhoda and Atieno would attend her graduation. It would be the first time her mother and father would meet Luka's family. They had enjoyed meeting Luka a week before he left for the United States. While Luka and Kamau sat outside on the verandah, Wanjira informed her mother that marriage plans were on hold until Luka's return from America and Njahira, though actually saddened by the turn of events, knowing full well how hurt her daughter was, had privately thought this waiting period might be good for the couple, even as she nursed a private fear that things might not turn out as the young couple might like. Two years can be a long wait, she thought, and many traps lie along the way, especially for a good looking and bright young couple like Luka and Wanjira, so far away from one another. To Wanjira she said, cheerfully, teasing her, "*Hii*, I can see why you have chosen him, Wanjira. He is *a man!*" Wanjira laughed loudly, pleased by her mother's acknowledgement that Luka was a handsome, brilliant and highly personable choice. But all she said to her mother was, "Didn't I tell you, Mami? Now you've seen him yourself, with your own eyes."

Wanjira, Wangu, and three other women from the Box held a joint graduation party two days after the formal event. It was held at Wangu's aunt's house in Kileleshwa, one of those beautiful homes that came with a swimming pool and luxurious grounds with finely trimmed lawns and beautiful flowers. A year earlier Wanjira and Luka had spoken of the beautiful Kileleshwa homes as they walked to and from the Arboretum, and she had said she would love to live there someday. "We'll live there Wanji, if that's your wish," he had said, and she had laughed loudly and hit him fondly on the back. That was before their relationship had reached the stage of planning a home together, but she had said, afterwards, "Kileleshwa, or Westlands." Those are my favourite places, so remember that, Luka O".

This evening she missed him, wondering what he was doing out there in "Exile," a faraway land, away from her and their friends. Most of them were here tonight: all his buddies from the Law Faculty, and their friends, and the crowd known to her and the other women who had organized the party, and their various friends and relatives, many from out of campus. There was a lot of dancing and merry-making, and the graduates felt proud of the great *Power to Read* conferred upon them by President Moi only two days earlier. A bit of Wanjira wished the old man, Mzee, had lived long enough to be the one to pass on this baton, this power, this license. But such is life, she reminded herself. Things do not go as we want them to, not ever, but they do work out in the end.

Luka was on her mind even as she danced, drank a few glasses of wine, and generally had a great time this evening. He had telephoned her the night before her graduation, and wished her well. He said over and over again how very proud he was of her for clocking an Upper Second! She was one of only a handful of students in her faculty who had obtained this Honours level. Her thesis was highly recommended, and her adviser thought it could, with modifications and revisions, become a book on the study of children's literature in Kenya. A book! That was beyond her expectations. She was pleased and flattered.

Only one student in the entire Faculty of Arts, the brilliant Simon G, as they all called him, had earned First Class Honours, and everyone knew he was headed for big things, as all First Class holders in any faculty always proved. Samuel, her first friend on campus and tennis coach, earned an Upper Second as well, and all indications were he had a promising career as a lawyer, following his expected entry into the School of Law in another year.

At some point in the evening Wanjira stepped outside for some fresh air, and to think a little bit. Unknown to her, Ben, Luka's close friend and Rugby buddy, had been watching her all evening, and now followed her out to the verandah, where some smokers were sitting, chatting away, the fumes from their mouths going upwards, while their mouths emitted soft sounds as they emptied them of the smoke. Ben had a soft spot for Wanjira, and had been one of Luka's greatest supporters when others thought he was doomed in trying to make the relationship with Wanjira work. Now he sat next to her on the steps in the backdoor of the kitchen, and put his arms around her.

"Take heart, Wanji. Take heart."

"Thanks, Ben." She leaned against him, and his shoulder felt warm and strong, as did his arm around her. They sat in this position for a while, and then Ben said, "Wanji, I'm here if you need someone to talk to. And don't worry about Luka. That fellow's fine, and he'll be back before you know it. In the meantime, it's good that you can have a good time, and relax. You must live!"

"Of course, Ben, of course. Life goes on!" She had started to use this aphorism in recent weeks as a kind of self-help mantra, and it seemed she used it many times in the course of the day, quietly, to herself. Tonight she was in a mellow mood, and for a while Ben's shoulder felt like a wonderful place to be, until Wanjira suddenly began to wonder what was happening. Something in her response to Ben, and his words, suddenly jolted her, and she sat up quickly.

"I've got to go in, Ben. Really." Her voice was strong, matter-of-fact.

"Why? Is anything wrong, Wanji?"

"No, Ben, I've just got to go back inside. Come dance." She held out her hand, and he rose to join her inside the house. The moment had passed, and Ben followed, wondering about just what had happened out there. He had felt something about Wanjira that a friend should not feel toward his buddy's girl, and he thought she too had felt something, but no harm done, he thought. No harm done.

A few days later Kairu came to collect Wanjira's things from the halls of residence, accompanied by Wagio, his fiancée. Their wedding was set for later that year, and both looked calm and happy. She was a marketing manager in an advertising firm in town, and had been a year behind Kairu at university.

Wanjira was surprised at how much she had accumulated in the last few years—books, more clothes, shoes, and two pieces of furniture she loved: a small bookcase, and a reclining chair she had bought at a second-hand store in Hurlingham. It was her favorite reading chair and she had surprised herself at the almost harsh manner in which she had refused to leave it for a woman across the hall who had come to "book" the chair a few weeks earlier. It was common to do this, and departing Third Years often left some favourite items to special friends as parting gifts, but this young woman was not even Wanjira's friend. "No way, Teri," Wanjira had told her, "Too many memories. I can't let it go." Teri had seemed disappointed. "Greedy girl," Wangu, who was with her at the time, had said after the younger woman left. "Some people have such bad manners," She had added, and she and Wanjira had burst into loud, wicked, laughter.

A few more gatherings with her friends, in various homes of friends or relatives, and it was time to leave *Chuo Kikuu*. The halls would close in a few days, and the women made the most of the short time left. Parties became the order of every evening, and one could drop into any room, such was the goodwill and friendliness of the departing Boxers, already beginning to feel nostalgic for their days in the residence halls. Some already had places of their own, especially those with parents who could advance them the rent for the first two or three months. Others, like Wanjira, would live temporarily with family members while they waited to be hired and become salaried professionals. Most would need to wait for at least three months before venturing out on their own. Wanjira had two interviews lined up with two newspapers the week after she was due to leave university. The future looked bright, if also tinged with the sadness of Luka's absence. He had sent her application forms from his university, and she planned to fill them out and send them back as soon as possible for America, now that it held Luka, beckoned, and who knows, studying there could turn out to be a good idea. The world seemed full of possibility for the new graduate, if it also held a few thorns, twists, and turns in its path.

Wanjira left the Box on a beautiful, sunny, Saturday morning in early June. All around her other university women were doing last-minute preparations, visiting friends along the corridors to say good-bye, loudly answering calls from siblings, cousins, and boyfriends waiting for them down the hall, or in their cars at the residence halls parking place. Wangu had left the day before; she would live with her aunt in Kileleshwa for a few months, and she and Wanjira had plans to meet later that evening at the home of a mutual friend in Buruburu. Samuel had taken the night bus to Mombasa two days earlier and expected to return to Nairobi in a month for a brief visit. Everyone else she knew was either gone, or leaving that same morning, and for a brief moment Wanjira felt a strong sense of loss, and a deep pain seemed to fill her soul. Tears filled her eyes, and all she could say was, "Luka!" She wished he was there with her, teasing, talking, helping her with her move, planning the day with her. "*Mwiiro wa ngoro ndukinyaga,*" she found herself thinking. She had often heard her mother and other women saying this to each other as consolation whenever things did not turn out as expected. *The heart's desire is never fulfilled.* "Luka's not here, but life goes on!" she said loudly, defiantly, speaking into the void that was now her former room. She stamped her foot on the floor in despair and rage at everything that had interfered with all the plans she and Luka had made.

With her *Kiondo* comfortably hanging from her left shoulder and handbag in her right hand, Wanjira surveyed her room one last time. She was ready, but, oh, she quickly unplugged her radio cassette player from the wall and put it into her *kiondo*. Her luggage was light, for everything else had already been safely delivered to Kairu's place in Harambee Estate.

"Ahsante!" Thank you! Wanjira knew the room was listening. Her voice was shaky, yet strong.

With her keys handed over to the residence hall clerk, there was nothing else for Wanjira to do but step out into the light of the mid morning, walk briskly down the hill, past the all too-familiar, fondly remembered, tennis courts, past St. Andrews, past St. Paul's, and across the highway, to the bus stop. She was a lovely sight to behold that morning: a shapely young woman in well-fitting blue jeans and light brown short-sleeved blouse, and a pair of brown leather sandals that showed neatly manicured, red painted, toes. Anyone looking at the confident-looking young woman headed to the bus stop would have noticed her poise, and perhaps remarked on the way she held herself with a straight-backed dignity. No-one, however, would have known that Wanjira's insides were in turmoil, or that a knot of fear and anxiety had settled into the pit of her stomach in the last few days as she contemplated the crossroads she had reached in her life.

A few minutes later Wanjira was on Bus Number 22, headed to the Eastlands on its way from Kabete. She was on her way.

Printed in the United States
113094LV00005BA/292-369/P